A Sweethaven
SUMMER

A Sweethaven
SUMMER

COURTNEY WALSH

Guideposts
New York, New York

A Sweethaven Summer

ISBN 13: 978-0-8249-4519-0

Published by Guideposts
16 East 34th Street
New York, New York 10016
Guideposts.org

Distributed by Ideals Publications, a Guideposts company
2630 Elm Hill Pike, Suite 100
Nashville, TN 37214

Library of Congress Cataloging-in-Publication Data has been
applied for.

Cover and interior design by Müllerhaus Publishing Group
www.mullerhaus.net

Cover photo by Shutterstock

Printed and bound in the United States of America
10 9 8 7 6 5 4 3 2 1

DEDICATION

For my mom, my cheerleader and champion. Thank you for sharing with me a passion for books, and thank you for always believing in me.

And for my dad, who, upon hearing my plan to study theater in college said, "You really should do something with your writing." I thought, "What writing?" And then went on to discover what God had already shown him. Thank you for being an example of wisdom and common sense...and for praying the boys away from me all those years. (I got a good one!)

ACKNOWLEDGMENTS

Writing your first novel can be a daunting task. The main thing I've learned is that it takes a small army, and fortunately, I have a great team on my side. I would like to thank the following people for the key roles they played in getting this book in print. What would I do without you?

My husband, Adam. You are, without a doubt, my favorite person in the world. I am inspired by your creativity and grateful for your willingness to read my work even though you're not "my target audience." You support me, stabilize me, believe in me, love me, and put up with me. And for that, I am eternally grateful.

Sophia, Ethan, and Sam. You remind me what's really important, share in the excitement of this journey, and make me smile every single day. God has big plans for you. I'm so blessed to be your mom.

My amazing agent, Sandra Bishop, who believed in me in the most inspiring way. I owe so much to you, my friend. Thank you for putting up with my neurosis.

Deborah Raney (my Deb), my mentor and my friend. I know God put you in my life at the most perfect time (and in the funniest way), and I thank Him every day for you.

My wonderful friends and critique partners who've read various incarnations of this story: Gwen Stewart, Carla Stewart, Mindy Rogers, Ronnie Johnson, and Cindy Fassler (Mom). Your feedback, encouragement, and thoughtfulness are so greatly appreciated.

Rachel Hauck, always encouraging. Thank you for not laughing when you read the first draft.

Dr. David and Beth Schleicher, whose generosity introduced me to the cottage community of Michigan, and in turn, gave birth to this story in the first place. Oh, and thank you for delivering my babies.

Jeane Wynn. What can I say? Your friendship is a beautiful blessing.

Beth Adams and Lindsay Guzzardo, two incredible editors who took a shot on a newbie. It has been pure joy working with you and shaping these books from day one! Thank you for your patience, your attention to detail, and your excitement for this novel.

Rachel Meisel. I am so thankful for the time and care you've put into this novel. Working with you has been a highlight of this entire process. Thank you.

Dianne Craig. They say, "To teach is to touch a life." It's so true. Sixth grade was a long time ago, but your encouragement and belief in me at that pivotal time in my life has stuck with me all these years. Thank you.

And of course, my Lord and Savior, Jesus Christ. Thank You for putting this dream inside me and then making it come true. Discovering my purpose and Your plan for my life has been among my greatest joys. I am most blessed to be Your daughter.

PRAISE FOR *A SWEETHAVEN SUMMER*

"This book captivated me from the first paragraphs. Bittersweet memories, long-kept secrets, the timeless friendships of women—and a touch of sweet romance. Beautifully written and peopled with characters who became my friends, this debut novel is one for my keeper shelf—and, I hope, the first of many to come from Courtney Walsh's pen."

—Deborah Raney, award-winning author of the Hanover Falls series and *Love Finds You in Madison County, Iowa* (2012)

"A Sweethaven Summer is a stunning debut. I fell in love with the characters and the charming lakeside town of Sweethaven and didn't want to leave. With a voice that sparkles, Courtney Walsh captured my heart in this tender story of forgiveness and new beginnings. It's certainly a great beginning for this talented author."

—Carla Stewart, award-winning author of *Chasing Lilacs* and *Broken Wings*

"A Sweethaven Summer is a sweet debut, filled with characters whose hopes, dreams, and regrets are relevant and relatable. A great book club read!"

—Susan Meissner, author of *The Shape of Mercy*

"*Courtney Walsh has created a town I want to live in. From the first chapter, the characters became my friends, jumping off the page and into my heart. I didn't want it to end. A masterful word painting,* A Sweethaven Summer *is a story of loss, regret, forgiveness, and restoration. Novel Rocket and I give it our highest recommendation. It's a 5-star must-read.*"

—ANE MULLIGAN, senior editor, Novel Rocket

"*This is a heart-tugging story of hope amid loss, and ultimately grace and acceptance. Novelist Courtney Walsh weaves a captivating tale that taps into the universal desire for belonging and happiness. This delightful debut novel has a bit of mystery, a bit of romance, a beautiful setting, and an intriguing cast of characters. A lovely, satisfying read!*"

—MEGAN DiMARIA, author of *Searching for Spice*

"A Sweethaven Summer *shines with moments of hope and tenderness. With interesting characters, a delightful setting, and a compelling plot, this is one of those stories that stays with you—like the precious pages of a scrapbook. Even after the story ended, I found myself wanting to visit Sweethaven again.*"

—TINA ANN FORKNER, author of *Rose House* and *Ruby Among Us*

But if the while I think on thee, dear friend,
All losses are restored and sorrows end.

—WILLIAM SHAKESPEARE

April 1987

When Suzanne hugged the oversized scrapbook to her chest, a whirlwind of memories flittered by like leaves kicked up in an autumn breeze. Lumpy and full after five years, the square book had become priceless to her. Photos and ticket stubs, notes scribbled on scratch paper—they'd all been attached inside the pages of that album every summer since eighth grade.

She could almost smell the air, heated by the crisp summer sun. If she closed her eyes, she could conjure the wooden planks of the dock stretching out into Lake Michigan, covered by a deep blue sky. The lighthouse she'd painted every year since she was twelve still showed up in her daydreams.

Would her secret taint those memories?

She called Jane, Lila, and Meghan her very best friends, yet even they didn't know the secret she'd carried with her on the road out of town.

The pages in front of her begged her to come clean—to tell the truth, after all this time. After the months of surface phone calls and brief letters—after pretending everything was okay. But scrapbooking a lie would defile the book. They'd all written their confessions. They'd all been honest.

Now, as she stared at the pages, she knew it was time to tell the truth. She flipped past Jane's admission that she hated her body and Lila's painful recounting of a relationship with an indifferent mother. Meg's scrawling handwriting confided her horror at being the only nondrinker at a high school drinking party last summer. She'd gone with a boy and sipped the same beer the entire night because she was afraid of getting drunk. Suzanne smiled as she read the tiny notes in the margins of happy pages.

Confessions.

They were all such good girls.

All except Suzanne.

These were their secrets. They'd shared them with her on the pages of this journal they'd kept. But they weren't kids anymore—and even their darkest secrets didn't compare to the bombshell Suzanne was about to drop.

The scrapbook had been her idea. She'd always been the artist, after all. But now, looking at the blank page in front of her, she wished she'd never made the suggestion. She had been so young, how could she have known it would come to this?

She set down the book and grabbed her art supplies from the bin behind her desk. She removed the lid, and the welcoming colors of the paint greeted her. She'd always been happiest when she was painting. Maybe that's why she thought a scrapbook was a good idea. A book to chronicle their summers in Sweethaven. A way to remember all that they'd experienced—to save the memories.

She flipped through the first summer's pages. Jane's tribute to *Flashdance* and Lila's layout about how she imagined "She's Got a Way" was written for her. Silly, meaningless tidbits that captured history and the innocence they'd all lost since then. As the years went on and the four of them grew up, the entries became more detailed. More heartfelt. They grew closer every summer, so the journal became more private. Full of admissions of their true feelings. Their deepest secrets. Their biggest dreams.

Their scrapbooking parties became tradition at the end of August. Armed with stacks of photos they'd each taken, they overtook Meghan's kitchen table for an entire weekend and relived the high and low points the previous months had brought.

Childhood dreams radiated from the pages in her hand. Dreams that weren't likely to come true now. Still, Suzanne carried a sliver of hope in her pocket.

It had been eight months since she'd seen her friends. She'd send the scrapbook to Jane, who would stash it in the bottom of her suitcase and bring it with her when she arrived in Sweethaven at the beginning of June.

Suzanne knew she needed to be truthful in this entry. Her last entry. The one that explained why she wasn't coming back. Why she had to stay hidden. Why her parents had all but locked her in her bedroom, making up excuses as to her whereabouts.

Like Quasimodo in the Bell Tower, Suzanne was an outcast. And even God couldn't *really* love an outcast.

But after eight months, she hoped—she prayed—that her friends could. At least one of them. She knew she could make it if she had just one true friend.

Suzanne scanned her paints until she found a small bottle of hazy blue and held it in her hand. She flipped through a few sheets of paper and settled on five different patterns, then cut them into small blocks and glued them to the blank page. Once the squares were in place, she diluted her paint with a few drops of water and began brushing a thin coat over the paper so the patterns showed through. If only she could swipe such a hazy covering over her secrets.

She stood and walked across the room, then positioned herself in front of the oversized, full-length mirror. She held her awkward Polaroid camera midair in hopes of capturing her own reflection.

Snap. Whirr. The camera spit the shiny, wet photo from the thin slot at its bottom and into her hand. She shook it back and forth until finally the image appeared. She stared at the girl in the photo. Seventeen years old. So much hope. Such big dreams. Dreams of being a real artist. Dreams of galleries and classes and a love story she could tell to curly-headed grandchildren.

Her sense of entitlement to wish for such things had dwindled. The path before her—a path *she'd* created—didn't give her the right to happy dreams and girlish wishes.

Using double-stick tape, she adhered the photo to the page she'd just painted. Beside it, she pressed down a solid-colored square, then used a fine-tipped black marker to write her thoughts.

For obvious reasons my parents are forbidding me to come back to Sweethaven this summer. The way they're talking, I may never be allowed to come back. Or leave my room. It's okay because I turn eighteen in a few months and then they can't keep me locked in the house anymore.

I've embarrassed them. I've shamed them. I've let you all down. I might not be able to keep going with the scrapbook, but you guys keep it up, okay? Don't let me ruin something that's been so good for all of us.

I don't know what I'm going to do, but as soon as I figure it out, I'll let you know. I promise.

I love you guys, and I'll never forget our summers in Sweethaven. I'll write when I can.

Love,

Suzanne

She held the page in the air and decided it needed something extra. Using a detail brush, she added pink curlicues and orange flowers to the edges of the page. By the time she was done, she was quite happy with her entry. Happy with everything except what she had to write. Happy with everything except the protruding belly on the girl in the photo.

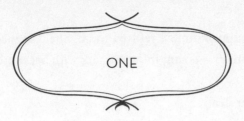

ONE

Campbell

The church smelled like flowers and dead people. Dead person. Just one. Her mom. The visitation the night before had sent her into an unexpected daze. She'd smiled. Thanked people for coming. Pretended she'd be okay.

She stood at the back of the sanctuary, her black skirt clinging to her waist and thighs and then flaring out slightly. Mom had always liked that skirt. She'd even borrowed it once to go on a date. One of the few Campbell had ever known her mother to agree to. It had always been just the two of them—and Mom seemed okay with that. Now, though, Campbell wondered if her mom would've fought harder if she'd had someone in her life. Would she still be dead if she'd had more to live for?

Surely a strong-willed daughter wasn't enough.

Inside, her anger wadded tight at the injustice she'd suffered, losing her mother when neither of them was ready for it.

Orphaned at twenty-four.

It had only been a week ago that Mom had called and asked her to come over.

"I have some things I want to talk to you about, hon."

Campbell could tell by her tone—a tone that radiated finality—that Mom was squaring things away. Getting those proverbial ducks in a row. Campbell almost refused to go. She'd argued she had to work—do laundry—do anything but talk with her mother about the inevitable.

About her death.

But Mom had one-upped her. "We need to talk about your father."

The words hung between them as Campbell tried to think of a response.

Mom had refused to talk about her dad, only saying they were better off this way, and despite their close relationship, Campbell had always wondered about him. Who was he? Where was he? Did he know about her?

Campbell pushed Mom's front door open, expecting the delicious aroma of hazelnut coffee and freshly baked chocolate chip cookies. Instantly, she knew something was wrong. She called out to her mom but was met with silence.

"Mom?" She called her name again, then walked through the living room and into the kitchen where she saw her mother, lying still on the hardwood floor, her legs bent in an unnatural position, her arms limp at her sides.

"Mom!" Campbell dropped to the floor beside her and found only a wisp of breath on her lips.

Several minutes later, Campbell watched as the paramedics hoisted her mother onto a stretcher and then put her in the back of the ambulance, unsure of how or when she'd even managed to dial 911. Before he closed the door, one of the men gestured for her to get in. She did, almost robotically. Moving as though in slow motion, she braced herself for the ride to the hospital.

For days, Campbell begged her mom to wake up. Begged her to come back so they could have that conversation over coffee. She had too many questions for Mom to really be gone.

Now, she'd never know what Mom planned to tell her about her father.

Campbell shook the thoughts away and perused the sanctuary, astonished by the number of people who had turned out to pay their respects. The entire staff of Liberty East High School now sat solemnly in the pews. Church friends. Former students. Even the mail carrier who had delivered their mail as far back as Campbell could remember sat on an aisle, his head bowed in reverence as he waited for the service to start.

So many people whose lives had somehow been touched by her mother.

"You wouldn't believe this if you saw it, Mom," Campbell whispered under her breath.

Not wanting to make small talk, she pretended to be interested in the program. She wanted to regain her composure. Sometimes the smallest thought popped into her mind, and her eyes involuntarily filled with tears. A glance toward the front of the sanctuary told her this wasn't a dream. No, she actually stood there, in the back of the church, waiting for her mother's funeral service to start.

Pastor Scott walked through the foyer and stopped beside her. His kind eyes were familiar after so many years in his church. Even as a rebellious teen when she'd begged to sleep in, her mother had insisted on their going to service. In the end, her faith hadn't done her any good. God couldn't heal Mom. Or wouldn't heal her. And worse, He'd stolen her away at the most inopportune time.

While Campbell hadn't felt ready to finalize things with Mom, she had to admit, she had questions. Not only about her father's identity, but about Mom's childhood—her past. Things Mom had always kept to herself. Things Campbell had stopped asking about for fear of hurting her.

If only she'd risked it.

Anger pelted her heart like a hailstorm.

She pushed it aside.

"You doing all right?" Pastor Scott put his arm around her and squeezed.

She nodded.

"Okay, we're getting ready to start. I'll go in first and you can follow like we talked about." He left her standing in the foyer in her black skirt and gray blouse. Would she ever wear the colors of spring again? Would she ever want to?

Black felt so appropriate.

After the pastor took his place on the stage, it was her turn. As if she were a bride, Campbell began the trek down the aisle. She kept her eyes focused on Pastor Scott, a man, she felt embarrassed to say, she'd imagined as her father on more than one occasion.

Just as she'd done with her third grade gym teacher. Her mother's male colleagues. Pretty much any man Mom's age with blond hair and a lanky frame, like her. She didn't get her features from Mom, so they must've come from her dad. Whoever he was.

She reached the front of the sanctuary, avoiding the teary eyes of the crowd, and sat in the pew. She peered down at her long-fingered hands resting in her lap. The blood had left them, leaving them white and cold. She rubbed them together to warm them. It didn't work.

Pastor Scott glanced at her and then smiled that soft smile. He'd have been a good father to her. She'd have called him "Daddy." He would've loved her and told her she was beautiful; told her she wasn't an accident. Just a surprise. He'd have made her feel better when the teasing started, told her those kids didn't know what they were talking about. He would have. But he didn't. He couldn't. He wasn't the one.

Why had Mom waited so long to come clean about her dad's identity?

She looked at the enlarged photo of her mom, radiant and smiling, that stood on an easel near the front of the church. She couldn't imagine her mother taking that secret to the grave. Campbell deserved to know—surely Mom had planned to explain everything.

Campbell had asked a few times, but her mother had always said there was no need for her to know. He wasn't in their life because he wasn't good for them. Was he in jail? Was he a serial killer? She'd never know.

And every time she'd brought it up, she sensed a hurt behind her mother's eyes. As though Campbell implied she hadn't given her enough or that she needed a father because she had a lousy mother. That couldn't have been farther from the truth.

Campbell tried to focus on the service. She chided herself for allowing her mind to wander at her own mother's funeral.

Six pallbearers carried the shiny wooden box to the front, and everyone turned their attention to the pastor.

"Today we say good-bye to a woman we all knew and dearly loved. I don't have to tell you what a bright light Suzanne Carter has always been in this church, in the high school, in the community."

She *had* been a bright light. Campbell's chest tightened in an emotional tug of war. The part of her that wanted to smile lost to the part that wanted to cry.

She dabbed her cheek with a tissue and tried to compose herself. She had to speak in a few moments. Nausea rippled through her stomach like a stone plunked in calm water.

Pastor Scott continued saying nice things about her mother. A woman everyone loved. Talented. Humble. A friend to all. A devoted mom. A tutor. An art lover.

He left nothing out.

His gaze moved across the sea of faces and landed on her with a slight nod. She felt her eyes widen. Time to stand. Would her legs hold her weight?

"Now we'll hear a few words from Suzanne's daughter Campbell."

She grabbed the pew in front of her and pulled herself to her feet on wobbly knees. Her stomach had hollowed, and moisture coated her cold palms. She smoothed her skirt and begged her feet to carry her to the stage.

Up the three small steps she went with a prayer of thanks she hadn't tripped. She took the pastor's spot behind a wooden pulpit and peered over the crowd that had gathered to say good-bye to her mother. They all expected her to say something appropriate. Expected brilliance. It's what her mother would've delivered.

She cleared her throat and pulled the microphone a smidge closer to her mouth. It fed back, its tinny ring cutting through the silence. She clung to the sides of the pulpit as though its wooden frame gave her the ability to stand.

"You all know what a wonderful person my mom was." She'd practiced her speech in her head. She should've written it down. Standing there, with faces staring back, well-practiced words escaped her.

"She...uh...she loved you all as if you were part of her family. You were her family. *We* were." She smiled and glanced at the photo of her mother. "Mom had a way of putting people at ease. A way of making you feel like you could do anything. I think that's because *she* could do anything. She must've figured we were all as competent and graceful as she was."

Campbell's eyes scanned the crowd. Mom's best friend Tilly sat near the front, nodding her support, a sweet smile on her face.

The entire high school had the morning off to attend the service in honor of her mom. So many of her former teachers and many of Mom's students now sat attentively, looking at her.

She cleared her throat and tried to remember what had come next when she'd rehearsed this in front of the bathroom mirror that morning. Mom's paintings caught her eye. "My mother was an artist. I think she always has been. She described herself as 'different,' but it was that artistic eye that separated her from the masses. It transformed the way she saw the world. The way she taught me to see the world." She nodded at the thought. "She believed in people— even though it sometimes hurt her."

Mom had always taught her to believe the best about people. The older Campbell got, the harder that had become.

A lump formed in her throat, and she coughed to clear it. "We knew Mom was…dying." The word jumped out at her and she had to look up at the ceiling to keep from crying. "But no matter how much time you have to prepare, it never seems like enough. She lived a wonderful life, cut short much too soon. She wouldn't want us to dwell on that, though. She would want us to live more deeply—more passionately— more beautifully. And *that* is the best way I can think of to honor her memory."

Even as she said the words, she wondered if *she* could live the passionate life her mother had dreamed for her. Every ounce of her passion had been sunk in her photography—not in people or relationships. Somehow, she imagined her mother wouldn't approve.

"Art is a wonderful thing, Cam," she'd say. "But you have to fill up your creative tank. It's the people in your life who do that."

She'd purposely kept her remarks brief, and once again, she begged her legs to transport her across the floor and to the safety of the solid pew beneath her.

Sniffles mingled with the piano as the chorus of "It is Well" rang through the vast room, filling the air with a heavy sadness.

"The song isn't sad," her mom had insisted. "The writer is rejoicing."

"I know where the song came from, Mom. The writer was grieving. He'd just lost his four daughters when their ship to England went down."

"Exactly. And even in that tragedy, he sang 'It is well, it is well, with my soul.'" Mom sang the line herself, then smiled. "Pretty easy to trust God when everything's going your way. Much harder to do that when your life is spiraling out of control." Mom shrugged then as if she'd said the simplest thing ever, but Campbell couldn't help but think it sounded a lot easier than it actually was.

Would things ever be well with her soul again?

Pastor Scott ended with a short prayer. Heartfelt and peaceful. Maybe Mom sat overhead on a cloud next to Jesus. Surely she would continue to watch over her only daughter. Would God allow that? Is that how things worked in heaven?

The pastor walked down the stairs and stopped at the edge of her pew, waiting for her to stand at his side. He offered his arm, even though he wasn't—and never would be—her father. The kind gesture moved Campbell almost as much as the realization that this was it. Time to say good-bye. One last look at the coffin and she mustered the strength to stand. She turned to face Pastor Scott.

He nodded as if to tell her she'd be okay. She weaved her own long arm through his, and they started down the aisle. Then, as if she were watching from a distant place in the room—as if she'd left her body—she headed toward the back of the church. As she walked, she scanned the room. A sea of recognizable faces.

Except for one man.

Tall. Lanky. Older. Gray hair atop a long face. A stranger.

She caught his eye, but he quickly looked away. At the floor. Out the window. Anywhere but at her.

Who is he?

She reached the end of the aisle and followed Pastor Scott into the foyer.

"We can head right over to the cemetery if you're ready," he said.

Campbell had made arrangements to ride with the pastor and his wife to the burial. There had been talk of a car to take her—alone—to the cemetery, but she refused. What could be lonelier than an empty car ride to a cemetery?

"Almost. Do you know who that man is?" She nodded in the direction of the stranger.

Pastor Scott followed her gaze and then shook his head. "Not sure. Maybe an old friend? Colleague?"

Campbell frowned. She expected to know everyone at the funeral. And with the exception of this one man, she did.

She stood in place until Pastor Scott's wife emerged from the sanctuary, followed by the rest of the crowd.

"You ready?" The pastor waited.

Campbell glanced back at the old man, but he'd gone. She scanned the lobby. There was no sign of him. No sign that a stranger had ever been there, paying his respects.

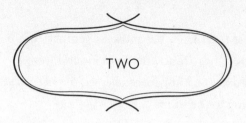

TWO

Campbell

Sitting in the driveway of her mom's house on Tee Street, Campbell couldn't turn the car off. Couldn't go inside. Would it still smell sterile and medicinal or would Mom's real scent have returned? Lavender and clean cotton. The perfect mix.

She hadn't been back since the night she'd found Mom on the floor. Then for a solid week she'd only gone between the hospital and her own apartment. Now, she had to go into the house where her mom had lived. And died.

Red flowered sheets still flapped on the clothesline out back. She'd have to figure out what to do with the house. But not today. Today, she couldn't think about selling it. She loved it too much.

And Mom had loved it.

That night, the chocolate chip cookie night that never was, Mom would've told her what to do about the house even when Campbell tried to stop her—not wanting to face the fact that her mom wouldn't be around forever. She would've broken it down so Campbell understood exactly how to list it and what to list it for. Or what it would take to keep it. She wouldn't have left anything out.

If only Mom had had more time.

Campbell finally turned the key and shut off the engine, but she sat for a few more minutes, her head on the steering wheel. Tears fell from her cheeks and dotted her black skirt.

A river of tears later, her muscles aching from bunching them up, reason took over. Tantrums were for children.

She wiped her face and forced herself out of the car. Up the walk. Until she came to the tulips.

"I'm planting these for you, Camby-Jay," her mother had said when they first moved in. "I know tulips are your favorite." At eight years old, Campbell determined her favorite flower after carrying a tulip bouquet in Tilly's wedding.

"What color are they?"

"White." Mom smiled. "Clean and crisp. They'll be perfect."

They bloomed the next spring after the last frost, and Campbell had been so proud of the one she picked.

"Not for picking," Mom said. "Just for looking."

Now Campbell's breath caught at the silky whiteness of the tulips. She picked a trio of them. Today she needed them on the kitchen counter more than they needed to be in the yard.The weathered arched door—a flea market find—boasted a Welcome sign her mother had painted herself with a light blue coat of watered-down paint, leaving the chipping, distressed look she loved so much.

"It'll add so much charm to the house," she'd said. "I'll feel like I'm at a beach cottage or vacation home."

Campbell didn't argue. She'd learned to trust her mother's artistic instinct. And her mother taught her to trust her own. She was grateful for that.

She stood in the doorway of the empty house—keenly aware of the absence of her mother's infectious laugh. How many nights had they sat on that old couch, indulging in popcorn and eighties movies? *Pretty in Pink. The Breakfast Club. Sixteen Candles.* Mom had covered Campbell's eyes during all the questionable parts, laughing and claiming that her baby still wasn't old enough to know about these things.

Campbell smiled at the memory.

In the entryway, Mom's gray sweater hung on a hook next to the door. Her "house sweater" as she called it. "I'll only wear it at home, Camby, I promise." But she didn't. She wore it everywhere. The ratty old thing became a permanent fixture on her mother's small frame.

Campbell picked it up, put it to her nose. Inhaled.

Clean cotton and lavender. Another long sniff. The smell of Mom.

The flea market sweater she'd tried to talk her out of buying now seemed like a familiar friend. Mom loved the history attached to the things in antique stores and flea markets. "Junk," Campbell had called it.

"You never know who this belonged to, Cam," she'd said, holding the sweater in front of her. "Could've been a famous author or"— she feigned a gasp—"an artist." Her eyes had grown wide and then she'd examined the wristband. "Is that a splotch of paint?" She grinned.

"Or it could've belonged to a mass murderer or"—Campbell feigned a similar gasp—"an accountant." She rolled her eyes at her mom, but it did no good—she'd already bought the ugly thing.

She shrugged her own jacket off and wrapped the ratty sweater around herself, poking her arms through the worn sleeves. She caught a glimpse of herself in the mirror. Ridiculous, yet somehow…perfect.

The house creaked in protest to its emptiness. Even the walls seemed sad at Mom's passing. She'd cared for the house so diligently, made it into a home. *Their* home. Tiny but tidy. Neat and artsy. Homey. Cozy. Theirs.

Hers.

Soon to be someone else's.

In that moment, she wanted to stay—to curl up on the couch and spend forever in the house that smelled of lavender and clean cotton.

She stumbled into the kitchen. The sight of the full coffee pot stopped her, and her breath caught as she realized the finality of pouring it out. The last pot of coffee Mom ever made.

It's just coffee. She picked up the pot and held it over the drain, but something stopped her from dumping it down the sink.

Thoughts of her mom standing in that very spot watching the coffee brew drifted through her mind. She took a deep breath and exhaled. Still, her eyes stung, tears threatening. She returned the carafe to the coffee maker.

For days she'd sat in the uncomfortable, vinyl-covered hospital chair holding Mom's hand, begging her not to die. The nurses flitted in and out of the room, testing, fixing, poking, prodding.

They always asked if she needed anything.

She always shook her head. "No, I'm fine."

No greater lie had ever been spoken, of course. She was anything but fine. Would she ever be fine again?

The lump she'd fought for days intensified at the base of her throat, mixing a cocktail of bile and pain. One stray tear. Then another. She swore she wouldn't cry. Even though Mom was in a coma, Campbell had to believe she could still hear her, and she didn't want to risk making her sad.

Mom's hand in hers looked thin and frail. Even the skin appeared almost translucent next to hers.

"Mom, you're all I've got." The weight of the statement hit her like a slap in the face. In a matter of minutes, she could be alone. How could this happen? How could a God she thought loved her let this happen?

Mom didn't respond. Campbell wished she would wake up—give them a chance to say the things they hadn't. Or at least a chance to say good-bye. ·

Campbell flipped through a mental Rolodex of almost-relationships she'd had over the years. Ashley Robinson. Grades two through six: best friend. Grades six through twelve: worst enemy. College to present: inconsequential person. She hardly ever thought of Ashley's betrayals anymore. The pain they caused. The permanent damage.

Scars are healed wounds, but they still show on the skin.

Jason Timmons—boyfriend: one month. Wade Cooper—boyfriend: two months and three days. Travis Berkley—boyfriend: record-breaking seven months, two weeks, and four days. Almost eight months. Almost heart stealer. Almost.

Mom told her she had to stop pushing everyone away. "For once, just believe the best about someone, Cam." She'd tried but failed. She couldn't let them in. She didn't believe them.

She grabbed a soda from the fridge and carried it into the living room. She sank into an arm chair and propped her feet on the coffee table, kicking her black heels off and pushing them over the edge and onto the hardwood floor where they landed with a thud. The clock told her it was almost one on the day she buried her mother. Now what? How would she spend the rest of the day? The week? Her life?

Amid her mother's flea market treasures, Campbell snuggled into the chintz cushions of the sofa and clicked on the TV. Not because she had any interest in it, but because she hated the lonely silence of an empty house. She flipped through the channels. Nothing.

Thoughts of the conversation Mom had planned on having that night bobbed around in her mind.

Her cell phone buzzed, forcing the thoughts away. She fished it from her purse and clicked it off without looking at the caller ID. Apologies and sympathy didn't interest her now.

She stared at her feet for a long moment, and only then did she realize the coffee table under them wasn't familiar. Instead of the usual coffee table, an old trunk with a farmhouse quilt draped over it sat in front of the couch.

Where'd this come from?

She pulled the quilt off of the trunk and popped open the lock. Musty basement smell filled her nostrils, obliterating the serenity of her mother's sweet scent. She coughed. A small quilt was folded on the top of the contents inside the trunk. She lifted it out, revealing stacks of canvases, not unlike those that filled Mom's art studio.

These were different, though. Striking. Magical.

She flipped them over, one by one.

Sweethaven Sunset. Sweethaven barn. Sweethaven dock.

Sweethaven?

Campbell glanced around the house, looking for other new additions. Things that hadn't been there the last time she'd visited.

She walked into Mom's bedroom, trying to shut out the emotion that knocked at the door of her heart. The queen-sized bed had been made up with its red and white quilt and topped with pillows. She headed into the bathroom—fewer memories there.

A white-framed mirror hung over a pedestal sink. She splashed water on her face and caught her reflection. She hardly looked like her usual self. Her blue eyes had lost their luster, and her skin looked pale. Her cropped blond hair was matted to her skull like an unattractive helmet. The mascara she'd carefully applied that morning had worn away, leaving her lashes to fend for themselves. Unsuccessfully.

Behind her, a shelf decorated with seashells and photos caught her eye. She hadn't noticed them before. A framed photo of her and Mom had been propped on one side of the shelf, but on the other side, something unfamiliar. She squinted at the foreign photo until she recognized her mother at the center of the group of four girls— probably thirteen years old—sitting on a long dock, their backs to the ocean. Or was it a lake?

The frame, made of seashells, had a date etched in it. 1983. Mom's long brown hair hung around thin shoulders, and a red polka-dot bikini top showed off her tan. Long and lanky arms draped around other thin shoulders attached to smiling faces.

Who were these girls? Mom hardly ever talked about her childhood. Instead, she told vague stories with few details.

And why had her mother never mentioned this place before? It must be real. The painted scenes matched the photo.

Walking through the house, she found similar framed photos, though the girls seemed older in each one.

She returned to the living room and flipped each frame over, facedown. Unhinged the backing from the frames and pulled out the photos. Each one had been labeled in a young girl's handwriting.

The Circle. 1983.

The Circle. 1985.

The Circle. 1986.

1986. The year before Campbell had been born.

She studied the photo. Four teenage girls sat on the same dock in each shot. Same pose—her mom always at the center, eyes beaming, so full of life. Girls who would now be women, and who didn't know her mother had died.

Girls who knew her mom when she got pregnant.

Pulse racing, she rummaged through the rest of the trunk. At the bottom, she found a wooden box. She pulled it out and carefully removed the top.

What if there were clues to her father's identity here? She'd convinced herself over and over that it didn't matter. Every daddy/daughter dance. Every major milestone and life event. The thought of one day walking down the aisle. It didn't matter. She didn't need a father. She had Mom. But now...

Now she had no one.

Inside the box, Campbell found an oversized packet of papers. She pulled them out. Pictures and phrases and sentences and snippets decorated the pages. A stack of them tied together with a ribbon. Why did her mother have what appeared to be only a portion of a larger scrapbook? Where was the rest of the album? Had it been torn apart in anger? Carefully separated with tenderness? She found a note attached that read:

Suzanne,

We wanted you to have the whole scrapbook, but we knew you'd never keep it if you weren't coming back. We decided to divvy up the pages. Here's some we thought were your favorites. Will you write? Call? Anything?

Love you,

Jane

Jane's note gave no reason.

If they'd documented everything, shouldn't there be a page somewhere that revealed her father's identity?

Campbell untied the ribbon and looked through the pages on her lap. Images of her curly-headed mother abounded. All of the journaling talked about a place called Sweethaven. One page showed a map of Michigan, a heart drawn around a tiny spot near the lake.

Our Summer Oasis. Photos of the girls standing beside a tall wooden Sweethaven sign at the city limits filled the pages. Campbell read the handwritten journaling: *We hated it here until we met each other. Now we wait nine months for summer to get here. We spend most of our time in Meg's cottage because her mom makes the best food. The rest of the time we spend on the beach. Or in the Commons. Or in the Main Street Café. We love our Sweethaven Life.*

The handwriting resembled Mom's artsy script.

Why had Mom never spoken of this town? Sweethaven was a blip on the map at the center of the layout. A small gold star marked the spot in Michigan, north of her home in the Chicago suburbs.

She flipped to the last page.

Summer 1987. Broken Circle.

A Polaroid photo had been stapled to the left-hand side of the page. A sheet of notebook paper with her mother's handwriting had been stapled to the right-hand side. A painted collage background told her that Mom had certainly crafted this page. Campbell ran her index finger over the familiar cursive. Even her mother's handwriting comforted her. She leaned in closer to the page. Her pregnant mother, frozen in time, stared back at her.

She looked so young. Only seventeen, her belly round like a basketball stuffed under a too-small shirt. Her long brown ponytail hung to her shoulders. She held the camera in one hand and took the photo of her reflection in a long mirror.

Campbell scanned the words on the page, and realized it acted as her mother's good-bye.

She'd never seen a picture of her mom pregnant. Mom said her grandma wouldn't allow any to be taken. The shame had been too great. Not something to celebrate. Translation: *she* wasn't something to celebrate.

Campbell lifted it and a dried, brown-edged, yellow rosebud

fell out. Had her father given her mother this rose? Had the two of them been kept apart in a tragic, Romeo and Juliet kind of way? She flipped through the pages searching for any mention of a boy's name. Nothing.

But this scrapbook was incomplete. What about the other pages? The pages the other women had? Would they connect the dots and spill the truth?

Campbell didn't have to look far to find the identities of the other three girls. The second page stretched across two sheets of worn cardstock. At the top, the title: *The Circle*. Underneath were four columns, with a photo of each girl in front of a cottage with a different house number and a brief introduction.

Mom stood on the porch of a steep-roofed cottage wearing a terrycloth one-piece shorts outfit and a wild ponytail. Campbell zeroed in on the handwritten note beside the photo.

My name is Suzanne Carter but my real friends call me Suzy-Q. I am one of the founding members of the Sweethaven Circle and spend my summers in this cottage, located on Juniper Drive. We just started coming to Sweethaven this year after my grandmother passed away. She left the cottage to my father. I like Bazooka Joe bubble gum, White Rain hairspray, and I'm obsessed with Michael J. Fox. (He's so cute!) If I hadn't met the other members of The Circle, Sweethaven would be totally lame. Oh, and I'm starting eighth grade in the fall. (Gag!) At least I'll have the summer to look forward to!
Yours Sincerely,
Suzanne Marie Carter

Campbell smiled at the thought of her mom as an almost eighth grader. She had no idea then how short her life would be. Only forty-two years.

The other introductions were similar. Jane Anderson had been coming to Sweethaven her entire life. She had other friends but made mention of her "kindred spirit" Suzanne—someone who understood her better than anyone else. Her "regular home" in Iowa wasn't nearly as interesting. Lila Adler lived in Macon, Georgia, but traveled all the way north to Michigan to "give Daddy time away from the real estate business." And Meghan Barber, a redhead with bright freckles across her nose and cheeks, had only recently moved to Sweethaven full-time. "To escape the 'dangers' of Nashville and because my mom made me."

These girls had been close to her mother. They'd watched her grow up. More importantly, they knew her when she'd made that terrible mistake…the one that led to Campbell's conception. Those girls—women now—had known Campbell's grandparents. They might even know who her father was.

Guilt shook her. Would it hurt Mom to know she was already thinking about finding her father? Only hours after her funeral?

She skimmed page after page of the papers that had been tied together with bright red ribbon, but she found no mention of a boyfriend. There were entries about a Blossom Festival. An entry about the old carousel on the boardwalk being restored. Even one page about Meg's mom's famous cheesecake. But not one word about a boy who might be her father.

What if all the secrets had been preserved by one of the other girls? What if the other pages lay somewhere in Sweethaven? In one of those cottages? What if someone—after she'd spent years wondering—could tell her where her long legs and blond hair came from?

What if she wasn't alone after all?

The phone rang, startling Campbell back to reality. She stared at it, not sure if she should answer Mom's phone. Finally, after three rings, she walked into the kitchen and picked up the receiver.

"Hello?"

"Suzanne. It's so good to hear your voice. I was just callin' to check in on you. How're you feelin', darlin'?"

Oh no, Campbell thought. *Someone who hasn't heard about Mom's death.*

"I'm sorry, this is Campbell, Suzanne's daughter."

A pause on the other end.

"Hello?"

"Oh, yes, sweetie, I'm still here. I'm sorry. Is your mother home?"

Campbell sighed. "I hate to be the one to tell you this, but she passed away two days ago." The words nearly stuck in her throat.

The Southern woman on the other end of the line let out a faint gasp. "Oh, hon," she said, "I'm so sorry. I hadn't heard."

Campbell stared at the ceiling—something that always kept her tears from escaping. "Who am I speaking with?"

"I'm an old friend of your mom's," the woman said. "Adele Barber."

Campbell frowned. *Barber.* She walked to the living room and picked up the scrapbook pages on the couch. *Meghan Barber.*

"As in Meghan Barber?"

"That's my daughter," Adele said. "So your mother *did* tell you about Sweethaven." Adele sounded relieved.

Campbell started to respond and considered pretending she knew everything—she'd get more information that way—but she'd never been a good liar.

"Actually, no," she said. "I just found some photos and scrapbook pages. Do you know where these other women are? And your daughter?"

Adele cleared her throat. "Maybe it's best if we meet in person," she said. "Can you come up here? To Sweethaven?"

"I don't think that's a good idea," Campbell said. "I've already been off work for a week." That part was true. She didn't mention she'd called her boss at *The Buzz,* the Internet tabloid site where she worked, and taken the rest of the week off.

"I see."

"So, my mom's friends don't know she's gone?"

"No, darlin'. I don't see how they could. The girls haven't spoken in years."

Campbell frowned. "Why not?"

"It's a long story. I was hopin' your mama would get in touch with them before she passed away."

"You knew she was sick?"

"I did. She came to see me not too long ago. Wantin' to make amends, I suppose. Wantin' some advice. I'm sad she didn't get to say a proper good-bye."

Confused, Campbell glanced around the kitchen, not wanting to get off the phone, but not sure what else to say. Maybe her mom had planned to tell her a lot more than just who her father was that night. Maybe she planned to tell her about Sweethaven.

The outgoing mail pile still sat in the organizer on the edge of the counter. In it, a stack of small envelopes caught her eye.

She picked them up and flipped through them one by one.

"Huh," she said. "It looks like my mom planned to get in touch with them. I just found three cards, one addressed to each of them."

"Oh dear." Adele's voice wavered. "She just ran out of time."

"Why didn't she tell me about any of this?" Campbell wondered aloud.

"I'm sure she had her reasons, hon."

Campbell studied the envelopes. Should she mail them? Read them? What would the women do if they heard from her mother? Would they call? Write? Then Campbell would have to tell them each they were too late. Her mother was gone.

"I have to go," she told Adele. "I'm sorry."

"I understand, hon, but you write down my number and call me if you need anything," Adele said. "And when you're ready, my door here in Sweethaven is always open."

"Thank you." Campbell hung up, confused, as more questions swirled around in her mind. She considered reading the cards intended for her mother's childhood friends, but something about that felt wrong.

She glanced at the clock. The mail hadn't come yet. Without giving it another thought, she stuck all three envelopes in the mail box just outside the front door.

Even if she was gone, her mother's friends had a right to know what she had to say.

She shut the door and braced herself for the questions that could come her way in the next few days.

For once, she'd be the one with the answers.

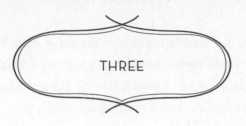

THREE

Jane

Three o'clock already? Jane sighed. Where had the day gone? She looked at her to-do list and crossed out *Fold laundry*. Still staring at her were *Cook Dinner, Do Bible Study Lesson,* and *Make "North Wind" costume for Sam's kindergarten class play.* She'd agreed to volunteer at the school one day a week, but it seemed like the projects always waited until the very last minute.

She looked at the piles of folded clothes stacked on the kitchen table. At least she'd gotten that done.

She hurried to her minivan and backed out of the driveway, pulling next to the mailbox as she reached the road. A stack of bills and junk mail waited for her. She tossed the pile on the front seat and drove toward the school.

Her cell phone chirped from the pocket in her purse. Keeping one eye on the road, she rummaged to find the phone before it stopped ringing.

"Hello?"

"Hey, hon." Graham. Wednesday, 2:45. He'd be working on his sermon for Sunday morning. Jane rarely heard from him at this time of day.

"Hey. Is everything okay?" Jane clicked on her turn signal and pulled into the school parking lot.

"Just calling to check in."

He'd started checking up on her years ago, and even though she was fine now, he still kept it up. She didn't mind.

"I'm fine. Just waiting for Sam to get out of school."

"I meant to call earlier, but I got wrapped up in what I was doing. I think I'm on a roll, but I'll be home for dinner." She could hear a smile in his voice. He loved coming up with a good sermon—it's what made him tick.

"Good. We'll see you then." She tossed the phone on the front seat and took her place at the back of the carpool line at the elementary school. Once she picked up Sam, she'd have to run up the street to get the girls at the junior high/high school, but in spite of the rush, she found herself ten minutes early.

She picked up the mail and thumbed through it. Electric bill. Cable bill. Credit card application. She tore that one up and stuffed it in the trash can at her feet. A small envelope fell from the pile. One look at the handwriting and a gasp escaped her lips.

Suzanne. How long had it been? She did the math in her head. Twenty-some years. Had it really been that long?

Hmmm. No return address. Just a Chicago postmark. Inside was a small card. Hand-painted watercolor flowers graced the front panel. Jane ran her finger over the card, taking a moment to admire it. It looked like it should be in a frame. Leave it to Suzanne to make her own cards. She'd always been the creative one. She flipped it open and Suzanne's beautiful handwriting greeted her like a long-lost friend. Simply seeing the familiar script brought back the ache of nostalgia. Suzanne refused to be ordinary in any way—right down to her penmanship. She could make a quickly scribbled check to a pizza place look like a masterpiece. In her youth, Jane had foolishly prayed for good handwriting after seeing Suzanne's for the first time.

God had answered her prayer, years later, and now Jane wondered what He would've done if she'd prayed for something that actually mattered.

Like friendships that didn't fade away as quickly as the changing seasons.

Jane's wistful smile faded into regret. They'd been so close—how had she let so much time pass without so much as a Christmas card? Even after everything they'd all been through, she shouldn't have allowed the distance—or the past—to come between them. She didn't even know where Suzanne lived anymore. She focused her attention on the words in front of her.

Dear Janie,

It's been too long. I think about you so often and wonder how you are. I walked by your cottage just last week. I could almost hear your laughter inside.

Jane blinked twice and found it difficult to open her eyes again. Suzanne had been back to Sweethaven?

Sweethaven.

Jane's heart constricted. There was too much history. Too many memories of The Circle. Of Alex.

Alex.

The thought brought tears to her eyes, but she held them back. She swallowed the lump in her throat and forced her emotions to stay put. She looked around at the line of cars outside. She needed to keep it together.

I miss you, Janie. I miss our friendship. I miss those carefree summer days down on the Lake, burying our toes in the sand and working on our suntans. I've made so many mistakes in my life, but one of my biggest was losing touch with you.

A knock on the car window startled her. She looked up to find the vice principal, Darla Gray, motioning for her to move the car forward. She mouthed the words "I'm sorry" and pulled ahead three places. She heard the bell ring and wondered if she should wait to finish Suzanne's letter until later—once Sam was in the car she wouldn't be able to concentrate. She didn't want to rush through it; it felt like an unexpected treat in the middle of the week. She folded it closed, but curiosity got the better of her. Why would Suzanne choose now to get back in touch? After all this time? Why the change of heart after she'd been so deliberate in leaving?

I don't know everything you've been through in the past twenty years—even Adele won't go into details, but I do know that there's still something magical here in Sweethaven, and I wish I could bottle it up and take it everywhere I go. Don't you miss it, Janie? Don't you miss walking down the street and knowing everyone? Don't you miss picking out your fruit at the farmer's market and the smell of grilled burgers every night? Don't you miss the four of us—all the fun we had?

Jane stopped. They'd all pretended to hate that their parents dragged them to Sweethaven every summer, but once the four of them found each other it became the thing she looked forward to throughout the entire school year. Real life here in Iowa became the thing to dread.

Even now, she knew Sweethaven promised the kind of life most people only dreamed of. Simple. Warm. Inviting. And yet she'd cut Sweethaven out of her own life like a malignant tumor.

It felt like it all happened so long ago, but if she thought about it, she could put herself right back on that beach with her friends. She could smell the air, the suntan lotion mixed with the sweetness of summer—a light sweat and mosquito repellent. She hadn't thought of it in so long.

I know I am at fault for what happened. I know if I hadn't left maybe we all could've worked through everything and we would still be a part of each others' lives today. Maybe. I guess some questions are bound to go unanswered.

Jane realized she was shaking her head as she read. Suzanne's leaving had nothing to do with the rift that had separated them. Like aftershocks of a monumental earthquake, things just kept happening to drive them apart.

I just wanted you to know that I love you, and I will always love you. And I'm sorry I didn't get in touch sooner. See, Janie, I've got cancer—and, well, it doesn't look like I'm going to win this battle.

Jane gasped, then squinted through cloudy eyes.

When I get to heaven, I'm going to look down on you and make sure good things come your way. I'm writing in hopes that you will come to Sweethaven for the Blossom Festival. Meet me there. Eat a funnel cake with me for old time's sake. And we can catch up and I can see you in real life one more time before I see Jesus.

Suzanne was dying?

Jane wiped away a tear. Her throat swelled around the lump that had grown. Swallowing suddenly seemed an impossible task. If only she had her sunglasses. She checked her eyes in the rearview mirror and blinked to force the tears away.

I wish things had turned out differently for all of us. I wish I'd come to my senses sooner, and hadn't missed out on so many years of knowing everything about you. Take care of each other, Janie. Please. I hope I see you in May.

And I hope you always remember Sweethaven.

Suzanne was dying. And she wanted her to come back there.

Her friend had no idea what she asked of her. Jane swore she'd never go back to Sweethaven.

No matter what.

Sam popped the door open, startling her back to reality. She wiped her eyes one more time and tucked the card in her purse. Now that she knew what it said, it felt very precious.

"Hey, Mom." Sam struggled to heave his backpack and lunchbox into the van.

Jane wondered how he managed to make a private school uniform look so disheveled.

"Hey, buddy, how was school?"

"It was the best day ever, Mom."

Jane smiled at him in the rearview mirror. He said that every single day. He leaned forward.

"You okay, Mom? Your eyes look all red."

"I'm good." She put on a smile. "Get buckled, mister."

Jane thanked God every day for Sam. Their little miracle baby.

With his dark brown curls and scattered freckles across his nose, he epitomized the word "joy." His delight in everything he did infected the rest of them. God knew exactly what they'd needed. She sometimes wondered if He sent Sam specifically for the purpose of bringing oxygen back to her lungs.

She glanced up at him in the mirror and saw he'd already lost himself in a book. She loved that about him. Suzanne would've loved her children. They would've loved her. She'd have been Auntie Sooze. And Jane would've been Auntie Jane. It's what they'd always planned. Grow up. Buy houses next door to each other. Spend holidays together and summers in Sweethaven.

But none of that had happened. And now it was too late.

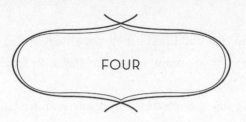

FOUR

Jane

That night, after the kids were in bed, Jane took Suzanne's card out and held it in her hand, aware that it could very well be the last connection she had to her friend. She couldn't go to the Blossom Festival, but she could call. She had a list of questions. What had Suzanne done with her life? How had things turned out for her? And her daughter? How old would she be now—twenty-four? An adult. And Jane had only ever seen her once.

"I think they're all down for the count," Graham said, entering the kitchen. He stopped when he saw her standing against the counter staring at the card. "What's that?" A look of concern crossed his face.

Jane handed it to him. Though he'd never met Suzanne, he knew all about her. He knew how they'd all grown up together in that tiny town—a sort of safe haven that seemed to shelter them from the rest of the world. She'd made sure to tell him because they were so important to her. Yet, if they were so important to her, how had she let them all slip away?

"You should go."

His words jarred her from her sorrow. "What?"

"You should go back."

She stared at him, then shook her head. "No. Graham, I can't."

The raw lump that had filled her throat all day stifled her ability to swallow. "There're too many reasons to stay away from Sweethaven, and you know it."

Graham paused. Sometimes his resolve annoyed her. How could he have moved on and forgiven? Why was he so *good*?

"Do you want to see if you can track down the others? At least see if they're going before you make a decision."

Just like that, he'd steadied her again.

"I can't see Meghan making this trip—and Lila? She won't go back either, Graham. Suzanne's going to be at the Blossom Festival alone."

"They might surprise you."

She shook her head.

He wrapped his arms around her and pulled her into a hug.

She savored his strong arms around her and noticed she'd been completely disarmed at his touch. How did he do that?

He wiped a stray tear from her cheek with his thumb, then kissed her forehead. "Let me know if I can help, okay?"

She nodded.

"I'm going to bed. Don't stay up too late."

"I won't."

With the house quiet and her to-do list out of sight, Jane's mind started to meander through her childhood—stories that almost always included Suzanne. Her friend had shown her what unconditional love was, at a time when she needed it most. Her mind drifted to the summer of 1983.

The smells of cotton candy and buttery popcorn floated in the air, blending perfectly with the breeze off the lake. The happy music from the carousel at the amusement park echoed across the beach as the horses spun round and round. Jane licked her ice cream cone, wishing for just one ride.

The park bench bit into her legs, but inside the melody of the carousel matched her heartbeat.

"How's that ice cream cone, Fatso?"

"It's gonna go straight to your big old butt."

Jane shrank in her twelve-year-old skin as she glared at the two girls standing in front of her. She'd been friends with Leanne and Lori last summer, but this summer something had changed. They stood, hands on hips, staring at her, as the blue moon ice cream melted all over her hand.

"Eat up, Porky."

Tears stung Jane's eyes, and she blinked to keep them from falling.

"At least she isn't gonna need a plastic surgeon for her face." The voice came from behind Jane. She spun around and saw a skinny brunette with a curly ponytail staring at the two girls. "You *must* know what it's going to cost to fix those cartoon noses of yours?"

"Who are you?"

"I'm Jane's friend. And you're not—so get out of here."

Leanne and Lori, as if on cue, rolled their eyes and sauntered off in the direction of the Boardwalk.

"I'm going to ride the carousel," the dark-headed girl said. "Wanna come with me?" She wore an orange bathing suit and a pair of white terry-cloth shorts.

Jane turned away. The girl sat on the park bench beside her.

"Finish your cone and then we'll go." The girl twirled a strand of hair and made an I-know-what-you-want grin. She blew a large pink bubble with her gum and let it pop on her face.

"I'm not going on a dumb carousel." The ice cream stuck in her throat, almost gagging her. Blue moon was her favorite and now she watched it turn to liquid in her hand.

"Don't let those stupid girls get to you," the girl said, pulling the sticky gum from her lips. "You don't need them anyway. You've got me now. Once I'm your friend, I'm your friend for life."

Jane watched as the girl pulled her legs up on the bench and crossed them in front of her.

"What's your name?" Jane licked her ice cream just before it dripped on her hand.

"Suzanne. And you're Jane."

Jane frowned.

"My mom knows your mom. They met at some tea or something. My dad's the pastor at Sweethaven Chapel this summer." Suzanne looked at the cone in Jane's hand. "You're dripping."

"Oh." Jane licked the blue ice cream off her hand and tossed the cone in the garbage.

"I would've eaten that, ya know."

"I licked all over it." Jane scrunched her face.

"So? I don't believe in germs." Suzanne grinned. "You ready for the carousel or what?"

Jane pressed her lips together. "Thanks for that."

Suzanne's eyes widened. "For what?"

"For sticking up for me." Jane looked away. "No one's ever done that for me before."

Suzanne grinned. "That's what friends are for."

Jane sat up straighter in the kitchen chair and realized she'd been crying. She wished she'd kept the entire scrapbook. She wished she had those photos—the four of them on the day they met, surrounded by all four souvenir tickets and their journaling about that day, written only a few months later at the end of the summer. By that point, she felt like she'd known Suzanne, Lila, and Meg her entire life, and none of them could wait to return to Sweethaven.

Maybe she could convince Suzanne to meet her somewhere else. It wouldn't be this weekend, but soon.

But what if Suzanne didn't have the time? What if she was too frail? This weekend could be the last chance to see her.

No, she couldn't go back. She'd promised Alex. Suzanne was right—Sweethaven did have a certain magic to it, but for Jane, the magic had died a long time ago. Now, with Suzanne dying, the last bit of enchantment seemed to float away.

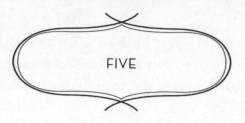

FIVE

Lila

Lila waved good-bye to Priscilla. In her black Lexus, she headed toward home, where she would begin to assess Priscilla's latest changes. Designing the décor in the woman's plantation home had originally excited Lila, but the more she worked with the woman, the less she enjoyed this job.

She'd opened her own interior design business years ago, back when she and Tom first started having trouble getting pregnant. She realized then that she needed something to occupy her days—and sipping tea with Mama's friends wasn't going to cut it.

She grabbed the mail and pulled into the driveway. Vast and spacious, the house seemed to taunt her barren womb every time she walked in. They'd bought the house with the intention of filling it with children.

Now in her forties, she wondered if they should consider downsizing.

Tom's parking space was empty. His flight was due in over an hour ago, so she expected him anytime. She'd fix dinner. They'd eat. They'd ask each other about their days. He'd go into the living room to watch basketball, and she'd go to the study to work. After a couple of hours, she'd head to bed, stopping by his recliner to wake him.

This was her life.

She turned off the ignition. As she pushed open the door, Lila smelled a mixture of lemon and bleach. The cleaning lady had been there that morning, and once again, Lila had forgotten to ask her to dust the blinds in the study. She'd have to make a note to have her do it next week.

As she sorted the stack of mail a plain white envelope fell onto the floor.

She picked it up and turned it over. She opened the envelope and pulled out the card inside. On the front was a beach scene, hand painted and signed by someone with the initials *SC*.

Suzanne.

It had been years. Over twenty years, but Suzanne's art seemed to have a voice that transcended time. So many of her paintings had been of their favorite places in Sweethaven.

She opened the card, but before she could read it, the garage door sprang to life.

Tom.

He entered through the back door, his tie loosened around his neck. Seeing him in that uniform always caused her heartbeat to quicken—no matter how great the expanse between them.

He frowned as he met her eyes. "What's wrong?" he asked.

"Nothing. I was just about to read this." She held up the card.

"What is it?"

"It's a card—from Suzanne."

"Suzanne Carter?"

As kids, Tom and his friends had seized every opportunity to terrorize the girls. They'd dug night crawlers from rich, black soil, waited until the girls weren't looking, and then placed them in whatever spot would garner the loudest scream. Lila had endured crickets, frogs, a raccoon tail they swore they'd cut themselves—all at the hands of those boys. Ironic she'd ended up falling in love with Tom after that trauma.

She hadn't thought about it in years.

"Seems strange she'd be writing after all this time. After leaving the way she did." If she thought about it very long, jealousy would overtake her. Getting pregnant had been a burden for Suzanne, the same way *not* getting pregnant had burdened Lila.

"Yeah." Tom grabbed a bottle of water from the refrigerator and took a long drink. "Are you gonna read it?"

She opened it and read the words slowly. "'Dear Lila. It's been so long—too many years have passed and I should've written ages ago. I hope you are well. I hope you are happy. I am sure you are just as beautiful as ever.'" She paused for a moment, as if she expected Tom to agree with Suzanne, but he said nothing.

"'I've had a lot of time lately to think about my life, and I realized that when I thought of happiness, I kept thinking about our summers in Sweethaven. I kept thinking about the homemade ice cream in the Commons and the fireworks on the Fourth of July. I kept thinking about you—about the four of us. About how easy and simple and wonderful things were back then.'" She looked at Tom. "She certainly knows how to romanticize things, doesn't she?"

He shrugged. "Maybe not. There is something special about Sweethaven."

"I guess so." She turned her attention back to the card. "'I do have regrets, though. I'm sure you can imagine. I regret so much of what happened the last summer I was there, but most of all, I regret the fact that I allowed our friendship to dissolve. I have so much more to say, but sadly, I am running out of time.'" Lila realized there had been a question in her voice. She scrunched her eyebrows together.

"'It's cancer.'" Lila stopped, surprised at the sorrow that welled from somewhere down deep. "'The doctor isn't giving me much longer.'"

Through clouded eyes, she kept reading.

"'Do you still go to Sweethaven? Do you still spend your summers standing on the beach, digging your toes in the sand? Do you find the time to let the wind mess up your perfectly styled hair? Do you watch the kids on the carousel or maybe even go to those crazy dances they used to have in the Commons? If you don't, will you come back for the Blossom Festival? It's still the first weekend in May. It might be my last chance to say good-bye. I pray you come. I pray you find that magic—that magic we all felt there. I pray you can find it in your heart to forgive the sins of the past, and when you think of me, I pray you'll find a way to smile at all we once shared. I love you, Lila. Suzanne.'"

Unable to speak, she whispered Suzanne's name. It hung in the air between them, tangible, thick, and dense as fog.

"Cancer," Lila spat. "I can't believe it. She's so young."

"Cancer doesn't seem to care," Tom said, shaking his head. "Do you want a glass of wine?"

Lila nodded and he poured.

"I'm sorry you can't go." He handed her the Chardonnay.

"Why can't I?"

"Doesn't Priscilla need you here?"

Lila frowned. "I think this is a little more important, isn't it?"

"Is it? You haven't spoken to Suzanne in over twenty years." Tom removed the tie from his neck and put it on the counter.

"But she was one of my best friends, Tom."

"A long time ago."

"You know how close we all were."

"I know. But I also know how long it's been since you last saw her."

She stared at him. She and Suzanne had their differences, as all friends did. They'd come from two different worlds, and a part of

Lila envied Suzanne her carefree ways. She'd only realized how jealous she'd been of Suzanne when it came up in therapy.

First Suzanne had stolen Jane from her. Doting Jane who'd been her best friend since second grade. Losing Jane's undying attention annoyed Lila, but not worse than the realization that Suzanne had won *her* over too. While Lila envied Suzanne's low-pressure, I-can-do-anything-I-want-to attitude, she couldn't deny that Suzanne had drawn her in from the moment she gave her a hand mirror she'd found at a flea market.

"Just imagine how many other beautiful faces have looked in this mirror," Suzanne had said. "It made me think of you."

"Looks old." Lila took the mirror and turned it over. The glass had brown stains around the edges.

"But it's neat, right?" Suzanne's eyes widened.

Lila fought the urge to toss it off the way she brushed off every other kind gesture. "Thanks," she said. "It *is* really neat."

"I'm glad you like it," Suzanne said. "Even though it's old."

Lila held the mirror in front of her, catching her reflection. Suzanne pushed her face next to Lila's and grinned. "Yep. We're stunning," she said.

When Lila laughed, the pain of the morning skittered away. A morning of trying to please Mama. No one else had ever done that for her before.

Had Tom forgotten that?

She glanced down at the card. It got her thinking about the long summer days they'd spent at the beach. Lila smiled at the memory. Suzanne had always been the fun one—the first one to explore Old Man McGuffrey's barn. The first one to jump in the lake in spite of frigid water. She'd always been daring and audacious, and the rest of them took their cues from her.

Suzanne had given her the courage to stand up to her mother. One simple question was all it took.

"What do *you* want, Lila?"

Lila stared at her.

"You've never even thought about it, have you?" Suzanne shrugged as if she'd just stated the obvious, but the question sent Lila's mind reeling.

Suzanne grabbed her hand. "You've gotta figure out what you want to do, and start doing that." Suzanne flashed a smile and squeezed her hand.

Suzanne's words gave Lila courage she'd never had before. Enough courage to confront Mama later that afternoon.

"Mama, I'm sorry I can't go to the Harbortown interview this weekend." The pageant had been on Mama's radar for years.

Mama's eyes darted up from her magazine and settled squarely on Lila's face. The shock of it was enough to scare Lila back into the pageant spotlight, but she tried to appear brave. "I don't want to do pageants anymore."

Mama's glare shook Lila to her core. One penciled-in eyebrow peaked higher than the other, and she stood straight and grand like the oldest oak tree in Sweethaven.

"We're leaving in ten minutes."

"I'm not going. I wasn't making that up, Mama."

Her mother inhaled, her nostrils flaring. "You will go upstairs, change into something presentable, and we will drive to the Harbortown interview without another word of this nonsense."

The evenness of Mama's tone sent a shiver up Lila's spine. "I'm through discussing it," her mother said. "As long as you live here, you'll do what I say. Now get upstairs and put your dress on. The pink one with the thick straps."

That was that. Lila would compete in the Harbortown Festival

Pageant. She would then compete in every other pageant Mama entered her in, leading all the way up to Miss America. It's what Mama wanted.

It's what she would do.

Lila held Suzanne's card in her left hand, her right hand now massaging her forehead. As if she could knead the sorrow away.

This could be her last chance to say good-bye. Surely Tom would understand.

"I'm going to go," she announced as she stood from the table.

His face fell.

"These are my oldest friends."

"Your friends are here." Tom crossed his arms.

"I need to do this, Tom. Why can't you just understand that?"

He threw the empty water bottle in the garbage and walked out of the room.

She stared at the card then walked into the bedroom and caught Tom's eye in the bathroom mirror. He stood at the counter, shirtless.

"I'm leaving in the morning."

He pulled a gray T-shirt over his head, walked past her into the bedroom, and sat on the end of the bed to put on his running shoes.

He looked up from his shoelaces, and for a second she thought he might challenge her—give her an ultimatum or argue why she should stay. Instead, he shook his head and she watched him walk out of the room and heard the front door slam.

Lila sat on the edge of the bed and stared at the closed door of her walk-in closet. Behind it, she knew her floral luggage sat on the top shelf.

She heaved her suitcase down and dropped it to the floor. If she hurried, maybe she could be gone before Tom returned from his five-mile run.

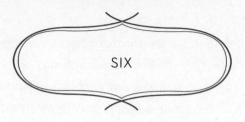

SIX

Campbell

If the map on the old scrapbook page was still accurate, I-94 North would take her straight to Michigan and deposit her almost directly in Sweethaven, but it wouldn't answer all the questions swirling around in her head.

Her decision to leave town the day after her mother's funeral might have been a rash one, but she needed the distraction to shake the image of her mother's flower-covered casket. To stop the replaying of "It Is Well," which had been running through her mind since Tuesday morning.

She glanced at the open book on the passenger seat as she drove in the direction of the little town.

The pages of the scrapbook showed four inseparable girls who lived for their summers in these cottages. One of the pages outlined the history of Sweethaven, but instead of reading like a page from a school book report, this layout gave a colorful description of the small town where her mother spent her summers.

Photos of the Sweethaven landmarks were arranged on the right-hand side of the page in a vertical line. A lighthouse. A carousel. A diner with a red and white awning. The beach. To the left, various samples of handwriting shared interesting facts about the little town.

Sweethaven became a village in 1834 and a city in 1891. In the early 1900s, people started the tradition of spending their summers in

the cottages and houses to be near Lake Michigan. Some of the rela-
tives of those earliest founders still live here today—either year-round
or during the summer. Someday our parents will pass their cottages
to us and we'll all bring our kids here to grow up on the banks of the
lake just like we did.

Campbell smoothed a hand over the page. If her grandparents
had a cottage, who owned it now? Did these girls—now women—
still spend their summers in Sweethaven? Had they stopped the
scrapbook altogether because of Mom's pregnancy?

Because of her?

She knew she'd ruined her mother's life back then, but she never
considered that she might have stolen her friendships too.

The most pressing question of all, though, still begged an answer.
Who was the boy—the man, now—her mother had loved? Who was
the one she could claim as her father?

And why hadn't he claimed her as his daughter?

Campbell glanced in the rearview mirror at the large bag she'd
crammed in the back seat beside Mom's trunk. Apparently, she'd
packed for a week, though she had no idea why or what would keep
her in Sweethaven that long.

A father. A father could keep her there forever.

She scrolled through her iPod till she found Norah Jones. Mom
had loved her as much as she had. They'd bonded over the cool,
jazzy sounds and long discussions of art and photography and their
future as gallery owners.

Now, Campbell had no reason to dream that dream. She had no
desire to make it come true without Mom at her side.

The time passed more quickly than she expected. Just after 11
a.m., she saw the sign: Sweethaven—Two Miles. According to the
directions, she got off at Main and turned left.

She opened the car window and inhaled. The sweet, distinct scent of lilacs, Mom's favorite, filled the car. Springtime, a time of new beginnings, begged to burst forth, and Campbell felt inclined to let it.

As she entered the small town, her tires *clunk-clunk-ker-plunked* over the brick road beneath them, almost as if she were entering a third dimension. Old-fashioned street lamps lined either side of the street separated by oversized bushes, blossoming with bright pink flowers.

"Wow." Their beauty nearly took her breath away.

It wasn't until that moment she realized she should've called Adele and let her know she was coming. In her excitement, she hadn't even remembered to bring the woman's phone number. Thankfully, her address was in the scrapbook, assuming she still lived in the same cottage.

Brick buildings flanked both sides of Main Street. Striped awnings advertised Sweets in Sweethaven, a quaint bakery, The Sweethaven Art Gallery, and at the end of the block, The Main Street Café.

Odds were good they had coffee.

Campbell pulled into a parking spot and stopped to stare at two old men sitting on a black park bench. Their faces showed a valley of wrinkles, and on their heads were bright green John Deere base-ball caps. A woman walked a dog down the sidewalk. Two children zipped by on bikes.

Perched inside her car, she held her camera to her eye and snapped a string of photos. Everything in Sweethaven seemed worth documenting. She'd been in town for two minutes and already this place had bewitched her with its beauty—its ability to transport her back in time.

A bell over the door rang her arrival at the Main Street Café, and the guy behind the counter glanced in her direction.

Her heels clicked on the knotty pine floor as she took in her surroundings: exposed brick on two of the walls and a tall, wooden counter at the right.

"Be right there," the guy said.

"No rush."

As he steamed milk in a metal cup, she looked around the café. Original artwork lined two of the orange walls, and shafts of natural light poured in from windows encased in thick white molding.

"What can I get you?" He snapped a lid on the drink he'd just finished and set it on the counter for the woman waiting in line. Now his attention rested on her. She noticed his dancing green eyes. Eyes that expected her to answer—not stare.

"Oh, sorry," she stuttered. What she wouldn't give for a calm and collected version of herself. "I'll just have a medium vanilla latte if you've got it."

"Whipped cream?"

"No thanks."

"Didn't think so." He grinned and punched numbers on the register.

She raised an eyebrow.

"Just a guess." He hit enter on the cash register. "It's $2.50."

"Seriously?" She'd pay almost twice that much for that drink at the coffee shop on her corner back home.

"Sweethaven blood isn't as rich as Chicago's." He grinned again.

"Chicago?" She handed him a five-dollar bill.

"Am I right?" He made her change and then moved away from her to start on the drink. "I know you're not local. The scarf thing on your neck is a dead giveaway." The noisy machine shot back to life as he steamed the milk for her latte. No sense responding. He'd never hear her anyway. Instead, she glanced at herself in the mirror behind the counter. The black scarf hung loosely around her shoulders. It did look a little pretentious in the casual environment of the Main Street Café.

She moved underneath a sign that read PICK UP HERE just as he covered her cup with a lid and set it in front of her.

"Is that a medium?"

"Large."

She pushed the drink back in his direction. "I ordered a medium."

"You look like you need a large." He took a bar rag and ran it over the nozzles of the steamer, cleaning off the milk from her drink. "Don't worry, I didn't charge you for a large. It's on me."

"Really? Thanks." She took a sip. "Whipped cream."

He smiled again. Perfect teeth sparkled in her direction.

"Yeah. You looked like you needed that too." He winked and walked back to the counter.

Caught off-guard, she stood in the same spot for at least a minute. He hadn't insulted her, but his implication that he knew what she needed twisted her insides. No one knew what she needed—not even her.

"You can't assume the worst about everyone, Camby," Mom's words rushed back. "I know so many genuinely nice people. Why not start off your next relationship trusting the person instead of forcing them to prove themselves to you? Believe the best, Cam."

Mom had meant well, but she'd also been burned one too many times believing the best about people. She hadn't dated many men, but the last guy—Joe Pancini—had scammed her into a pyramid scheme that claimed a good chunk of her money. She'd been too trusting. It didn't matter that she hadn't ended up needing her retirement after all.

But maybe Campbell had swung too far in the opposite direction. Possible? Maybe.

And this guy probably didn't mean any harm. He was just a little cocky. Or was that confidence? She couldn't quite tell.

Campbell walked to the end of the counter and waited for his attention.

"How's your drink?"

She set the cup on the counter. Curiosity got the better of her. "What'd you mean by that?"

"By what?"

"I look like I need a large. I look like I need whipped cream. Do I look that bad?" She scolded herself for asking. Her insecurity bled through like a wound through gauze.

He shrugged. "My mom always says 'sometimes it's a whipped cream kinda day.'"

Her face warmed into a smile. "And you think I'm having that kind of day?"

"If I had to guess." He opened the cash register and shuffled some bills around. "Do I have to guess? Or do you want to just tell me?"

She took a sip of the whipped cream–covered latte and then propped herself on a tall stool at the counter.

"Good, isn't it?" He closed the register and ran a towel over the same spot he'd wiped only moments before.

"It is good, actually, but I'll be cursing your name when I'm doing an extra thirty minutes on the treadmill tomorrow."

"Ah, but you'd have to *know* my name in order to do that." He grinned.

"True." She took another drink. It really was better with whipped cream.

"It's Luke." He held out a hand in her direction.

"Campbell." She took his hand and squeezed. An innocent handshake shouldn't cause stomach gymnastics.

"Campbell, huh? Like the soup?" He let go of her hand and tucked the towel back in his apron.

She rolled her eyes, laughed. "Yeah, like the soup." She'd been hearing that since kindergarten—usually sung to the tune of the commercial.

"What brings you to Sweethaven?"

Mystery. Intrigue. Trying to figure out where I came from.

"Oh, just needed to get out of the city," she said.

"Do you want something to eat? It's on me. First time in Sweethaven discount. We've gotta do what we can to get people to come back." He smiled again. Could she resist?

"No thanks, just the coffee. I should run."

Disappointment ran across his face and then disappeared.

"I've got people to find. Well, one person anyway. I'm hoping it'll lead to more people."

"Can I help?" He looked sincere.

"Maybe." She reached into her bag and pulled out the pages of the scrapbook.

She set them on the counter and glanced at him. His eyes had zeroed in on her. Something about his expression set her off-balance. Could be the sparkling green of his irises or the wave in his sandy blond hair. Or the compassion she seemed to find waiting in his gaze.

He broke the stare and she straightened her scarf, suddenly self-conscious of her attire.

"I found this." She drew his attention to the pages.

He turned the scrapbook around and looked at the pictures. Recognition crossed his face.

"You know them?" Hope filled Campbell's chest.

"Sure. Well, I know of them. And I recognize the cottages." He pointed to the one on the end. Redheaded Meghan stood in front of a tidy house with sprays of flowers planted on both sides of the stairs leading to the porch. A black lab lazed at her feet. "This one on Elm Street is where I grew up."

Campbell frowned. "Where you grew up?"

"That's my sister Meghan."

"Adele is your mom?"

He smiled. "You know my mom?"

Campbell shook her head. "She called my mother yesterday. Do any of them still come here?"

"Where'd you say you found this?"

Hope started to trickle away. How much should she risk telling him—a perfect stranger with kind eyes?

"It belonged to my mother." That much shouldn't hurt.

His eyebrows lowered. "Which one is your mother?"

She pointed to Mom's picture. "Suzanne Carter."

"I've heard people talk about her over the years. She hasn't been back here since before I can remember."

"I'm guessing twenty-four years." She ran a hand through her hair. "That's when I was born. I think that's when she stopped coming. Stopped seeing her friends. Stopped being Suzanne and started being Campbell's mom."

He leaned across the counter. "You say that like it's a bad thing."

Uh-oh. Grief, like a sneaky devil, had slithered in. Nipped at her. Hissed. Whined. Expected a response. She swallowed the bulge that had grown in her throat, hollowed her belly, and she looked away.

"She died four days ago." She couldn't make eye contact. "Breast cancer. We buried her Tuesday."

He stilled at the confession. "Ohhh," he said. "So that's why you needed the whipped cream."

In spite of her sadness, she smiled.

"I'm sorry." He let his hand rest on hers, not for long, just a brief count to two. Maybe three.

She shook the grief away, focused on the task at hand. Find a father. Find *her* father. Stay distracted. Don't think about Mom.

"Who'd you come to Sweethaven to find?" Luke asked.

She sipped her latte. "I was hoping maybe these girls—these women—might have some answers for me."

"I hate to be the one to tell you this, but these women—none of them come to Sweethaven anymore." Luke watched her.

"But the book says the cottages are passed down from generation to generation. They come every summer."

"They did—but they…don't. Anymore." He folded his hands on the counter.

"Oh."

"But talk to my mom. She might know where to find them."

The image of the three letters she'd found came to her mind. Why hadn't she written down their addresses? She'd expected all three women to come calling, but she had no idea what the notes even said. Now she had no way to get in touch with any of them.

Except Adele.

"Okay. I'll start there." She stacked the scrapbook pages on top of each other, making a neat pile, and tied the red ribbon around them again.

"What is it you're hoping to find?" His question hung in the air between them, daring her to answer.

After a long pause she answered. "My father."

His eyes widened. "Well, then, I hope you find what you're looking for." A smile crossed his face, lopsided, sincere.

How long had it been since she'd witnessed a sincere smile?

She looked away. Perhaps something divine had intervened—

had led her to the Main Street Café, for coffee and her first lead, bringing her one step closer to finding an answer.

To finding her father.

She glanced back at the handsome guy behind the counter. "Thank you," she said, and it struck her in that moment—she meant those two words. Probably more than he'd ever know.

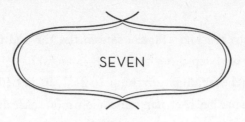

SEVEN

Campbell

Campbell left the café and, armed with the map Luke had drawn on a napkin, headed straight back down Main to Elm, turned left, and drove up Elm Street two blocks to 418.

"Then just park the car and she'll meet you at the door. I swear she can smell company a mile away," Luke had said.

"Your mom sounds like a good person," Campbell said.

"Well, she's a character, that's for sure."

As she drove past The Sweethaven Gallery, she admired the artwork in the front window. She thought of her mom's canvases in the back seat—of their dream to open their own gallery one day. She'd have to visit that place before she left.

The neighborhood along Elm had full, mature trees and charmed her instantly. Campbell recognized a huge barn on the right from one of her mother's paintings. The Sweethaven Commons. A sign near the front door told her she was right. According to the scrapbook, the Commons was housed in the old Byron Colby Barn. It looked different than the one in the photo. Newer. Richer. But charming just the same.

The left side boasted a row of clapboard cottages, all with neatly trimmed yards. Flowers burst over terra-cotta pots and vases, lining porches and flagstone walkways. Pots hung over porch railings decorating various homes, each one as welcoming as the next.

When she reached 418, she slowed the car and parked across the street.

She had never done anything so rash in her life. Mom had raised her to use her common sense. Common sense didn't condone knocking on a stranger's door with a handful of scrapbook pages. What was she thinking?

She inhaled then unlatched the car door and stepped onto the brick road, willing herself to be strong. She'd never find the answers if she didn't take a risk.

The flagstone walkway, lined with tulips, caught her eye, drawing her gaze downward. A sweet butterfly perched on one of the petals. She bent down for a closer look. It seemed to stare at her. She fought the urge to cup it in her hands and take it home with her. She wished she had something so beautiful to carry in her pocket.

A noise behind her startled her to an upright position.

"Hello?" A white-haired woman with ample hips and a kind face stood at the edge of the yard. She wore white cotton capris, a white shell covered by a pale pink button-down, a floppy sun hat, and tennis shoes. Gardening gloves graced both hands.

"I'm sorry. Hi." Campbell walked toward the woman, extended a hand. "I'm—"

"Campbell Carter, as I live and breathe." The woman laughed and then pulled her into a tight hug. "Oh my stars and bananas!" The lazy lilt of her Southern drawl floated like a summer song.

"You really favor your mama, darlin'. Oh, your sweet mama, God rest her soul." She removed her gloves, took Campbell's face in her hands, and stared at her for a long moment.

Campbell's awkwardness washed away and she looked straight into Adele's eyes, where she found the warmth and compassion of a mother waiting for her.

The woman dropped her gloves on the ground by her feet. "I think you need some sweet tea. Me-maw made the very best sweet tea, and I happen to have some. I'm famous for it. Don't you even try and say no." She shook a finger in Campbell's direction. "Go ahead and sit down. We'll chat." She motioned toward two rockers with a small table between them on the porch. Before she disappeared in the house, the older woman turned and stared at Campbell for a long moment.

Campbell did as she was told, and within seconds, Adele had returned with two tall glasses of sweet tea.

"I've never had sweet tea before."

Adele gasped. "That's a travesty," she said. "I have to tell ya, hon, I didn't think you'd come. After we spoke on the phone, I imagined you'd go back to your life and forget all about this nonsense." She leaned forward and put a hand over Campbell's. "But I'm glad you didn't."

Campbell smiled. "I wasn't going to come. But the more I read these, the more curious I became." She produced the scrapbook pages from her bag.

In Adele's hands, the pages looked like precious documents, treasures that should be behind glass at a museum. "Do you know what you have here?" Her eyes welled with tears.

Campbell shook her head.

"All their memories. Their stories." She closed her eyes as if she needed a moment to regroup.

"Not all of their stories. It's not complete. There are chunks missing."

"I know, darlin'. When your mama didn't come back that summer, they wanted to abandon the book altogether. This beautiful book of all their memories. Just sitting on the shelf in Meghan's room. I couldn't stand it. So, I got the three of them together and

I forced them to look through it with me, dividing up the pages so they could each have a stack to keep. I'm glad your mama kept hers all these years."

Campbell sipped her tea and stared out across Adele's yard. She hadn't mustered the courage to ask the one question she most needed answered. She didn't have the heart to tell Adele her reasons for coming weren't for "posterity's sake," as the book suggested, but to find something much more important.

Campbell had come to find her father.

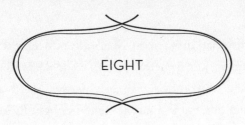

EIGHT

Adele

Adele watched Campbell drive off to a local store to pick up a few things, in spite of her offer to provide anything she needed for the night. Sounded like an excuse to her. No matter. The girl needed a little alone time, and that was just fine by her. She couldn't blame the poor thing.

Once the car pulled out of sight, Adele sighed. So, Campbell Carter had found the scrapbook. And she had questions.

She wasn't the only one. When Suzanne had shown up on Adele's doorstep only months before, Adele had fought the urge to bombard her with questions of her own. Questions that had gone unanswered for so many years.

She'd been making molasses crinkles when there was a knock at the door. It was rare for Adele to have unannounced visitors— especially in the winter.

Suzanne's long brown hair had hung in waves around her shoulders, flowing out of a multi-colored stocking cap Adele imagined she'd made herself.

The little girl she'd known and loved all those years ago had grown into a beautiful woman. Adele pulled her into a tight hug, and in a flash the memories came back: The day Meg came home with new friends after she'd spent months hating her for moving them to Sweethaven from Nashville. The scrapbooking slumber parties Suzanne had insisted on. Meg's announcement that Suzanne wasn't coming back to Sweethaven—that she'd abandoned them all.

"Hi, Adele." Suzanne's face brightened. She'd always had a vibrancy about her, but in that moment, her light flickered.

"What is it, darlin'?"

Suzanne sighed. "Can I come in?"

Suzanne carried an oversized bag on her shoulder.

"Would you like some coffee? Tea?" Adele led her into the living room.

"Those are awfully grown-up drinks, Adele." Suzanne grinned as she took a seat in the blue armchair.

"Hot cocoa it is." In the kitchen, she filled the tea kettle with milk and set it on the flame. As she put the carton back, she glimpsed Meg's photo on the side of the refrigerator. Her daughter should be here. She should be the one talking with Suzanne over warm drinks.

Adele brought a steaming mug to her young friend. "Feels like a whipped cream kind of day." She handed Suzanne the mug and sat on the sofa across from her. "What is it, darlin'?"

Suzanne sighed. "Cancer."

Adele gasped. Just like her Teddy. "I'm so sorry."

"Don't be. I'm at peace with it now." Suzanne sipped the cocoa.

"But you still have your hair."

"Chemo wasn't an option for me." Suzanne looked tired. Especially around the eyes. "So, I am living it up while I've still got the time."

"Oh, sure you are, and that's why you're here to see me—the life of the party." Adele laughed. A forced laugh. She wondered if Suzanne noticed.

"I wanted to talk to you about why I left."

"I know why you left, darlin'. Meg showed me the picture."

Suzanne's face reddened, and she looked at her feet. "I didn't have a choice, Adele. My mom wasn't going to bring me up here with a new baby. It was bad enough that our friends at home found out about it. But Sweethaven was my mom's favorite place to pretend. She could be picture-perfect with her pastor husband. But I was a failure." She set the drink on the coffee table. "I really let them down."

Poor girl. She'd been carrying this pain for years.

Adele took Suzanne's hands in her own. "You listen to me. I will not judge you. My good Lord Jesus tells me not to judge. I am only here to be your friend."

"Thank you." Suzanne pulled away. "I know the girls were mad at me. They didn't really know my parents. I think they were mad I wouldn't tell them everything, but I was just so ashamed." Even now, all these years later, she wrung her hands, eyes focused on the floor.

Shame. Powerful demon, that one.

"They were upset, I suppose, but they loved you, Suzanne. They would've been there for you. I would've been there for you."

"Adele, the people who were supposed to protect me the most couldn't even be there for me. They kicked me out. Told me if I didn't marry the father, I shouldn't come back. My child wasn't welcome in their home."

Adele cringed. She'd suspected Suzanne's parents—especially her mother—had been unsympathetic, but she had no idea how badly it had hurt Suzanne.

Suzanne fidgeted with the edge of a pillow at her side. "I went to Jane. I would've told her everything that night, but I couldn't. Bad timing. I didn't want to push my problems on her. A few months later, I got a stack of scrapbook pages in the mail. I figured it was her way of saying they'd all decided they were finished with this foolishness."

"That could be, sweetheart, but isn't it just as likely they wanted you to know they couldn't continue without you? The Circle was broken. *I* am the one who insisted they divide that scrapbook, darlin'. I felt like that book needed to be with each of you, and the only way to do that was to give everyone a portion of the pages. They picked your pages so carefully, making sure to get the ones they thought you'd love most."

Suzanne shook her head, almost as though it hurt to imagine she'd gotten it wrong for so many years.

"I need a favor."

"Anything, hon."

"I need you to send these cards to the girls after I'm…"

"Suzanne." Adele touched Suzanne's knee. "No."

"Yes, please. You're the only one I trust to do this."

"Darlin' listen. I know a little something about regret, and I can tell you if you don't find these girls yourself and say good-bye, you will regret it. And so will they."

"Too much time has passed, Adele. I wouldn't know where to start."

"You could start with 'hello.' You don't know what they've all been through, hon."

"Exactly, and I wasn't there for any of them. I left. In their minds, I died a long time ago."

Adele sat back in her chair. "That's just not true, Suzanne."

"Can you honestly tell me if I called Meg right now we could just pick up where we left off?" Suzanne stared at her, but Adele said nothing. "Can you?"

"I can't tell you much of anything about Meghan these days, I'm afraid. We haven't spoken in a long time."

Suzanne's brow furrowed. "What do you mean?"

"She left Sweethaven a few years ago, and I haven't seen her since."

Suzanne crinkled her forehead. "I don't understand."

"It's a long story, but it would be better if you tried to reach them yourself."

"Please, Adele. I don't have a lot of time left. I need to spend it all with my daughter. I am praying the girls will understand."

"I have a better idea. Why don't you all come up here for a weekend? You can get everyone back together. You can introduce them to your daughter. You can tell them how much you love them face to face."

Suzanne sighed. "I don't know."

"Come on, darlin'. A reunion is long overdue. I vote for the first weekend in May."

"Blossom Festival." Suzanne smiled. "It does seem perfect, doesn't it?"

"So you take those cards home and rewrite them. Invite everyone back for the Blossom Fest."

As she spoke, her stomach fluttered with anticipation. Would Meghan return if her dying friend invited her?

"But I don't want Campbell to come."

"Why ever not?"

"I want to tell her about this place, but not everything. Some things would just hurt her. I won't let that happen."

"She's a grown woman now, Suzie-Q. Don't you think you oughtta let her decide what she does and doesn't want to know?"

Suzanne shook her head. "She's felt enough rejection over the years. Her father has his own life. My family—well, you know how that all turned out."

"But your history is her history." How could Suzanne deny her daughter the beauty of this little town? "Just think about it."

"If she gets a hold of the scrapbook, she will be at your front door within a day," Suzanne said.

"Fine by me. I'd love to meet her."

"Adele. It's a bad idea. Sweethaven is part of my past. Not part of Campbell's future."

"Sweethaven has a lot to offer, my dear. And I think that daughter of yours might benefit from a little bit of this town's magic. Don't you?"

Adele sent her home with a box of molasses crinkles and prayed she would make it to the first week of May. Now, she mourned the loss of her young friend and wondered why so many things in life seemed unfair.

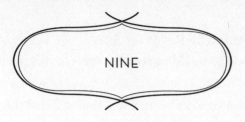

NINE

Jane

Jane gripped the steering wheel until her knuckles turned white. Five hours in the car with nothing to do but think.

Alex. She forced his face away every time it danced through her mind. She had to or she'd start crying.

Twice she'd called Graham to explain why she needed to come back home. Both times he'd talked her into getting back in the car and continuing on to Sweethaven.

"Are you worried I can't handle the kids?" he asked, his tone light.

"You know I'm not."

"Good, 'cause I've got it under control. The cottage is empty, hon. You could use the time to yourself."

Time alone seemed like the last thing she needed right now. This trip had already dredged up pain she'd long since buried— and she hadn't even reached the town limits yet.

She exited the interstate and turned left on Main. A wave of familiarity washed over her. She inhaled deeply and let out a slow breath. Maybe she should've packed a paper bag. Just in case. She wouldn't go down to the Boardwalk. Or even glance in the direction of the beach. Would that be enough to keep the pain at bay?

She picked up her cell and dialed home but hung up before it rang. She could do this. She needed to do this. Graham had offered to come with her. In an unexplainable moment of strength, she'd refused.

She regretted that now.

As she drove down Main Street, she noticed some of the changes they'd made over the years. Old-fashioned lampposts. New brickwork that matched the original. No wonder tourists flocked here for the seasonal festivals. The Reindog Parade each winter. The Venetian Festival over the Fourth of July. And the Blossom Festival always on the first weekend in May. This weekend.

She could almost smell the pink blooms on the crabapples that lined both sides of Main Street. The vineyards would be open, offering samples of their very best wines, and an old-fashioned carnival would be held all weekend down by the Boardwalk and the carousel. How appropriate for Suzanne to suggest this weekend for a reunion.

But then, cancer didn't care what season it was.

She turned on Elm toward Adele's cottage. Always warm and inviting, Adele Barber had been the glue that held them together on more than one occasion, the mediator in their silly arguments. Adele's freshly baked chocolate chip cookies seemed to cure all the world's ills. Suzanne's and Lila's mothers were busy with their luncheons and social functions, Jane's mom had younger children to tend to, but Adele had nothing but time to get into their business. Even after Luke was born. Meg pretended to hate it, but the rest of them wouldn't have had it any other way.

She pulled into the driveway and admired the potted plants that flanked Adele's front door. Clothes on a clothesline in the side yard waved in the wind.

She turned off the engine and said a quick prayer. As excited as she was at connecting with her old friends, it was another wretched day that haunted her. She prayed that, for now, she wouldn't have to face the old demons that lurked in the shadows.

She grabbed her purse and opened the car door. The sooner she could get this over with, the better.

As she stepped out of the car and slung her purse over her shoulder, a silver Mercedes pulled over and parked in front of Adele's house. Surely Adele didn't have a silver Mercedes. She tried not to stare, but quick glances didn't award her any knowledge, and there didn't seem to be any movement inside the car.

Seconds later, the door popped open and a blond woman with a thin frame appeared.

Lila. She wore oversized sunglasses, a crisp, white button-down, and a pair of black dress pants. As Lila stepped away from the car, Jane saw pointy heels peeking out from the bottom of her pant legs. Jane glanced down at her own tennis shoes and looked away.

Lila walked to the end of the driveway and removed her glasses. "Aren't you gonna say anything?"

Jane closed the car door and took a step toward her old friend, then took Lila's hand. Her mouth went dry as cotton and she struggled for words. "I can't believe it's you."

"You're gonna cry, aren't you?" Lila hugged her.

Jane pulled away and studied Lila's face. She looked almost exactly the same, only a bit older. Jane ran her hands through her hair—anything to make herself more presentable. "It's so good to see you here. How long has it been?"

"Too long. I haven't been back since Tom and I got married. How about you?"

Jane's face fell.

"I'm sorry, Janie. Forget I asked." Lila turned away.

"Do you think Suzanne and Meg are here yet?"

Jane's heart leapt. What if Meghan had already arrived? She glanced at the bay window at the front of the cottage. What if she sat inside peeking at them through barely parted curtains? "I suppose there's only one way to find out."

* * * * *

Campbell

"Whoever could that be?"

Campbell followed Adele's gaze up the hill, where she saw two women standing on Adele's front lawn. After a brief walk to the farmer's market with Adele's old dog Mugsy, Campbell still didn't have any answers. These two women could change all that.

"I'm not expecting anyone till tomorrow." Confusion laced Adele's tone.

"But you weren't expecting me either," Campbell said.

Adele reached an arm around her and squeezed. "But you're family now, so you're welcome any time."

The warmth of her voice, her touch, reminded Campbell of her mother. How nice to feel wanted again.

Would her father want her too? Maybe he didn't even know she existed. Had Mom even told him? If not, that would explain his absence from her life.

And make her feel a little less rejected.

Adele picked up the pace, practically dragging Mugsy in the direction of their house. The poor mutt whimpered at the strain.

"Come on, you old coot." Adele yanked the leash. "My girls are home."

"I'll take her, Adele, you go on ahead." Campbell might not be a dog person, but even she felt sorry for the poor animal.

"Thank you, hon." Adele bustled up the sidewalk, hurrying to meet her company.

The dog's panting slowed, and she settled into a nice trot at Campbell's side.

From a distance, Campbell couldn't make out the facial features of the short, plump woman Adele pulled into a warm embrace. She didn't actually know any of the girls well enough to determine who it was, but she gathered it wasn't Meghan because this woman's hair wasn't the fiery red of Adele's daughter. She guessed the other woman, tall, thin, and blond, was Lila Adler. That meant the first woman must be Jane.

Hope sprang in her chest. These women could lead her to her father.

Mugsy whimpered as they reached the driveway.

"Fine, Mugs, you can get off the leash, you big baby." Adele took the leash from Campbell. She unhooked it and sent Mugsy back to the garage. "Campbell, these are your mom's friends, Jane Atkins and Lila Olson."

Campbell studied Jane's face until she finally found the teenager behind the wide eyes and cropped dishwater hair. In every way, the woman epitomized a soccer mom.

Jane stepped closer, and Campbell saw the tears in her eyes. "Campbell! It's so nice to meet you after all this time. I had no idea you'd be joining your mom for this trip, but I'm so glad you're here."

Campbell's eyes stung as she swallowed hard, not knowing what to say. She turned to Lila, who pulled her into a stiff hug and patted her back. "It's so nice to meet you both."

"We are the lucky ones." Lila turned to Adele. "Where's Suzanne and Meghan? Are they both inside looking through old scrapbook pages or something?"

Campbell watched Adele. Her eyes filled with tears.

Lila's smile faded, her eyes darting between Campbell and Adele. "What's going on, you two?" She looked at Jane, whose face had gone stark white. She looked away.

Adele glanced at Campbell and then turned to the two women in front of her. "Girls," Adele said, "she's gone."

Jane shook her head. She pulled Campbell into a hug.

"I am so sorry, hon," she said.

"Just like that?" Lila asked. "We didn't even get to say good-bye?"

Awkwardness hung in the air. Finally Campbell said, "The funeral was Tuesday."

"But the letters..." Jane's took a step back.

"I found them on the counter at my mom's house. I think she was planning to send them last week—maybe even before that—but she took a turn and ended up in a coma." Campbell willed her voice to remain steady.

"I'm sorry. I'm so sorry." Jane still shook her head, her mouth agape.

"This is so unfair. We came here to say good-bye to her. We deserved that much." Lila wrapped her arms around her waist and stared at the ground.

Adele stepped forward. "I think Suzanne was hoping for a joyous reunion, and I think that's what we should give her. You're right. We didn't get to properly say good-bye, so we're going to have to have a memorial service of our own."

Jane nodded. "I think that's a great idea."

Adele and Jane exchanged a look and then Jane wrapped an arm around Campbell, rubbing her back like a mom does. "You look a lot like her."

"You think so?" Adele cocked her head. "I wasn't seeing it right away."

"I think it's the eyes. They smile and dance just like Suzanne's. Suzanne always had the best eyes. I was so jealous of her long, dark lashes. I got stuck with these short, blond things."

Lila straightened. "They make stuff to help with that, Jane. It's called mascara."

"It's good to know you haven't changed, Lila," Jane said.

A split second of tension hung in the air, and then Lila's face broadened into a smile. Jane covered her mouth with her hand and laughed.

Campbell smiled. "I'm really glad you both came."

"Come in, come in. Let's have some tea." Adele walked toward the house, Jane and Lila on either side and Campbell following close behind. "I'm makin' my world-famous pork chops tonight. Can you stay?"

Adele laced her arms through theirs, squeezed.

"I think so. I won't be in town for long, but I can stay for your pork chops." Jane turned around and looked at Campbell. "They're world-famous, ya know."

Campbell laughed. She liked her mom's friends already.

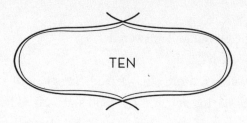

TEN

Campbell

Inside, Campbell listened as the conversation danced from Adele to Jane to Lila and back again. She waited for a lull and then pulled the old scrapbook pages out of her bag.

"Do you know anything about these?" She looked at her mom's friends.

Jane's eyes widened. "Oh my." She gingerly took the pages. Her eyes filled with tears. "The Circle." She carefully flipped through the pages.

"Do you have pages like this?"

Jane nodded, her attention still on the scrapbook. "I do."

"And you do too?" Campbell asked Lila.

"Somewhere. I think they're in my hope chest."

Jane glanced up from the pages and met Lila's eyes. "You don't know where they are?"

Lila shrugged. "I'm not very sentimental, what can I say?"

Jane held her gaze for a long moment and then returned to the pages in her hands.

"Do they tell more of the story?" Campbell asked. "More about The Circle, my mom…who my dad is?"

The surprised expression on Jane's face dashed Campbell's hopes in a nanosecond, but before she could respond, Campbell's phone buzzed in her purse.

Great timing.

She fished it out and answered.

"Campbell, it's Tilly."

Tilly Watkins, Mom's best friend. She glanced at the three pairs of eyes staring at her, then stood and walked into the next room, holding one finger up as if to say she'd be back in a minute.

"Hi, Tilly. What's up?"

"I was just calling to check on you mostly. I didn't get a chance to talk to you after the funeral."

Campbell felt guilty for leaving without so much as a word to Tilly—a woman who was like the aunt she always wanted and never had. In some ways, Tilly was the only family she had left.

"I'm good," she said. "I'm actually in Michigan."

"What are you doing there?"

"I found some of Mom's old stuff. I guess I just wanted to see where she grew up."

"She grew up in Chicago, hon." Tilly sounded confused.

"But she spent her summers here. In a little town called Sweethaven. I'm there now."

"That's right. She did mention it a few times."

"She did?" Jealousy twisted in her gut. Mom had told Tilly about this place but not her?

"Just in passing. Mentioned a charming little beach town where she spent some of her summers. What do you think of it?"

"It's like she said. Charming."

"Hon, I know it's the last thing on your mind, but I wanted to ask you if you'd given any thought to the house and the will?"

Campbell frowned. "What will?"

Why would Mom have a will? She didn't have anything worth leaving to anyone—and she didn't really have anyone to leave anything to, except for Campbell.

"Yes. You should probably call her lawyer when you get a chance. They may need you back tomorrow for the reading."

"Thanks. I'll call him. I guess if he thinks it's urgent that I come back, I'll cut my trip short."

"I'm sure we can work something out. You take care of yourself, Cam."

"I will."

Campbell returned to the kitchen and felt like she'd just walked into a cloud of awkward. The phone call couldn't have come at a worse time—she'd posed the question about her father and then walked out of the room. Judging by the looks on their faces, they'd been discussing it—and the pit in Campbell's stomach told her their answer wasn't a good one.

She returned to her seat.

"Sweetie," Jane said. Adele handed her a tissue. She dabbed at her eyes and then wadded it in her hands, tore pieces from it, and stacked them in a pile.

"You don't know, do you?" Campbell stared at her folded hands.

"None of us do. Your mom never told us. It was part of why we all stopped talking, I think." Jane frowned. "I was so hurt that she didn't tell me." Her eyes glassed over. "Sometimes I wonder if I hadn't been so jealous of her secrets, would I have made a point to stay in touch? Would she have?"

"Jane, stop beating yourself up," Lila said. "People grow up. They go their separate ways."

Jane looked at her, and Campbell could see by the expression on her face that their lack of communication had been due to more than the typical "drifting away" that happens as you age.

"Can I look through your pages? Would you mind?" Campbell

had to at least look at them. Her curiosity would never leave her alone if she didn't.

"Sure you can. Mine are buried in my luggage. I brought them with me. How silly is that?" Jane laughed. "When I got your mom's letter, I had to get them out again. How about if I bring them tonight to dinner?" She smiled. Sniffed. Wiped her eyes again.

Campbell nodded. "Sounds good."

"I'll see if I can find mine. Mama probably threw them away. You know she has no tolerance for anything sentimental," Lila said.

"I appreciate that," Campbell said. She forced a smile, but sadness had settled in her heart. If none of them knew—why stay? Sweethaven had nothing to offer a girl looking for the father she felt she'd never have.

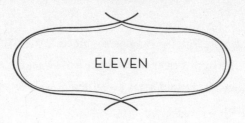

ELEVEN

Adele

While Adele prepared the pork chops, she kept her ear tuned to the conversation going on between her young guests.

Campbell—on a hunt to find her father. Jane—to make peace with the past. Lila—still carrying the pressure of being an Adler.

Would any of them find what they were looking for?

Sweethaven held the answers for all of them, though she wondered if they'd be too stubborn to see it. Still, she couldn't ignore the fact that in spite of her excitement over having the girls in her house, a sense of dread had been following her around ever since she found out about Suzanne's death the day before.

Adele knew Suzanne's letter could potentially draw Meghan home. She hated to see this reunion tainted with her own insecurities. She reminded herself Meghan most likely wouldn't make it back anyway. Why was she worried?

But knowing the possibility existed planted a balled-up knot low in her stomach.

"I think I'm going to go lay down for a while." Campbell pushed her chair away from the table and stood.

Adele turned and saw the sorrow in the girl's eyes. When Jane and Lila admitted they didn't know her father's identity, they'd shattered Campbell's very reason for being in Sweethaven. Adele saw that plain as day.

"All right, hon. Take as long as you need." Adele watched her go.

Jane ran her hands over the wet glass of sweet tea in front of her. "Did you know McDonald's has sweet tea now?"

Lila gasped.

"Don't get me started on McDonald's sweet tea. Some things you can't franchise and good sweet tea is one of 'em." Adele laughed.

"You tell her, Adele," Lila said.

"You girls want some scones? I just made 'em fresh this morning." Adele set a saucer in front of each of them. The smell of the blueberry scones wafted to her nostrils. She hoped her girls would feel as comforted by them as she always was.

"What about you, Adele? You have to eat with us." Jane's smile looked forced.

"Don't you worry about me. I plan on joining you." Adele laughed.

Lila took a bite and closed her eyes. "These are incredible. You should open a restaurant."

"Or a coffee shop." Jane took a sip. "I bet Sweethaven would love it."

"I have my antiques to keep me busy."

"What antiques?" Jane covered her mouth with her hand as she chewed.

"Why, *I* am a business owner, girls. I have a little antique shop out on the edge of town."

"Adele, that's wonderful. You were always so great at finding the real gems in those junk places." Lila scrunched her nose.

"I beg your pardon? Junk is about as handy as a back pocket on a shirt. My shop is full of honest-to-goodness treasures."

"I'll take your word for it."

Silence hung in the air, and Adele felt her smile fade.

"How've you girls been?"

Jane smiled, but she didn't fool Adele. "Good. Real good. We're all doing really well now."

"I'm glad to hear it." She sat across from Jane. "If it's the truth."

Jane's eyes welled with fresh tears. So many tears the woman had cried through the years.

"Sad about Suzanne." A trail of moisture dashed down her cheek. Adele set the tissue box in front of Jane.

"It's unfair that she didn't get to say good-bye." Jane pulled a tissue from the box. "Why didn't she send the letters *before* she was gone?"

"I think that's what she was tryin' to do, hon. Campbell found a trunk with all the Sweethaven stuff in it. Paintings she'd done, the scrapbook, photographs. I think she was planning to tell her daughter everything about this place—maybe even the name of her daddy."

"You can't hardly call him a daddy," Lila said. "He sure didn't do right by Suzanne."

"If he even knew." Jane patted her cheeks dry.

Lila frowned. "You think she never told him?"

"She didn't tell you girls, right?" Adele said. "Maybe she was too embarrassed to tell him too."

Jane shook her head. "I wish she'd have trusted me with her secret. That girl deserves to know who her father is."

"That she does. Poor Suzanne. I don't think she ever stopped feeling ashamed."

Jane nodded. "I would've loved to see her one more time."

"I had so much to say to her," Lila said. "Starting with 'How could you leave us like that?' and ending with 'I still love you.'"

"I know, darlin'." Adele sighed. "What are we gonna do about this scrapbook?"

Jane met Adele's eyes. "I'd love to see it all together again. It's been so long."

"It's pretty important, isn't it?"

"It's everything." Jane played with her tissue, rolled it between her hands.

"But you know it's not going to give Campbell any clue about her daddy," Lila said. "We all tried to find some hint when Suzanne left."

Jane glanced at Lila. "You remember how shocked we all were. Suzanne didn't even have a boyfriend. It was so unlike her. If it had been in the scrapbook, we'd have found it. One of us would've."

"You girls must have your suspicions." Adele leaned back in her chair.

Jane quieted. "Do you think he could've been someone we knew?"

Adele shrugged. "You'd know better than me, hon. I've wracked my brain tryin' to figure it out. Wondered if maybe it was someone older—married even?"

Jane's face twisted. "You think?" Her eyes glossed over as if she'd just gotten an idea.

"What is it?"

"Suzanne took an art class at the community college that summer. It could've been someone in the class. Or even the professor."

"Jane, do you really think Suzanne would've gone for an old guy?" Lila scrunched her face.

"Why else would it have been such a big secret? And as far as we know, the relationship ended because Campbell never met him."

"And it must've been pretty painful for Suzanne if she didn't talk about him at all." Adele watched the two girls. "Maybe we should come up with a list."

"It'd be a pretty short list, Adele," Lila said. "Someone in her class at the community college. That's about it."

"Or the professor," Jane said.

"Or anyone she might've met while she was there." Lila sighed.

"Was there anyone here you girls hung around with that summer?"

Jane shrugged. "The same boys we'd been hanging around with since we were twelve, but we would've known if Suzanne had something going with one of them. We saw them every day."

"And nothing ever seemed strange or awkward?" Adele leaned forward.

Lila shrugged. "Not that I noticed. It had to be a guy we didn't know."

"We should start with the community college idea. That's Campbell's first lead." Jane sat up in her chair. "At least it's something, right?"

"It's something, but I don't know how helpful it'll be," Lila said.

Jane sighed. "Try to think positive, would you? Maybe back then we just gave up too quickly. We should tell her. And then do some digging to see if we can come up with any other ideas."

Adele folded her hands on the table. "I agree. If she doesn't have a lead to follow, that girl's going to go straight back to Chicago—and something tells me more than anything right now, she needs to be here."

Adele had a feeling all of Campbell's answers were right there in Sweethaven.

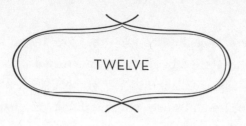

TWELVE

Campbell

Campbell spent an hour in her room thinking about Jane and Lila and missing Mom even more than before. It all came back how unfair it was. Why had God taken her mom before they had a chance to say good-bye?

Why? Why? Why?

The smell of pork chops—the world-famous kind—wafted up the stairs and into the room. Her stomach growled and she realized she hadn't eaten a real meal in a couple of days.

Was it only two days ago they'd buried Mom? She'd left in such a rush, but it felt like days had already passed. If she stopped and thought about it, she knew she'd break down.

She heard a knock on the front door and then a man's voice filled the entryway. Luke. Her stomach flip-flopped, and she ordered it to behave. She wasn't here to start a fling with a local boy. Just to find her father.

Romance would only complicate matters.

Still, she double- then triple-checked herself in the mirror and applied a fresh coat of lipstick. Exhaustion showed on her face. She looked closer at the whites of her eyes.

Bloodshot like the eyes of a person who hadn't slept in days. Fitting.

The garlic-tinged smell of the home-cooked meal led her to the kitchen where Adele bustled from the stove to the sink and back again. Luke sat at the table, his long legs crossed at the ankles.

"Can I help with anything?" Campbell took a step into the room and focused on Adele, but that didn't keep her from feeling the weight of Luke's stare.

"Oh, darlin'. What kind of hostess would I be if I allowed my guest to work in the kitchen? Sit down. Would you like some lemonade?"

"I'm fine, thanks."

"This is my son, Luke—"

"We've already met, Ma," Luke said, interrupting.

"Oh?"

"Earlier today." Luke pulled his feet out of the middle of the kitchen and pushed the chair next to him away from the table. "Hey," he said.

She smiled a hello and sat down.

"Well, okay. Good, you're already acquainted, I suppose." She directed the comment at Luke, then turned to her. "You really should have some lemonade. It's just the right balance of sweet and tart. Taken me years to get it right."

"I will in a little while," Campbell said.

Luke still stared, unnerving her.

"You changed," he finally said. "No more scarf." His grin hung sideways.

She shrugged. "More comfortable this way." She smoothed her hands over her jean capris and loose floral blouse. Did he think she'd changed because of his comment? Why did that matter to her?

The front door popped open.

"Hello? I'm back." Jane's voice rang out before they saw her. When she appeared, an oversized bag hung on her arm. "I brought the pages. " She glanced at Luke. "Oh my goodness." She held a hand to her mouth. "Look at you." A giggle escaped.

He stood, towering over her.

Her eyes followed him upward, and she shook her head. "I can't believe how grown up you are. What are you now—twenty-five?"

"Twenty-seven."

"Twenty-seven. Unbelievable. I haven't seen you in…gosh, years. Since your high school graduation. You went off to that fancy college and never came home for the summer anymore."

He pulled her into a hug as she wiped tears from her cheeks. Jane and her tears. Was it just the reunion or did she cry all the time?

"Would you like some lemonade?" he asked as Jane sat next to Campbell.

"Sure, thanks. Campbell, this boy was born when we were all fifteen. He was the cutest thing. I think we even babysat you a time or two. Suzanne and I." She laughed. "I think I rocked you to sleep."

"Now you're just embarrassing me." Luke set the glass down in front of Jane. "You ready for some now, Cam?"

His familiarity caught her off guard. Mom always called her Cam. Or Camby. Lots of people shortened names, she told herself. It didn't mean anything.

She nodded.

The door opened again and Lila's voice rang out. "I'm here." Her sing-songy Southern tone carried into the kitchen. She appeared in the doorway and, like Jane, gasped when she saw Luke.

"Isn't he gorgeous?" Jane giggled again.

"I can't believe how grown up you are. Like, a real man."

Luke's face flushed pink, and he shook his head. "Maybe I need to get my dinner to go—this looks like the kind of party I don't want to crash."

"Don't be silly," Lila said. "You're family. Don't let us chase you off. I'm sure you're used to being surrounded by beautiful women." She laughed.

"Oh, not this one. Hasn't found anyone who meets his criteria," Adele said. "Or should I say, 'his requirements.'"

He glanced at Campbell, but she quickly looked away.

"Oh? What criteria is that, Lukey?" Jane smiled and sipped her lemonade.

"Lukey?" He chuckled. "No one has called me that since I was five, *Mrs. Atkins*."

"Now that's just mean." Jane laughed, her plump face lighting up at the playful banter.

"I'm just not anxious to rush into something just for the sake of having someone in my life," Luke explained.

"You really *are* a grown-up," Lila said. The large diamond on her finger caught the light from the window behind Campbell.

"I've tried to set him up with three or four different girls. Adorable girls." Adele stirred something on the stove.

"Vapid girls, Ma." Luke rolled his eyes. "The first criteria is that she has to have a brain."

They all laughed, but as Luke's smile faded, Campbell noticed his eyes danced in her direction. She reminded herself to keep her head on straight.

A phone rang.

They all stared at her until Campbell finally remembered she'd turned her ringer on.

"That's me. Sorry." She stood.

"Boyfriend?" Lila's eyebrows shot upward and Jane let out an "*Oooh*."

She escaped Luke's watchful eyes and stepped into the hallway. The caller ID said TILLY, and Campbell almost didn't answer. "Hello?"

"Hi, hon. I'm sorry to bug you again. Just wanted to make sure you got the text I sent."

"I got it. I haven't called the lawyer yet, but I will."

"Well, don't bother. I just got off the phone with him. He asked if I could get you to his office tomorrow. I guess he's got a big European vacation planned and they leave day after tomorrow."

"Oh."

"You sound disappointed."

"No, it's fine. I can make that work, I guess."

Tilly paused. "Cam, can I ask what it is you're doing up there? I've been thinking about you all day."

She sounded suspicious. And worried. Did she know something? Had Mom confided in her when she hadn't trusted her oldest friends? It was possible. Tilly had become more like family to them over the years.

"I had a few more days off. I figured I'd use them."

"That's it?"

Campbell sighed. "I'm hoping to find some answers, I guess."

Another long pause. "Answers to what?"

Campbell knew Tilly meant well, but she didn't want to burden her by making her feel like she had to be a surrogate mother in her mom's place. She could take care of herself, after all.

But if Tilly knew something…

"I found a trunk," Campbell said. "There're about a dozen paintings of this place, Sweethaven. Plus, photos of my mom as a kid and scrapbook pages she made back then. I thought," she paused, "I might find out who my dad is."

Now Tilly sighed.

"What's wrong with that, Tilly?" Campbell asked. "I have a right to know, don't I?"

"You know your mom would've told you if she wanted you to know. Didn't you guys talk about this when she was alive?"

"She said we were better off on our own."

"She had reasons for that."

"And I accepted those reasons, but now that she's gone, I guess, I feel more alone than I thought I would. I just want to know where I came from." Campbell tried to maintain her composure, aware that the others weren't too far out of earshot.

"Hon, I just don't want you to get hurt. Going off on a wild goose chase, trying to find a father and unearth all of your mom's secrets— it's just not a good idea."

Campbell heard the concern in Tilly's voice. Should she try to reason with her? To explain Mom *had* planned to tell her everything— she just ran out of time?

"Tilly, she didn't tell you, did she?"

"No, Campbell. And I never asked." She paused. "Call the lawyer, okay? Then get home where you belong."

She hung up, Tilly's last words ringing in her ears. Home. Where she belonged.

But without Mom, it didn't feel like either of those things anymore.

Was she crazy to hunt for a father she'd never known? A man who had quite possibly never wanted her? Was the search a bad idea?

But Jane and Lila wouldn't be in Sweethaven forever. This was her one chance to find out what she could, to hopefully find her father.

"Dinner, hon."

Campbell hadn't seen Adele pop her head around the corner. She startled at the sound of her voice.

"You okay?"

Campbell nodded.

"We're going to eat outside on the patio. You mind helping me carry a few things?"

"Not at all." She followed Adele into the kitchen, thankful for the distraction.

"I sent them all outside because they were eavesdroppin' on your conversation." She laughed, but when she saw Campbell's expression, she quieted. "Everything okay?"

"It's fine," she said, forcing a smile. "It smells wonderful."

"Thank you, darlin'." Adele handed Campbell a bowl of fresh fruit. "I'll follow you out with the rest."

Greenery and potted plants surrounded a long rectangular table on a flagstone patio out back. Mugsy perked up when Campbell popped the door open but quickly lay back down, disinterested. Luke sat on one side of the table, Jane and Lila on the other. Only two places remained. One next to Luke and one at the head of the table.

And she couldn't sit at the head of the table.

She set the bowl beside a platter of pork chops and potatoes. Two different cobblers rounded out the meal. Luke pulled the chair away from the table so she could sit.

"What a gentleman," Lila said, eyes on Luke. "Your mama taught you right."

"She sure did." Adele walked out of the house, another platter in her arms. She set it down and took her seat at the end of the table.

"She's gonna cry," Luke said.

She swatted his arm. "I am not." Her voice caught as she spoke the words. "All right, maybe I am, but I'm entitled to a few tears having these girls at my table." She turned to Luke. "You're just lucky we let you stay." She laughed as she stretched her hands toward Luke and Lila, sitting on either side of her. "Can we bless the food?"

Luke took his mom's hand and then held an upturned hand in

Campbell's direction. She looked at it and then quietly slid her own hand in his. His long fingers wrapped around her hand, warming her from the inside out. She tried to focus on Adele's prayer rather than the way Luke's touch sent her insides whirling. No sense being sacrilegious on top of everything else.

"Lord, I thank You for these children who've all come back home," Adele said.

Campbell bowed her head and stared at her empty plate. Luke's thumb ran over the top of her hand, breaking her concentration.

"I am so blessed to see them again, and my prayer is that they all find what it is they're looking for here in Sweethaven. Bless this food and help us to always be thankful to the One who provided it for us. In Your name we ask it. Amen."

The others echoed with their own "Amen," and Jane let go of Campbell's right hand. Luke squeezed twice before releasing her left hand. She glanced at him, keenly aware of the absence of his touch.

He radiated confidence. How did he do that?

They passed the dishes around the table. Silverware clanked and clanged as plates were piled with food, food that, judging by the smell and appearance, promised to be delicious.

"Who was on the phone?" Luke's question broke the silence with all the grace of an oversized ox.

Campbell cleared her throat and noticed the others stared in her direction.

"Lukey, leave the girl alone. She can talk to her boyfriend in private if she wants to." Lila winked at her.

She shook her head and sipped her lemonade. "It wasn't a boyfriend," she said. "It was a friend of my mom's. Same one who called earlier."

Luke sat up straighter. Did she imagine his relief?

"I may have to go back tomorrow is all."

Adele frowned. "I don't think that's a good idea, hon," she said. "You'll never find what you're looking for if you leave before you give yourself a chance."

Campbell's heart jumped. What was she saying? Did she know something?

"Adele's right," Jane said between bites. "If you leave, we won't get to tell you about the scrapbook. Did you bring your pages, Lila?"

Lila nodded. "I thought Mama had thrown them away, but I found them."

"Remember when Suzanne came over here with her nutso idea to start a scrapbook?" Jane laughed. "We all thought she was crazy."

"She *was* crazy. She knew none of us were artsy like she was. And scrapbooking wasn't exactly cool back then. I mean, who wants to sit in the house and scrapbook when we could be at the beach watching the boys pretend not to stare at us?" Lila's smile faded at the memory.

"But your mom had a way about her," Jane said, her expression wistful, as though she were remembering something. "Remember what she said, Lila?"

"She said, 'You guys will thank me for it later. When we're all old ladies and we come here with our grandkids you'll take out this scrapbook and tell them stories of Sweethaven way back when and then you will thank me.'" Lila sipped her tea. "Then she carried that book around with her all summer. Every summer."

"She was right. If she were here today, I would thank her," Jane said. "Those silly scrapbooking parties became the highlight of our summers."

"Speak for yourself," Lila said. "I can think of a few other high-lights, like the summer I won the Harbor City Pageant. The summer I got engaged."

"All in the scrapbook," Jane said. "I still scrapbook now for my kids."

"You do?" Lila said, eyebrows raised.

Jane nodded. "They aren't artsy like Suzanne's, but they're mine. And the kids love them. Seriously, Sam used to sit in his diaper on the landing of the stairs and flip through it, page after page of 'baby!' 'baby!'" Jane stopped. "I never would've done those books if it weren't for Suzanne."

"It's so nice hearing you talk about her." Campbell set her glass on the table. "It's almost like she's still here."

"Those scrapbook parties were something else," Adele said. "I knew I needed to stock the fridge and prepare for a sleepless weekend."

"Admit it, Mama, you loved having us here." Lila winked at Adele.

"That I did, sweetheart. I had to or I'd lose my 'coolest mom' title."

"There's really nothing in the book about my father?"

Jane and Lila exchanged a glance.

"Hon, the scrapbook isn't going to help you find your father," Lila said. "Your mom didn't put that in the book. We're pretty sure about that."

Campbell felt Luke glance at her, but she kept her eyes on the women across the table.

Suddenly she wished she hadn't said anything. They could know she wondered about her father's identity, but that was all. They didn't need to know the hours she'd spent daydreaming about meeting him.

"You must have a list of people you all hung around with. Maybe it's someone you all knew but didn't realize she loved?"

Lila laughed. "I hate to burst your romance bubble, but your mom wasn't in love with the guy—whoever he was."

Campbell frowned. "How do you know? I mean, if you don't even know who he is?"

She shrugged. "If it was love, she would've told us."

Jane swallowed and stared at her plate.

Campbell studied them both.

"Maybe Campbell's right, girls," Adele said. "Maybe you've missed something. Hon, we were talking earlier about an art class your mama took at the community college. Could've been someone from there? We'll put the pages together and see what we find."

Campbell's confidence had gone. Not only had her mother left her father's identity out of the book, but she'd been embarrassed about it. Not even in love with the guy.

A dead end.

Tilly's words rushed back. *Get home. Where you belong.*

Suddenly she didn't know if she wanted answers to her questions. Suddenly ignorance felt safer.

THIRTEEN

Campbell

After dinner, in the darkness of the cool May evening, Campbell sat on an outdoor loveseat, Mugsy quietly snoring at her feet. Jane and Lila still sat at the table, talking quietly about the old days, while Luke helped Adele clear the table. When he emerged from the house empty-handed, he spotted Campbell and walked toward her.

He crossed his arms over his chest and stared at her.

"What?" She glanced up at him.

"Wanna go for a walk?" His lopsided grin lured her in, and against her better judgment she stood.

"Should we bring Mugsy?" Campbell glanced at the mutt lazing at her feet.

"Nah, this dog is older than the hills." He led her out of the back yard and down the driveway.

Campbell laughed, falling into step beside him. "Your mom said that too. I like her. I think she's sweet."

"She is. Balances out Mom's saltiness." He smirked.

"Your mom is plenty sweet." Campbell tossed a glance back toward the house. "I wish I could stay."

"You're leaving then?"

She looked away. "Not much point hanging around. You heard them—the scrapbook doesn't have the answers I'm looking for."

"For what it's worth, I think you should at least try. Stay a few days. Blossom Fest—"

"I know." She smiled. "I hear it's a lot of fun."

"It's okay. You know, if you like tours of the orchard in bloom, a lit Ferris wheel on the beach at night, the parade and old movies in the park." He stared straight ahead. "Aren't you a photographer? Think of the pictures you could get."

"Had to throw that in there, didn't you?" Campbell glanced at him, falling into step at his side. "You sound like a tourist brochure."

He shrugged. "Whatever it takes to get you to stay. Besides, you still haven't seen all that Sweethaven has to offer. I could take you on a tour. You can bring your camera."

She hated to admit it sounded like the perfect way to spend a day. No deadlines. Nowhere to be. What kind of creativity would emerge without the pressure of an assignment?

But what about Mom's will? Tilly said they needed her tomorrow. And in a few days she had to be back for work. It would be best to take care of Mom's will, the house—everything—before then.

"Could you show me something now?" She tossed a look in his direction.

"Name it."

"I want to see where my mom grew up. I'm curious about the people who bought the cottage after my grandparents died." She glanced back the way they'd just come. Perhaps they'd passed the old house and she didn't realize it.

Luke cleared his throat. "Maybe we should do that when it's light out. You won't be able to see much now."

"No, this way I can sneak on by and no one will notice I'm there." She bumped into his shoulder. "Please?"

He slowed his pace and studied her eyes. "You sure you want to see it?"

She frowned. "Why wouldn't I?"

They stood at the corner of Elm and Juniper Drive. He glanced up at the street sign. "It's down this street." Luke turned the corner.

Even in the dim light of the streetlamp, Campbell saw his hesitation.

"What's wrong? Is it haunted or something?" She jogged to catch up to him.

"No, of course not. It's fine. I'll show you quick and then we'll head back."

Campbell walked up the slight hill of Juniper Drive until they reached the next block. Luke stopped before they crossed and pointed at a bungalow across the street directly in front of them. "It's that one."

She recognized it from the picture. Her mom had grown up there. So much of her life had taken place only feet from where she now stood, and Campbell didn't know any of those stories. She could almost see the four girls sitting on the deep porch well into the warm summer nights.

"Do you know who lives there now?" she asked. She wondered if Mom had carved her name into a wooden post in the basement or if her handprints were pressed in cement on the back patio.

Luke took a deep breath, but before he could respond the porch light came on.

Campbell gasped. "Oh my gosh. They're home."

"Maybe we should go," Luke said.

Campbell started across the street. What could the new owners tell her about the cottage's previous owners? Had anything been left behind, and if so, what had they done with those things?

There were secrets in that house, and Campbell had to at least try to uncover them.

From behind, Luke called to her, but she didn't hear what he said. Instead, she focused on the door opening in front of her. Excitement bubbled in her chest as she anticipated the potential answers.

But as she neared the walkway leading to the front door, her breath caught in her throat as a figure appeared in the faint light on the porch. A figure she recognized.

The name CARTER jumped out at her from the mailbox, and Campbell began to piece it together.

It was the man from her mom's funeral.

He met her gaze and stood, unmoving, at the top of the stairs. They stared at each other.

"Campbell." Luke's voice broke through her cloud of confusion as she tried to process what she was seeing.

"Is that...?" The words halted in midair. She couldn't say it out loud. Because if what she suspected was true, then her mother had done more than hide her past. She'd lied about it.

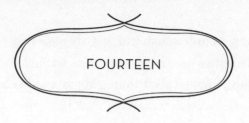

FOURTEEN

Campbell

Campbell's heart pounded in her chest, and she struggled for a deep breath. Luke grabbed her hand.

"Evening, Reverend Carter," he said.

The old man looked at them, his brow furrowed, his mouth agape. *This can't be happening.* This was her grandfather.

"Do you want to say anything?" Luke whispered, his face turned away from the man.

Did she want to say anything? Her head spun. She didn't know. What would she say? Would she start with "Why didn't you find me?" or maybe "Didn't you ever wonder what happened to your daughter?"

Heat rushed to her cheeks as she shook her head, unable to make sense of her thoughts. "I can't believe this," she whispered.

The old man took a step toward her, and in an instant she knew she did not want to talk to him. And she didn't want him to talk to her. Who did he think he was showing up at Mom's funeral? Why hadn't he found them? Why hadn't he come to them? What else hadn't her mother told her?

As he took another step, Campbell backed into Luke, who steadied her, his warm eyes watching. "You should've told me," she said.

His eyes widened, but she didn't give him a chance to respond. Instead, she pushed past him and ran back down the hill.

The sound of her feet pounding on the pavement invaded her

own mind. Her heart raced and she struggled for air, certain she'd never breathe normally again. She wished she could run forever—away from this place that held too many secrets and too much hurt.

* * * * *

Campbell returned to Adele's house, intending to gather her things and get back to the city where she belonged. Instead, she was met in the entryway by Adele, Lila, and Jane.

"I'm just here for my things. I've got to get back to the city. There's a will and…" Her voice faded as if the trail to her sanity had just gone cold.

"Darlin', what's wrong? You're white as a sheet." Adele stepped closer.

"Nothing. I just need to get home. They need me back home." Campbell looked away.

"You found everything you were looking for then?" Adele stood in front of the stairs, blocking Campbell's way.

"Well, no."

"Mmm-hmmm. Didn't think so. You sure you want to go leavin' already?" Behind Adele, Jane and Lila watched, their faces filled with pity and pleading.

"I'm not sure I want answers anymore." Campbell looked away.

Adele's eyes narrowed as if she were trying to figure out where her change of heart had come from. "You might find out a few things you hadn't bargained for, darlin'. You need to make up your mind now if you can handle that." She watched for Campbell's reaction, but Campbell schooled her expression to remain blank.

"Finding out my mother's father lives around the corner—I

hadn't bargained for that." Her bottom lip quivered, and she willed herself not to cry. Adele put an arm around her and led her into the living room.

"You didn't know about him?" Lila asked.

Campbell shook her head. "Mom said her parents died. In the crash right after I was born."

"Adele, did you know that?" Jane sat down on the sofa.

Adele sighed. "I did. Honey, your grandpa is a friend of mine. I didn't want to say anything because, well, y'all just got here and I thought we'd talk about it all tonight."

At that moment, Luke burst through the door, wild-eyed. His eyes met Campbell's, and he stared at her for a long moment—almost as if he were asking for forgiveness.

And she knew he hadn't done anything wrong. Not really.

"So you knew too," Campbell said to Luke. "That my grandfather lived in town."

His face fell, and he avoided her eyes. "I'm sorry, Cam. I tried to talk you out of it. I thought we'd hurry by. I didn't know he'd be coming out of the house." He met her eyes. "I'm really sorry."

She held his gaze for a long moment and finally looked away. It didn't make sense to blame him. It wasn't his fault her mom had lied to her. But then, blaming the dead wouldn't get her anywhere either.

She glanced at the clock. Nine thirty. She could still make it back to Chicago tonight if she left now. She could go to the reading and then spend the weekend getting the house ready to sell. The whole idea held no appeal for her, but she'd already found more information in Sweethaven than she'd bargained for. Campbell hated knowing that her mom had lied to her. It made her wonder if they'd really been as close as she thought they were—and that threatened to change her memories. Thinking about it scared her.

Maybe Tilly was right. Maybe coming here in this ridiculous hunt for a father was a huge mistake.

She had to face the reality that these women didn't know who her father was—and that alone was reason to go.

Her mind spun with images of the lanky man from the funeral. The pain she saw in his eyes that day was still there—she saw it when he looked at her that night.

And suddenly Campbell didn't feel like fighting for the truth anymore.

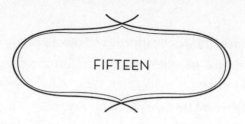

FIFTEEN

Campbell

Campbell gathered from the dresser the few toiletries she'd unpacked and stuffed them in her bag. The quiet of the guest room didn't offer any comfort. If anything, it wrapped itself around her like a straitjacket, taunted, tormented. Just like that, she was seven years old again, watching Alison Temberly walk past her house to the park, hand-in-hand with her tall, handsome father. In a second, the rejection had weaseled its way back in without her permission.

She'd come for answers and had gotten nothing but more questions. Her grandparents were alive and yet her mother never allowed her to meet them? Why? Was she really that selfish? Were they really that vicious? She was tired of thinking her mother must've had her reasons. Of course she did, but that didn't make them good ones.

That didn't keep her from hurting.

Campbell startled at a gentle knock on the door. She blotted under her eyes with the sleeve of her shirt and busied herself with packing. Or at least pretending to pack.

"Come in," she said.

Jane appeared on the other side of the door. "I came to check on you."

Campbell looked away.

"May I sit?" Jane motioned to the armchair in the corner.

Campbell nodded.

"Your mom and I were really close." Jane studied her feet. "I wish I could've said that more recently, but unfortunately, we fell out of touch."

"I'm sure it wasn't anyone's fault."

Jane's smile was almost patronizing, as if to tell her she didn't really understand. "I think Lila and Meghan assumed I knew she'd gotten pregnant, you know, before she told us. Before she sent that scrapbook page. But I didn't. I was so hurt that she didn't tell me, I think I missed her cry for help."

Campbell frowned. "What do you mean?"

"She came to me. When you were a baby. It was a Friday night and I had plans to go to the football game at my school. I remember because I was supposed to meet Graham there. Our first date." She smiled. "I was so excited." Jane closed her eyes, as if going to a different place.

Jane had been so nervous to see Graham Atkins. She'd spent over an hour in front of the mirror that night, then emerged from the house and prayed her old white Citation would start. She could not miss that game.

A voice cut her trek to the car short.

"Janie?"

The stark light of the street lamp out front cast a dark shadow on a girl standing next to an old green car. Jane squinted, trying—but failing—to place the vehicle.

"It's Suzanne."

"Suzanne?" Jane headed toward her and pulled her into a tight hug. "Where've you been? I tried calling."

Suzanne clung to her for a long moment until finally Jane pulled back and looked at her. "Are you okay?"

Suzanne nodded and wiped a stray tear from her cheek. "I had a baby." She smiled and cried at the same time.

"I know. Was it a girl or a boy?"

"A girl." Suzanne looked at the car. "Her name's Campbell."

"Aw, Suzanne, that's so pretty." Jane looked in the back window and spotted the sleeping baby that barely filled the car seat. Such a sweet baby with that one little tuft of hair on her otherwise bald head. "She's beautiful."

"Her middle name is Jane." Suzanne looked at her.

"It is?" Jane swelled with pride. Suzanne had named the baby after *her*?

"She's four and a half months already." Suzanne smiled at her daughter.

"How are you, Suzie?" Jane read the worn-out expression on her friend's face.

"I'm okay. I was thinking about you when I was driving so I thought I'd stop. I had your address in my book.

"I'm heading to a football game. Do you want to come?"

Suzanne looked away. "I doubt they'd appreciate a baby at a football game." She laughed. "Besides, it might be a little loud for her."

An awkward silence fell between them. Jane searched for words. She'd never struggled to find them with Suzanne before.

"How long can you stay?" Jane finally asked.

"Not long. I just wanted to say hi and introduce you to my baby."

"She's really beautiful, Suzanne. Do you want to come in? I can skip the game." Jane tried to sound sincere, but Graham's handsome smile skittered through her mind. The thought of missing their date turned her stomach, but he would understand, right?

Would Suzanne pick up on her eagerness to leave?

"No, no. I can't stay." Suzanne ran her hand through her long brown hair and for a moment looked a little lost.

"Are you sure?" She felt relief, then guilt when Suzanne turned her down. "I really can skip it. It's just—there's this boy." Jane smiled.

"I knew you'd probably have plans. You'll have to call and tell me all about him. I'm just glad I caught you."

"Suzanne, wait." Jane ran over to her car and fished through the mess in the backseat. She located the scrapbook, then walked back toward her friend.

"You should have this," Jane said.

Suzanne took the book from her, wrapped her thin fingers around the edges. "Oh, Jane, I couldn't. I don't think I'll be going back to Sweethaven. But the scrapbook should still go."

"No. It was your idea. It's your book. We all agreed. We did our pages from this past summer, but we left a couple of blank ones. For you to scrapbook your summer. The baby and everything." Jane smiled, but Suzanne looked troubled.

"I missed this," she said. Tears filled her eyes.

Jane studied her friend. "What's going on, Suzanne? What's wrong?" Jane laid a hand on Suzanne's arm.

"Nothing." She closed the book and hugged it to her chest. "I will treasure this always." She pulled Jane into a tight hug. "Will you tell Lila and Meg I love them?"

"What do you mean? We can all get together. Maybe we can come see you or something. You really don't think you'll ever come back to Sweethaven? It's not the same without you."

Suzanne paused, then looked away. "Things are kind of a mess right now."

Jane glanced at the sleeping baby in Suzanne's back seat. "Can I do anything?"

Suzanne shook her head. "I'm fine. Just gotta figure some things out."

A helpless feeling washed over Jane like a splash of ice water.

"I should let you get to your game." Suzanne opened the car door.

"Can I ask you one more thing?"

Suzanne turned and looked at Jane. "Anything."

Jane set her jaw and then blurted out, "Who's the dad?"

Suzanne studied the road with an odd intensity. "It's kind of complicated, Janie."

Suzanne's refusal hit her like a punch in the gut. "Okay." She considered guessing—throwing names out there and judging Suzanne's reactions—but decided against it. If Suzanne wanted to tell her, she would. No sense pushing the issue and making herself feel more like a fool. "Well, if you need me, I'm here, okay?"

Suzanne nodded again. "Thanks for the scrapbook, Jane. I really appreciate it. It'll keep us all together."

Jane smiled. "Call me when you get back home, okay?"

"Sure."

Suzanne closed the car door and waved before she drove away.

But she never called.

And Jane never saw her again.

Campbell watched Jane as she recounted that day. Clearly she blamed herself for not realizing how badly her mom needed help.

"Do you think they kicked her out that day?" Campbell asked.

Jane shrugged. "I don't know. As a parent, I can't imagine ever doing that to my daughter, but Cathy—your grandmother—well, she was pretty stubborn. She might've kicked her out just to prove a point."

"And they never worked things out?"

"I don't think so, hon. I always hoped they'd made their peace, but I guess not."

Campbell stood and began folding then re-folding the same

T-shirt. She couldn't understand why her mom lied to her all those years about having extended family, why she didn't make things right with her own mother. It contradicted everything she knew about her mom. "It's hard to believe. Mom and I were so close. I can't imagine her having such a bad relationship with her own mother."

"Suzanne obviously wanted to be a different kind of mom. She did a good job with you, Campbell."

Campbell zipped the bag, then met Jane's eyes. She allowed a weak smile. "But what about that scrapbook? If you gave it back to Mom, why didn't she have the entire thing?"

Jane sighed. "The following summer, it arrived on my doorstep. Your mom wanted The Circle to continue, and she knew it wouldn't if we didn't have the book. We tried, but it just wasn't the same without Suzanne. In the end, Adele talked us into splitting it up. That way, we each got part of the memories. We went through and each took out our favorite pages, setting aside the ones we thought your mom should have."

"But it'll never be complete again," Campbell said.

"Not unless Meghan sends us her pages."

"Or comes back." Campbell watched Jane's expression change.

Jane stuttered, fumbled for words.

"Why do you think she's not here?"

"I couldn't say," Jane said simply. "I haven't spoken to her in over six years."

"Can I ask why?" Campbell avoided Jane's eyes, scanning the guest room one last time for anything she might have missed.

Jane took a deep breath. "It's a story for another day, I think." She stood and looked at Campbell. "I keep wondering what would've happened if I'd stayed with her that night instead of going to meet Graham at the football game."

"You might not be married to him," Campbell said.

"Or I might never have lost touch with your mom." Regret cooled Jane's face. "I hate all these 'what-ifs.'" She turned to leave. "I'm sorry you're finding this all out right after losing your mom. It's so unfair."

"Life isn't fair." Campbell flipped the lid of the suitcase and zipped it up.

"Adele and Lila and I already started a list of possibilities. Who knows, maybe it *was* someone in that art class."

"Maybe."

"If you stay we could—"

Campbell cut her off. "I'll think about it."

She remembered Lila's speculation that her mother hadn't loved the guy. How it'd just been a terrible mistake—one that had cost her mother everything. Friends. Parents. A future. How different would things have been if she'd given Campbell away—or never had her at all?

The threat of having her heart broken, or running into her grandfather again, wrung out her insides like a sponge.

She'd lost her courage. She needed to go. She couldn't endure the pain of uncovering more of Mom's secrets. It had started to change the way she felt about her mother, and Campbell couldn't risk that.

She slung her bag over her shoulder.

"Good-bye, Jane."

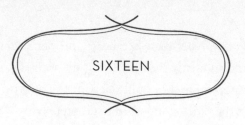

SIXTEEN

Campbell

The quiet of the car should've comforted her, but Campbell's thoughts somersaulted through her mind, making peace impossible. She'd made the right choice. Leaving Sweethaven—leaving her mom's friends and her not-dead grandfather—was the right thing to do. So why did she now find herself parked at the Boardwalk, admiring the full moon glowing behind the lighthouse? Why couldn't she drive straight out of town and keep on going until she reached Tee Street—her mom's house?

Campbell got out of the car and walked along the lake, reminded again that she was far from the city. She replayed the moment she stood face to face with her grandfather—a man she didn't know existed. He'd been there all along, only a couple of hours away. But he'd never tried to find them. He hadn't cared enough about her or Mom to right the wrongs of the past.

She shook the thoughts away, but she knew the pain of his rejection was nothing compared to what she'd feel if she discovered her father had abandoned her in the same way.

Leaving had to be the right thing.

She pulled her sweatshirt around her torso and hugged herself, walking back to the car. She turned the key in the ignition and hit Seek on the radio. A little music would drown out the thoughts bombardingher mind.

The tug of war between her head and her heart had left her exhausted, and suddenly the only thing she wanted was to get back to Mom's house, where she could sleep for the next three days.

But when the radio stopped on a station playing "When You Say Nothin' at All" by Alison Krauss, Campbell's eyes filled with tears. Mom's favorite song. The words didn't fit every sad situation that had come her way, but it didn't matter—it was Mom's go-to song, the one that always comforted her.

Mom had never been much of a singer, but it didn't stop her. Whenever she'd had a broken heart, Campbell could count on Mom smoothing her hair away from her face and singing that song until the pain finally started to dull.

She stopped the car in the parking lot and rested her head on the steering wheel.

"Mom, why didn't you just tell me what you wanted me to know instead of making me go figure it all out for myself?" A tear fell onto her jeans, leaving a wet dot just above her knee.

The song filled the car, like a much-needed hug from her mother that told her she could go on. She had questions and Sweethaven had answers. If she left now, she'd never work up the courage to come back.

Could she muster the strength right now to do it? No matter the cost of what she discovered?

"This is gonna sting a little," Campbell said as she put the car in drive. As she headed back toward Elm Street, she imagined what she'd say if she ran into her grandfather again, but quickly put an end to that line of thinking as Adele's house came into view.

The living room lights illuminated the front of the house, and two cars still sat outside. Lila and Jane hadn't left yet. Would they forgive her for taking off? Maybe they wanted no part of this drama.

But she had to try.

She walked up to the door and knocked. Seconds later, Adele appeared on the other side of the screen. She didn't say a word, simply opened the door and ushered Campbell back into the room as if she'd never left.

Jane's and Lila's surprised expressions faded into understanding, and they made room for her to sit with them. Luke shifted in his seat and avoided her eyes.

Adele took her hand and squeezed it. After several beats of silence, Adele said, "There are two options. We can call it a day right now. Or," her voice slowed, "if you're up for it, the girls and I were thinking we could get out the scrapbook pages and do a little detective work. See if we can't piece together who your daddy is."

Campbell stared at the three women, all wearing the same hopeful expression. Her insecurities faded as she realized they really wanted to help her. She hadn't imagined she could ever have a *daddy*. She liked the way it sounded. Her nod of agreement was met with three smiles.

"I'll go get the coffee." Adele disappeared into the kitchen.

"We'll go get our pages. Come on, Lila." Jane hopped up, grabbed Lila's arm, and exited the room, leaving Campbell and Luke alone.

He stood and took a couple steps toward her, forcing her gaze. She pressed her lips together and squared her jaw. Stubborn, her mom would say.

Luke took her hands and kept his eyes fixed on hers. "I really am sorry you found out that way. If I'd known—if I'd been thinking— I would've handled that differently."

The apology hung between them, waiting for her response. His stare unnerved her until finally she looked away. "It's okay."

"I promise if I think of anything else, I'll tell you right away."

She nodded.

Adele burst back in the room carrying a tray of coffee and assorted creamers. Jane and Lila were right behind her.

Luke glanced at them, then back at Campbell. "I should go. Thanks for dinner, Ma," he said. He hugged Lila, then Jane, then Adele. Then he stopped in front of Campbell and pulled her into a gentle hug. "Hopefully I'll see you tomorrow."

Her arms didn't move. They were locked at her sides. He pulled away, waved, and then walked out. Campbell heard the sound of the front door closing behind him, and a hint of sadness wound around her heart.

"What's that about?" Lila wore a knowing grin, her tone playfully accusatory.

"What do you mean?" Campbell crossed her arms.

"Are you blushing? I can't tell for sure, but I think you're blushing." Jane giggled. "He's so dreamy."

"I don't know what you're talking about." Campbell turned her cell phone over in her hand, staring at it as if she'd never seen it before.

"He's a good catch, hon." Adele put an arm around her. "But he's been hurt before, so he doesn't usually put himself out there. I think he likes you."

"Can I get some of that coffee, Adele? Coffee would be wonderful right now." Campbell stared at the floor.

"Good idea, hon. We could all use a little something warm in our bellies." Adele poured four mugs of coffee and handed them around to the others.

Lila nestled into an old armchair, Jane and Campbell on the couch. Adele stood until everyone had found a spot and then settled in a white rocking chair with a big cushion.

"This chair is so comfortable, Adele." Lila fixed the pillow around her.

"Well, it's probably worn to my backside, but you're right, it's a comfy one. I like everything in my house to be comfortable."

Perhaps Adele had been her mother's inspiration.

"It is, just like always." Jane hugged a pillow over her midsection.

Conversation lagged and silence filled the room. Campbell shifted and pulled her legs up under her. How could she convince her mom's friends to tell her everything they remembered? To divulge their secrets? Surely they'd known her father. Sweethaven wasn't a big town. Maybe they just needed their memories jogged.

"Tell us about her." Jane interrupted Campbell's thoughts. "Your mother. Your life."

Campbell glanced at Adele, who smiled but said nothing. "What do you want to know?"

"Everything." Jane pulled her legs up on the couch and settled in, as if Campbell had an entire night's worth of stories to tell. But Campbell was the one with questions. Like why hadn't her mother told her anything about them—or Sweethaven? Or that she had a grandfather?

"I wouldn't know where to start," she said.

Didn't her mom's friends know it was all she could do not to run screaming from the house? She had no tolerance for small talk.

Lila sat tall in the cushy recliner, her posture perfect, her chin just high enough to look down on the rest of the room. "What did she end up doing? Something with her art?"

Campbell nodded, the knot in her stomach loosening just a bit. "She taught at my high school. It was always just the two of us, but she still went back to school and became a teacher."

"What did she tell you about her parents, hon?" Jane's brow furrowed.

"Just what I told you. That they died in a car accident right after I was born."

Confused glances criss-crossed the room.

"Why would she tell me that if it wasn't true? Is my grandmother alive too?" Her voice broke and she chastised herself for being so weak.

"It's complicated, darlin'." Adele's smile failed to comfort Campbell.

"I deserve to know the truth. Don't I?" She looked at them, one by one, but no one responded.

* * * * *

Jane

Jane's heart broke when she realized Suzanne had lied to her own daughter. Had she planned to tell Campbell the truth about them too? How was it she'd slipped into a coma the very day she intended to come clean about the past? Jane knew Suzanne had had a rocky relationship with her parents—even more so after her pregnancy—but she always hoped they would work it out. Apparently, they hadn't. And their rift was serious enough for Suzanne to keep them from knowing their only granddaughter.

What had happened all those years ago to make her hate her parents that much? They'd speculated, but none of them knew for sure.

She could see Campbell's confusion—and they'd only just started talking. What else didn't she know?

Jane's heart sank. Campbell had deserved to know her grandfather still lived around the corner on Juniper Drive, and she also deserved to know her grandmother had died only a few years ago. She knew because she'd attended the funeral. She saw the way it broke the old man's heart to bury his wife—even though the woman had turned into a bitter, angry thing.

Adele fidgeted across the room. "Campbell, hon, there are some things we need to tell you. I imagine they are things your mama planned to tell you—and I do wish you were hearin' all this from her."

"It's okay, Adele. I need to know," Campbell said. "Even if it hurts."

Adele glanced at the coffee table. "Why don't we start with the scrapbook?"

Three piles of scrapbook pages sat on the table between them. Their memories, their past, their childhood stared at them, reminded them of all they'd been.

They'd all had such dreams back then.

"This isn't right." Lila looked at Adele.

"What's not?" Jane asked, afraid Lila would jump in before Adele had a chance to explain things to Campbell. Adele had a softness that Lila didn't.

"Where's Meghan for starters? Didn't she get a card? Can you call her, Adele?"

The questions seemed to stun Adele. "I—I—I could try calling her, I guess." The old woman glanced at Jane, whose muscles clenched at the mention of Meg's name.

"She's got two beautiful kids right here in Sweethaven, and when was the last time she saw them?" Lila crossed her long legs and stared at Adele.

"Too long ago. Almost two years, I think."

Lila shook her head.

Tension wormed its way through the room as the three of them danced around their unspoken secrets. Jane studied the floorboard, willing the grief back in its hole. She couldn't think of Meghan without thinking of Alex.

Finally, Adele stood. "I think I'll get more cream," she said. "Would anyone else like some?"

Neither Jane nor Lila responded.

"I'd love some, Adele," Campbell said.

In seconds, every good memory she had seemed to float away, carried off on a wave of sadness. Sadness that threatened to tear Jane in half. She stood. "I'm going to use the restroom." She walked toward the bathroom and tried not to make it look like she was escaping.

In the solace of the tiny pink powder room, Jane leaned over the sink and inhaled while she counted to ten.

Why did Lila have to be so thoughtless?

Jane forced herself not to cry. She shouldn't have come. She should've stayed home with her stack of pages and the comfort of Graham's arms. Feeling the grief hurt in a way she didn't have the capacity to handle. Jane had mastered the fine art of not completely feeling her emotions. If this continued, the heaviness might crush her.

"You're okay," she said to her reflection. "You can do this." One more deep breath and Jane went back to the living room. At the same time, Adele returned with a small pitcher of cream. "I brought extra in case anyone changes their mind," she said. She glanced at Lila. "Maybe we can focus on Campbell instead of digging up the past?"

Lila raised her eyebrows, trying to look innocent. "I didn't do it on purpose, Adele."

No, Jane thought. Lila never did it on purpose.

Adele gave Jane a quick hug, but Jane tightened at her touch.

"I think I'll have some more coffee," Jane said. As if the coffee could wash the pain away.

"Comin' right up, honey."

Finally, Jane forced a smile—the smile of a pastor's wife, used to living in a fishbowl—and turned her attention to the stacks of finished layouts on the table in front of her. Lila did have a point: nothing felt the same without their other friends. And as much as she hated to admit it, that included Meghan.

Had she gotten Suzanne's note? Why wasn't she here?

"Look at all those pages." Lila ran a hand over the stack nearest to her. "Mine have been here this whole time. I found them in my hope chest. Mama stuffed them in there like dirty laundry. I haven't seen them in years."

"You were all so artistic," Jane said.

"Not me." Lila glanced at her. "Suzanne was the real artist, although Meg could do a pretty mean graffiti wall." Jane and Lila shared a tension-relieving laugh and Adele covered her ears.

"I don't want to hear it," Adele said.

"Lila, you could always decorate a room like a work of art." Jane glanced at Campbell, who appeared to be tolerating their chitchat. "I'm telling you, I was the only one without any trace of artistic talent." Jane picked up Suzanne's pile and thumbed through the square layouts. "You can tell which of these pages are Suzanne's and which are the rest of ours at first glance."

"She definitely had her own style." Lila leaned forward, joining Jane as they pored over the first few pages.

"'Pure Delight.'" Jane laughed. "I remember this."

"Remember Suzanne insisted on using the word 'delight'?" Lila laughed. "I think we made fun of her for that for years."

"We'd throw it into sentences—"

"This corn dog is so *delightful*." Lila did her best Scarlett O'Hara imitation.

"I simply *delight* in the summer sun." Jane put on an accent to match Lila's.

"Suzanne got so mad." Lila's eyes sparkled as they told the story.

"Did she tell you about the summer we all met?" Jane smiled as she focused on Campbell. "Lila and I had been friends for years, but we didn't meet Meghan and Suzanne until we were almost thirteen. Suzanne rescued me from two mean girls and then convinced me to go for a ride on the carousel, remember, Lila?" Jane could still feel the sense of relief as clear as if she were sitting on that bench with a drippy ice cream cone today.

Lila laughed. "The summer it was restored. I remember. Suzanne made us keep our ticket stubs. For 'prosperity's sake.'" She glanced at Campbell. "That's what she called it."

Jane could still see Suzanne's grin as she stood up from the bench and challenged Jane.

"You ready for the carousel or what?" Suzanne took off in the direction of the carousel, and Jane tried to keep up with her. When they reached the line, Suzanne nearly plowed into Lila, who wore a pink belted dress and a white headband.

"Oh, sorry." Suzanne apologized.

"You really should watch what you're doing," Lila said, her Southern accent more pronounced than usual.

"I said I was sorry, geesh." Suzanne looked at Jane and shrugged.

"Lila, this is Suzanne. It's her first summer here."

"How wonderful for us," Lila said.

Jane glanced at Suzanne, who seemed completely unfazed.

When the carousel came to a stop and it was time for them to get on, a man handed them all tickets.

"I thought it was free," Jane said, turning it over in her hand.

"It's a souvenir," the man said. "Grand reopening."

The small gray ticket fit in the palm of Jane's hand. Fancy red letters spelled out *Sweethaven Beach Carousel. Grand Reopening. 1983.*

Sweethaven's only traditional wood-carved carousel. Jane closed her fingers over the ticket and glanced at Suzanne.

"I'm going to keep my ticket someplace safe. A scrapbook or something," Suzanne said. "That way I can always remember the day I met my first Sweethaven friend, Jane."

Jane stopped, then pulled the scrapbook pages onto her lap. She flipped through them until she found one with an enlarged photo of the carousel. She pointed to the right-hand corner. "She kept her word. All four tickets, neatly preserved."

Campbell took the page and read her mother's handwritten words: "'The day I met my first Sweethaven friend, Jane.'" She glanced at Jane, who wiped a tear from her cheek.

"That carousel was like freedom to me," Jane said. "Your mom had a way of pulling me out of my shell. It didn't matter what anyone else said because she was always on my side."

The girls zig-zagged to the other side of the merry-go-round, where Jane spotted the perfect baby-blue horse. She hopped up and slung her leg over the bright pink saddle, then grabbed on to the golden pole.

"So is this your new best friend, Jane?" Lila said, leaning forward.

"I just met her. Can't we all be friends?" Jane tried to talk quietly so Suzanne wouldn't hear her.

"She doesn't look like she'll fit in here at all."

Jane had gotten used to deferring to Lila. Her friend had the kind of personality that made it hard to do anything but what she wanted.

"I think she fits in just fine," Jane said. She couldn't remember a time she'd ever openly disagreed with Lila.

Lila shot her a look, but Jane focused on the unfamiliar happiness that bubbled in her belly.

Once they were all in place, Jane looked behind her. A redheaded girl with long legs and pale skin sat in an oversized sleigh being pulled by two hand-carved tigers. The girl stared, steely-eyed, in their direction. Had she been there this whole time? Jane hadn't seen her get on.

Suzanne followed Jane's gaze to the girl. Suzanne smiled, but the girl looked away. Just then the organ music kicked up and the carousel began to spin.

Jane gripped the shiny pole as if she were five again. The music bubbled up inside and her mind floated back in time. Hanging on for dear life, she swayed to the music, then threw her head back. A happy giggle escaped her lips and it didn't matter who heard. She followed Suzanne's lead, holding on tightly to her pole, while her hair swished in the wind. No worries. No cares. Just happiness.

When the ride came to an end, Jane and Suzanne followed Lila off, but the redheaded girl stayed put in the tiger-pulled sleigh. Jane assumed it was so she could ride the merry-go-round over and over again without waiting in line. Once they reached solid ground again, Jane couldn't keep herself from laughing.

They rode the carousel five more times that day, and eventually they even made friends with Meghan, the redheaded girl, who'd just moved to Sweethaven from Nashville.

Darkness fell as the four of them watched the sun set over Lake Michigan. In all the years she'd been coming to Sweethaven, Jane had never really made friends with anyone other than Lila. The kids she played with on the beach didn't really count, so she spent all her time with her family. Her mom said that's why they were there. To be a family.

Something told her things would be different now.

"Hey, look!" Suzanne pointed at a photo booth next to the carousel. "Let's do that!"

"I'm not going in there." Lila crossed her arms.

Suzanne grabbed Jane's hand. "You're in, right, Janie?"

No one called her Janie. She liked it. "I'm in!" She grinned.

"Meg?" Suzanne turned her attention to Meghan.

"Sure, whatever." She shrugged.

"Do you know how many people are in there every day?" Lila turned up her nose.

"Thousands. In Sweethaven. Population 152." Suzanne laughed. "Come on!"

Finally, Lila relented and the four of them crammed into the closet-sized photo booth.

That was the beginning. The beginning of The Circle.

Campbell shook her head. "She didn't tell me anything about this place. I guess she had her reasons for keeping it to herself. I mean, she had a reason for leaving here, right?"

"So you didn't know anything about us at all?" Lila stared at Campbell, who shook her head again.

"Wow." Jane said. "I can't believe she didn't tell you anything."

"Yeah, me neither."

Campbell's terse reply told Jane the young girl didn't care to walk down memory lane with them. She couldn't blame her. She'd just been hit with a bombshell and they'd yet to explain anything to her. It was thoughtless of them.

Campbell eyed them, suspicion behind her glare.

"Campbell," Adele said softly.

"I think it might've been complicated," Jane said.

"How so?" Campbell straightened in her chair.

The girl knew nothing. Not of them. Not of Sweethaven. Not of her grandparents or her father. How could they break all of this to her at once?

"It's pretty straightforward," Lila said.

Jane cringed. Lila wouldn't be gentle.

"What do you mean?"

"She left because she got pregnant." Lila rifled through a stack of layouts, found one, and handed it to Campbell. "Look."

Campbell glanced at the page and then looked at them. "I read this one. It was on top of Mom's stack."

Jane knew the layout. They'd received it in the mail, along with the scrapbook—when it was still intact. Suzanne's letter to them, a good-bye of sorts on a scrapbook layout, explained that her parents wouldn't let her come back. She'd disgraced them, and she'd be punished by staying home that summer, taking care of her new baby.

Punished. Harsh words for a daughter to read.

Campbell ran her hand over the Polaroid Suzanne had stapled to the page. The only photo they'd seen of her nine months pregnant. Maybe the only one that existed.

"I get it. She left because of me." Campbell stared at the page. "I figured as much. Being with me was her punishment."

"We don't know the whole story. Her parents weren't in Sweethaven that summer. We had a different pastor, and by the time they returned, Suzanne had already gone." Jane kept her tone soft, not that anything she did would soften the blow at this point.

The blood drained from Campbell's face. "She said they died right after I was born, but she never spoke to them or introduced me to them." She bit her bottom lip as if to keep from crying. "They didn't want me. Is that right? They kicked my mom out?"

"We always thought they gave her an ultimatum," Jane finally said. "She could stay if she gave her baby—if she gave you—up for adoption."

"And she chose you, darlin'," Adele said. "She chose you. And it was a hard choice, but you were worth it."

"Was I?" Campbell's tears came quicker now. She wiped

them away before they could run down her cheeks. "My grandma—what happened to her?"

Silence filled the room. How did they tell her? Adele and Jane exchanged glances, and finally Adele laid a hand on Campbell's shoulder.

"Your grandma died about seven years ago," Adele said. "She was very sick, but people around here swear her bitterness killed her."

"She was alive this whole time? She died when I was seventeen." Adele nodded.

"And my grandfather's lived here all along? Two hours away from us?"

Adele hesitated, then looked at Jane and Lila. None of them had words to comfort Suzanne's daughter.

Everything the girl thought she knew was a lie.

Lies her mother had told.

Were they wrong to tell the truth? Would it somehow ruin Campbell's memory of Suzanne?

No way around it now. The pain hovered overhead—familiar pain that sliced into Jane.

Campbell excused herself, leaving the three of them staring at each other, dumbfounded.

She'd come there for answers, but Jane wondered if she'd rather go back to not knowing the truth. Some secrets were too painful to dig up. Some feelings were too heavy to feel.

Maybe they shouldn't have told her anything. Were these painful secrets even theirs to share? If they kept this up, Campbell would regret ever coming to Sweethaven—ever meeting any of them.

Jane sighed. She'd imagined this so differently.

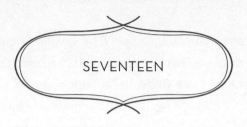

SEVENTEEN

Lila

Lila tossed and turned, punching the pillow then flipping it over. No use. No matter what she did, sleep eluded her. Finally, she gave in and went downstairs. Cold floors under bare feet sent a shiver down her spine.

The house, which should be providing relaxation and comfort, had done the exact opposite—sent new thoughts spinning in her already confused head. Memories she'd done everything to bury now flashed in front of her like a beauty queen's bleached white teeth under hot stage lights.

Her phone on the granite countertop in the kitchen showed no missed calls. No messages.

Where was Tom? Did he even care that she'd gone?

Maybe he had a trip. Maybe he had gone overseas. She hadn't bothered to look at his schedule before she left. She'd just gone. Impulsively. That was so unlike her. She hadn't even remembered to put her favorite hand lotion in her bag, the lotion that rubbed the wrinkles from her hands. The lotion that promised youth.

But she knew the truth. And so did Tom. She hated to imagine all the ways she disappointed her husband. No longer the picture of beauty, wrinkles had wormed their way into her once-taut skin. He'd never mentioned them, but she could tell things had changed between them over the years. Would he still marry her if he'd known this is what they'd become? Sometimes tragedy brought people closer, but not them. Theirs had torn them apart.

Had it gotten more difficult for Tom to spend time in their empty home, a home devoid of the sounds of children? Maybe they'd been torn apart by the constant reminder that they'd never have the one thing they always wanted.

A baby.

Not for lack of trying either. With Daddy's wealth, she had access to the best of everything. Doctors, fertility treatments, answers.

But a baby seemed the one thing Daddy's money couldn't buy.

It had driven a wedge between them. With every birthday that passed, she watched the dream get further and further away, like a boat sailing out to sea.

Tom had always wanted kids. He'd have been a great father too, but Lila sometimes wondered if this was her punishment for being such a selfish person.

Maybe God knew what a terrible mother she'd be. Maybe He was sparing her the failure, or sparing her children the therapy.

She spread the old afghan over her lap and lay on the chaise lounge in the front room. Moonlight spilled through the skylights, illuminating the space.

How had she gotten here? How had she allowed herself to become so pathetic? Such a caricature of a person. Beauty pageants and Junior League and social climbing had done nothing to fill the constant void that tormented her.

She pulled the blanket up around her neck, wishing it could offer her the warmth she needed. Wishing she didn't need strong arms to fall into. She'd spent her life pushing people's buttons and what had it gotten her?

Her eyes grew heavy and she struggled to keep them open, her mind drifting back to when she had the comfort of friends who'd accepted her for who she was. Only in coming back here did she realize how important that had been.

Lila's eyes flickered open and she shifted her position on the couch. As her eyes closed again, she relived that summer in her mind.

Blue Freedom Days in Sweethaven made the little town feel even more Mayberry-esque than usual. It didn't need a holiday to come alive, but for some reason, the mid-summer celebration plugged the town into an electrical socket and turned up the charm. Swarms of people filled the streets, all decked out in red, white, and blue.

Lila arrived near the flag pole to meet the others for the opening ceremony. She'd tucked her pink LeClic camera in her purse. Suzanne had already titled the scrapbook page they'd dedicate to this day: "Blue Freedom Through Our Eyes."

She watched as women set up booths to sell their jams, jellies, and homemade pies. Men showed off their woodworking projects. Artists displayed their favorite pieces around the perimeter of the square. At the center was the gazebo where the mayor prepared to kick things off.

She met up with Jane and Suzanne, but none of them had spotted Meghan.

"Let's move up. Meg will find us." Lila pushed her way through the crowd.

"Good afternoon, Sweethaven," the mayor began. "We have a long tradition here that goes back to my great-grandfather, one of the original founders of this fair town."

Suzanne scoffed. "He's not even trying to be sneaky about his name-dropping anymore."

"That tradition continues today. The Blue Freedom Days." Cheers went up from the excited crowd.

"There's Mrs. Barber." Suzanne pointed to the other side of the crowd where Meghan's mom stood in the very front, an American flag in her hand.

"Is Meg with her?" Jane followed Suzanne's finger, expectation on her face.

Lila glanced at the mayor and then gasped. "No," she said. "Meghan's on the stage."

The three of them stared behind Mayor Swanson where their usually shy friend stood, poised, in front of the entire town.

"What's she doing up there?" Suzanne waved in Meg's direction. Meg spotted them and lifted her fingers in a slight wave.

The Mayor continued. "This year, one of our very own, Miss Meghan Barber, will kick things off with her stunning rendition of our national anthem."

Lila looked at Suzanne and Jane.

"Meghan sings?" Jane turned her attention back to the stage.

"Apparently so," Lila said. "And her rendition is 'stunning.'"

Silence fell over the rowdy crowd. The mayor backed away from the microphone stand and motioned for Meghan to take center stage.

"She doesn't even look nervous," Lila said.

Seconds later, Meg's strong, raspy voice rang out through the Square. Like a country Pat Benatar, her magical voice flowed over the audience. No one spoke. Even the small children stopped chattering as they all listened to Meghan Barber, Sweethaven's newest sensation. She saw a man look at his wife, eyebrows raised, and mouth, "Wow."

When she finished, Meghan stepped back from the microphone and opened her eyes. A few long seconds passed and finally, as if on cue, the crowd erupted into cheers and shouts and applause.

Lila shoved her jealous feelings down deep and forced a smile. She'd had more practice than anyone in the art of the pasted smile. Afterwards, Meghan maneuvered through the crowd in their direction, stopping every few steps to accept more congratulations.

"Meghan!" Suzanne shouted. "You're amazing!" She threw her arms around her, and Meghan hugged her back, letting out an excited sigh.

"Why didn't you tell us you could sing like that?" Jane gushed.

"It wasn't my idea. My choir director recommended me to the mayor. He called when I wasn't home so my mom told him I'd sing. I think I sort of loved it." Meg covered her face with her hands and squealed.

"Maybe you'll be a famous singer someday," Jane said.

Lila shifted and looked away.

"Did you guys take a picture?"

The three of them exchanged horrified glances. They'd forgotten.

"We were so stunned. You should've warned us you were going to be onstage," Lila said.

"Let's take one now—of all four of you." Mrs. Barber came up behind them. "Hop up on the stage."

Jane, Suzanne, and Meghan ran up the stairs to the top of the gazebo, giddy like children. Lila followed behind. Sometimes her friends could be so juvenile.

Meghan's mom snapped one—two—three shots. "Just in case one of y'all closed her pretty eyes."

After the photos, they found a spot under an old oak tree at the center of the square where Mark Davis, Tommy Olson, Nick Rhodes, and Gunther Blackwell waited for them.

"We've got corn dogs for everyone." Mark handed them out to the girls.

"Well, aren't you sweet?" Lila said, taking hers.

"I try." He grinned.

Suzanne asked a passerby to take a picture of their entire group.

"Don't show that to anyone," Lila said. "My mom will kill me if she finds out I ate a corn dog." A delightful surge of rebellion rippled up Lila's spine.

"What's she gonna say when I take your picture with a huge funnel cake?" Suzanne laughed. "Let's go get them now. Come on, Lila."

Lila glanced up from her spot on the blanket. "Me? Why? Take Jane."

"Come on," Suzanne insisted. "Live dangerously."

As the two of them headed for the portable funnel cake trailer, Suzanne said, "I think Mark Davis likes you."

"What? No he doesn't." Lila pretended she hadn't noticed— even enjoyed—the extra attention from Mark, the son of a doctor and a lawyer who lived in Milwaukee.

"Lila, don't play stupid. I'm telling you to turn it down a notch. Jane really likes him." Suzanne stopped her now. They stood yards from the trailer, and the smell of the doughy fried cakes wafted across the Square.

"Jane and Mark are just friends. Besides, I can't think of anyone I'm less interested in."

Suzanne stiffened as something behind Lila caught her attention. She grabbed Lila's arm and dragged her toward the funnel cakes. "Let's go."

"What in the world has gotten into you, Suzanne?" Lila glanced to her right and felt the blood drain from her face. There, on a park bench in the center of town for everyone in Sweethaven to see, sat Lila's father, his arm draped around a younger woman wearing a sun dress and sandals.

"Daddy?" Lila noted the horror in her own voice.

He scooted away from the woman and cleared his throat. "Hi, darlin'," he said. "Didn't think I'd see you out here."

Obviously.

"What are you doing?" Tears burned her eyes but she blinked them back.

"I'm just having a little chat with my friend Sharon." Daddy stood.

"Where's Mama? Does she know you're having a *chat* with your friend Sharon?"

"Lila, let's not make a scene." Daddy spoke slowly, his Southern drawl more pronounced than usual. "Remember who you are. We can discuss this at length if you want to, but let's wait until we get home."

Lila blinked hard, trying to hold back the tears. "Daddy, everyone in town is out in the Square this afternoon. Everyone will be talking about us whether I make a scene or not."

Daddy took a few steps closer and closed the gap between them. "Listen to me, young lady, you are the daughter and I am the parent. I expect you to treat me with respect."

"I would if you deserved it," Lila spat.

The hot stinging of his palm across her cheek shocked her. She grabbed her face and gasped to catch her breath. Daddy's eyes went black. Then, slowly, his forehead loosened as realization set in. "Hon, I am so sorry…" His voice trailed off.

A small crowd had gathered, had seen her father strike her. Her face throbbed with pain and burned with embarrassment. She swallowed and lifted her chin, willing away the tears that threatened to fall. In the sea of faces staring open-mouthed and whispering, one came into sharp focus. Suzanne. Her eyes, calm and reassuring, reached out to her. Two steps toward her friend and Suzanne took her hand in a firm grasp and led her away.

"You hold your head up, Lila," Suzanne whispered.

Her cheek burned but her pride hurt even more.

Suzanne put an arm around her. "Do you want to talk about it?"

Lila hesitated. "He's being a jerk."

Suzanne nodded.

"Probably shouldn't have mouthed off to him. I said that to make him mad."

"I think it worked." Suzanne stared at her for a long moment and then the two of them burst out laughing.

"Don't tell the others, okay?" Lila looked away.

Suzanne crossed her fingers over her heart in an *X*, kissed them, and held them up at her side. "I promise."

Now, sitting in the lake house, Lila could still see the photos Adele had snapped that day. All three showed four beautiful girls, perfectly framed by the decorated gazebo. Mama had told her those girls weren't good enough for her. She'd said they were fine *summer friends* but that Adlers didn't associate with just *anybody*. Part of Lila had believed her. It had kept her from ever getting too close.

The clouds passed over the moon, casting a bright light on her face, forcing her eyes open. She'd learned so much that summer. Suzanne had shown her what it meant to be a true friend—by being one to her. She'd never breathed a word to anyone about Daddy. Lila had let Mama convince her that high society and *things* were more important than her friends, but she knew now that Mama was wrong.

She sat up, pulled the blanket tighter.

The truth threatened to reveal itself. The truth she'd avoided and pretended not to know.

She wasn't too good for her friends—her friends were too good for her.

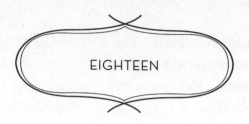

EIGHTEEN

Campbell

The next morning, after a hot shower and a bagel, Campbell sat in Adele's kitchen and sent Tilly a text. *Still in Michigan. Calling the lawyer now. I'll be in touch.*

She rifled around in her purse until she found Mom's address book. She'd had it with her at the hospital in case she needed to get in touch with anyone not in her own contact list. She opened the book and flipped to the *H* section.

Henry Tillman.

Mom insisted on alphabetizing by first name instead of last. "When I think of you, I don't think 'Carter,'" she'd said. "I think 'Campbell.'"

"Bad example since either way you slice it, I'm filed under *C*."

Mom frowned. "Stop being a smarty-pants."

Campbell dialed the number on the page.

"Henry Tillman's office," a woman answered.

"May I speak with Mr. Tillman, please?"

Would Henry Tillman even know who she was? Elevator music played on the line. She clicked her thumb on the kitchen table. Finally, the music stopped and she heard rattling on the other end as if he'd dropped the phone after picking it up.

Campbell held the phone away from her ear until she heard him.

"This is Henry Tillman," said a deep voice. She'd only met him once, but she had a clear picture of her mother's lawyer. Short. Stocky. Bushy black moustache over a tight upper lip.

"Yes, Mr. Tillman. I'm not sure if you remember me. My mother is—was—Suzanne Carter."

"Of course. I was sorry to hear about your mom. She was always such a delight."

"Thank you." Campbell swallowed. How did she ask her questions without sounding hopelessly ignorant?

"Will you be stopping by the office today?"

"No, sir. That's why I'm calling. I'm actually out of town for a few days, but I wanted to talk to you about my mother's home."

"What about it exactly?"

"I don't want to sell it." Saying the words out loud sent her pulse racing. What was she saying? He would think she was crazy. How could someone with her income even consider keeping that house?

"No, I wouldn't either if I were you. It's a nice little place for a single girl like yourself."

She chewed the inside of her cheek. "How do I go about paying for it? Do I need to do something legal to get it turned over to me? I've never had a mortgage." Campbell felt her face flush with embarrassment.

"Didn't your mom talk to you about this before she passed away?" Mr. Tillman sounded confused.

"No, she didn't. I'm finding there were quite a few conversations we should have had."

"Hon, the house is already yours."

"What? What do you mean?"

"Your mom owned the house free and clear, and she willed it to you. There's also a substantial bank account."

"My mom was a teacher, Mr. Tillman. We pretty much lived paycheck to paycheck."

"She didn't tell you about your benefactor?"

"My what?" Campbell chewed on her thumbnail.

"A benefactor is a person who supports someone else, financially or otherwise—"

"No, I know what a benefactor is, I just don't understand how I could possibly have one. Who was it?"

"She never told me. Just that she felt like the money should be yours, so she stashed it all away in an account for you. Listen, this is good news, Campbell. You don't have to worry about a house or money. You should be very happy. Let me know if I can do anything else for you, hon."

Hon. She let the fatherly endearment settle on her ears. He was not the kind of father she usually imagined, but a father of any kind was better than no father at all.

"Thank you, Mr. Tillman." She hung up and called Information for the number to the bank. Once she was connected, she waited for the banker to locate the mystery account.

How had her mother managed to keep this from her all these years? She'd struggled to provide for the two of them when she had a stockpile of money at her disposal. Why?

And who was this mysterious benefactor?

Her mind flipped through a mental rolodex of friends and family, but no rich uncle or wealthy guardian came to mind.

The only person that kept popping into her head was the one person who didn't have the right to give her a thing. The man who'd never wanted her and made that fact known to her mother— so much so that she ran away and never returned, never breathed a word of her hidden pain to anyone.

She didn't want or need her grandfather's handouts, and if she stayed in Sweethaven long enough, maybe she'd work up the courage to tell him so.

When the banker finally returned to the line, she told Campbell there was a branch in Harbortown. It would be better for her to visit in person.

Campbell thanked her, grabbed her bag, and headed to the car. After she punched the name of the bank into the GPS, she started off for Harbortown.

She drove for half an hour and located the bank as she pulled into town. After showing the banker her ID, she was given a printout of her account records. Her eyes widened as she looked at the number on the page.

"Are you sure this is right?"

"Yes. Would you like to make a withdrawal?" The banker stared at her.

Campbell blinked, unable to pull her attention from the amount of money they said belonged to her. She withdrew one hundred dollars and stashed it in her wallet.

Dazed, she walked back to the car, her wallet with the crisp hundred-dollar bill jabbing her like the pea underneath a dozen mattresses. Mom had had all this money, and she'd never spent a dime. It didn't make sense.

Campbell started the car and was driving through the parking lot when a sign for Harbortown Central Community College caught her eye. Jane had said her mom had taken an art class there. It had been the only clue Lila and Jane could come up with. Maybe they kept records. Maybe someone there could shed some light on her father's identity.

Before she could think twice, Campbell made a quick turn and drove down the block, parked her car, and found the office at the college. A wave of doubt crashed over her. What was she doing? Would she be okay with what she uncovered—if there was anything to uncover at all? Though every fiber of her being told her she wasn't prepared, and as images of her grandfather standing on his porch bombarded her, she methodically placed one foot in front of the other, choosing to keep walking forward.

Inside, a woman behind the desk looked up. "Can I help you?"

"I'm looking for a 1986 summer art class list," Campbell said.

"Oh." The woman started clicking the computer mouse. "Do you know the teacher?"

Campbell shook her head. She didn't even know if she had the right school.

"Well, there was an art class that summer, but…" She continued clicking the keys on the keyboard while Campbell's stomach turned somersaults. "That's what I was afraid of. No class list. Summer classes like that one are considered elective. They're often attended by people in the community, and, well, we just aren't the Ivy League out here."

"So there's no record at all of my mother being in that class?"

"'Fraid not. But you could talk to the teacher, Mr. Hanes. He still teaches here." She jotted down the teacher's information on a sticky note and handed it to Campbell. "If you hurry, you might catch him. He's in the theatre building on the second floor."

Campbell thanked her and hurried out onto the sidewalk, spotted the theatre, and went inside. The smell of sawdust filled the space, and she realized she was backstage.

A college kid dressed in black painted a set piece. He glanced up. "You look lost."

"Looking for Mr. Hanes."

"The art guy? He's upstairs." The kid showed her to the elevator.

As the doors closed, Campbell let out a heavy sigh. What was she doing? This was crazy.

But it could lead to the answer she needed.

What if her mom hadn't told anyone her father's identity because he was older, like a teacher? What if it was Mr. Hanes?

The elevator doors popped open. The walls had been decorated with student artwork, and Campbell imagined her mother, only seventeen, coming here to take her first college art class. She must've been so excited to study something she loved so much. She wiped her wet palms on her jeans and found Mr. Hanes's room, the door partially open. The room was empty, but the light was on.

"Hello?" She looked around but saw no one.

She walked down the hallway, peeking in other classrooms, but the floor was dark. Apparently everyone was out to lunch.

Campbell pushed the elevator button and waited.

"You looking for someone?" A man's voice echoed down the hallway. She turned and saw a tall, stout man with white hair and a white beard standing outside of Mr. Hanes's room.

"I'm looking for Mr. Hanes," she said.

"You found him." He held his arms out at his sides and grinned. "What can I do ya for?"

The elevator doors opened. Her last chance to escape.

Campbell stared at the doors, her heart racing, then turned and walked toward Mr. Hanes. "I just had a couple of questions."

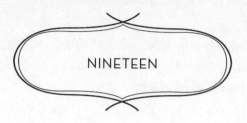

NINETEEN

Campbell

Mr. Hanes ushered Campbell into the classroom. The man, who bore a striking resemblance to Santa Claus, waited for her questions. What if this man was her father? No telling how charming and handsome he'd been twenty-five years ago.

"Sir, I wanted to talk to you about a student of yours. Her name was Suzanne Carter, and she took a summer class with you when she was seventeen."

He frowned. "I have a lot of students, Miss…what'd you say your name was?"

"Campbell Carter."

"So, this girl—she's your mom?"

Campbell nodded. "I was wondering if you might remember her." Campbell opened her purse and pulled out a scrapbook page. She pointed to her mom's photo. "That's her."

He studied the picture, but no sign of recognition crossed his face. "I'm sorry. I don't remember her. If I only had her one summer, that would've been a six-week class. Not much time to get to know my students."

Campbell took the page from him. "You're sure?"

"I am. Is she missing?"

"No. I was actually hoping you might know if she was dating any of the other students or…"

"Or?" His brow furrowed.

"If maybe you might've had some kind of…romance with her?" Had she really just asked that?

Mr. Hanes cleared his throat. "Miss Carter, I don't think I like where this is headed."

"I'm not accusing you of anything." Campbell's stomach churned.

"That's not how it looks from where I'm sitting. Men in my profession have to be especially careful to avoid these sorts of accusations. I can tell you in no uncertain terms that I was never involved with your mother or any other student." He didn't raise his voice, but Campbell didn't question his intent.

"I understand." She cracked her knuckles. "I'm really just trying to find my father. I needed to exhaust all my resources."

His face softened. "Well, no harm done."

"Do you keep your class lists?"

"We weren't computerized back then, but I have files that go back at least that long. I've got my own system, I guess." He walked over to a large metal file cabinet that had to be fifty years old. He yanked the bottom drawer open. "The eighties are on the bottom."

Campbell watched as he flipped through the files and finally held up a manila folder.

"Eighty-six," he said. He opened it and rubbed his beard. "Hm. Looks like there was only one boy in that class."

"Really?"

"Tony Angelotti."

Campbell rummaged through her purse until she found the small notebook she carried with her. "Does it say anything else about him?" Her heart raced.

"No natural talent," Mr. Hanes read from the sheet in front of him. "Guess he wasn't much of an artist."

Campbell smiled. "Thank you, Mr. Hanes. This is really helpful."

"My pleasure."

"If you think of anything else, would you mind giving me a call?"

"Sounds fair," he said.

Campbell jotted down her cell number and thanked him for his time.

She wished the elevator could transport her to a land free of embarrassment. What was she doing accusing random men of being her father? But she'd risk embarrassment all over again if it got her closer to the truth.

Tony Angelotti.

She drove toward Sweethaven, back toward the interstate that would lead her home. But as the Sweethaven lighthouse came into view on the horizon, Campbell started to see things differently. This man, the teacher, had given her a name. A new lead. And, she'd eliminated Mr. Hanes as a father. That was progress. She still had a faceless father, a mysterious grandfather, an unknown benefactor, and a bank account full of money, but she had one solid answer: the art teacher was not her dad. Maybe she could do this after all.

The short car ride back to Sweethaven had been a mental tug-of-war. She considered that it didn't matter where the money had come from. She should accept it and move on. But it did matter. The money felt dirty. Like a payoff. A bundle of *we're easing our own guilt* cash.

She drove to the beach and parked in the lot with the best view of the lighthouse. Mom's old trunk filled the back seat, but she reached the latch and propped the lid open as best she could.

She rifled through Mom's old things and found a Blossom Queen sash and tiara, a pennant for the Sweethaven High School football team, a dried rose, Mom's old Polaroid camera, a stuffed frog with a tag around his neck that read *You have to kiss a lot of frogs before you find your handsome prince.*

Mom never had.

Or had she? What if Lila was wrong and her mom really *was* in love with someone that summer? What if they couldn't be together? Maybe her grandparents had forced them apart. Maybe Tony Angelotti didn't meet their standards.

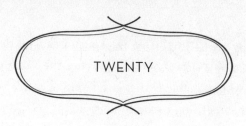

TWENTY

Jane

After she left Adele's, Jane had called Graham, certain he would agree that she'd done enough time in Sweethaven. She could take the scrapbook home and never have to come back to this place. But her husband, as usual, surprised her.

"Hon, you should stay. Didn't you say the Blossom Festival is this weekend?"

"Yes, but we have things at home. Church. Other things."

"Jim's covering for me Sunday. I'm bringing the kids up."

Jane's heart leapt. But as quickly as it soared with happiness it plummeted with fear. The girls hadn't been here in six years. Sam had never been.

"I don't know if that's a good idea, Graham."

"Too late, I've made all the plans."

Jane's pulse quickened.

"Do you really think the girls will be that into summer at the lake anymore? We don't even have Internet access." Why did she insist on carrying this cross alone? Was she the only one who could decide how their family grieved?

"They'll be fine." He paused. "Jane, I think our family needs this. We've been stuck in a holding pattern for six years. Maybe we need some closure."

What could she say? She hung up and realized she'd already started praying.

"God help me through this weekend. I cannot do this on my own." She'd awoken that morning praying the same prayer. Now, sitting at the kitchen table with a large mug of coffee, she felt more peaceful, as if something had shifted inside.

A knock on the door startled her. She walked to the entryway and saw Adele's white hair through the window.

"Hi, darlin'. I brought you a carrot cake." She held the cake holder out as an offering.

"Thanks, Adele, but I don't know if I can have that in my house. The way I've been feeling, I'd probably eat the whole thing myself."

"Cake's meant to be eaten, hon." She stepped inside and shut the door behind her. "Listen, I know it's not easy for you to be here—and that scrapbook houses a world of hurt—"

"No, the scrapbook houses a world of happiness."

"And that's why it hurts." Adele touched Jane's arm. The nearness of another person unnerved her. Times like this she wrapped herself in loneliness and retreated on the couch with a pint of Ben and Jerry's. Knowing Adele, she wouldn't get off that easily.

"The cottage is lovely, Jane."

"We've been renting it out summers," Jane said. "Making a little extra money."

"But you haven't been back since—"

Jane shook her head before Adele could say his name. *Alex.* "No, but Graham's bringing the kids up." She glanced around the cottage, out the window—anywhere but at Adele. Jane hated how weak she still felt, how volatile. One look and Adele would see the pain she worked so hard to bury.

"For Blossom Fest? Perfect. We can do a barbeque at my house."

"I don't want you going to all that trouble." She could smell the sugary sweetness of the carrot cake through the Tupperware.

"Don't be silly. I'll invite Lila and maybe Luke will come." Adele smiled.

"What about Campbell?" Jane searched Adele's face for a sign she'd simply forgotten to mention Suzanne's daughter.

"Of course, if she's still here. She seems ready to bolt back to the city at any second."

Jane sighed. "That's my fault."

"Why would you say that?"

"I went to talk with her after she went upstairs last night. I think I only made it worse. Can you imagine finding out you have a grandfather after all these years?"

"I think she has a lot goin' on right now. I'm still hoping she'll stay around." Adele smiled warmly. "What about you now? How are ya, honey?"

"I'm fine." She sat at the rickety kitchen table, which was distressed from wear and age.

"I don't believe you. I can see it in your eyes." Adele put a hand over hers.

"It's been six years. It should get easier." Jane purposely sat with her back to the window that overlooked the lake. The view made their cottage one of the best on the block—maybe one of the best on this side of Sweethaven. But Jane couldn't stand to take in that view. It mocked her. Reminded her of all she'd lost.

"Let yourself feel the pain. Only way to heal." Adele's eyes carried a sadness—an understanding. Perhaps anyone with children could imagine the horror of losing one.

"I won't keep you. I just wanted to bring the cake by. Would you stop over for dinner tonight? I sure am enjoying the company." Adele's face fell and for the first time, Jane recognized the loneliness in her eyes. The older woman had lost her husband a few years ago, and now that Jane knew she and Meg weren't on speaking terms, she saw a very different Adele. She'd always been so strong, but perhaps Jane had been too caught up in her own pain to notice Adele's.

"I would love to, Adele. What can I bring?"

"Your pretty self is all." She stood. "And maybe a smile if you've got one."

Jane walked her to the door. "Thank you for the cake. I'm sure it's wonderful."

"Believe me, these hips are wearin' their fair share of Me-maw's carrot cake." She laughed. "Enjoy it. I have a couple other stops to make, so I'll get outta your hair."

Jane closed the door behind Adele, and the silence of the cottage haunted her. She walked through the long hallway and into the master bedroom. The bed was made and the room decorated in a nautical theme. Her mother's doing. She heaved her suitcase onto the bed and unzipped the front pouch.

She pulled out a small scrapbook. The plain blue front hadn't been decorated, but knowing its contents brought tears to her eyes. She ran a hand over it but couldn't open it. Not yet. She couldn't see his face smiling at her. Not while she sat in this house. In this town.

She tucked it away and wiped a tear from her cheek.

She lay on the bed and her mind transported her back to one summer on the lake. Even as a kid, she'd never liked the water. Rightfully so, it turned out. It seemed strange now that the lake had been the backdrop for so many of her memories. One in particular flittered to the forefront.

Suzanne lay beside Jane on the dock with one toe in the water. Her red and white bikini showed off her skinny frame and tan skin. Jane twisted the drawstring on her shorts but refused to take them off. No sense sharing her newfound cellulite with the entire beach.

Lila fanned herself with a magazine. She looked like a movie star with her wide sunglasses and perfectly coiffed hair. Jane pulled her legs underneath her, sitting cross-legged on the dock and wishing she could disappear.

Meghan lay on her stomach, her red hair dumped in a messy bun on top of her head. She'd been quiet so long, Jane assumed she'd fallen asleep.

At the end of the dock, Jane spotted Mark Davis and one of his friends. She shifted on her towel. What did she look like next to her three skinny friends? She wished she could crawl into a hole.

She spent most nights staring down the street at Mark Davis's house, wishing he'd come out and talk to her like he used to when they were kids. It was silly, really. Boys didn't like her that way.

"There's your boyfriend, Janie." Lila hopped up and waved at them. "Hi guys!" Like a swimsuit model, she exuded confidence in that pink gingham bathing suit with her long, skinny legs and perfectly golden tan.

"He's not my boyfriend, Lila." Jane's heart raced as the two boys walked toward them.

"Want some lemonade?" Lila held up her cooler and Mark took it from her.

"Thanks." He took a long drink. Lila giggled and flirted. Both of the boys seemed taken with her. Who wouldn't be?

"You guys busy later? We're going over to Jane's." Lila shot her a look.

"Lila." Jane's parents wouldn't let her have boys over and Lila knew it.

"Yeah, that'd be great." Mark flashed a smile at Lila and then turned to Jane. "Haven't been there all summer."

Lila raised an eyebrow. "I'm sure Jane would love to have you over." She winked at Jane. "Jane, what's wrong? You're all red. Too much sun, maybe?" Lila giggled and turned her attention back to the boys.

The sound of a splash caught Jane off guard.

They all turned and saw that Suzanne had jumped in the lake, halting the conversation and saving Jane from more embarrassment. "Come on in, guys, the water's great." Suzanne swam away from the dock, and within seconds all of the attention had shifted from Jane to the water.

The others joined Suzanne, but at the thought of jumping in the water, Jane's stomach tensed. Ever since a wave pulled her under two summers ago, she'd stayed on dry ground.

Jane forced a smile. "I'm going to go home. I think I have to baby-sit today." She didn't wait for them to try and stop her. Instead, she gathered her things and started down the length of the dock, squinting in the bright summer sun.

Tears poured down her cheeks. She dug in her bag for a pair of sunglasses and prayed they would hide the pain she felt at her own inferiority.

Now, standing in the old cottage, Jane begged her mind to stop dredging up old memories. The therapist had said she had control over her thoughts, that she should "take every one captive." It sounded like nonsense to her. She felt helpless to stop the ping-ponging of painful memories. This was why she needed to go back home—to get out of Sweethaven.

She thought about how her life had turned out, how her husband had been exactly what she'd spent those lonely nights praying for. Everything hadn't gone south, so why did she find it so difficult to focus on the good things?

She wrapped her arms around her body and attempted to comfort herself as best she could.

Sweethaven might be a magical place, but for Jane that magic had died six years ago.… And it had tainted everything she thought she knew about the little town she used to love so much.

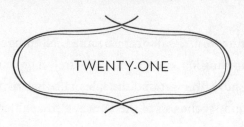

TWENTY-ONE

Adele

Adele picked up the crumb cake and walked out the front door. Her second delivery of the day. The sweets were a good excuse to check in on people, but Luke had accused her of snooping, and now she felt self-conscious about it. Did it show she cared or make her look nosy? The truth was somewhere in the middle.

Adele waved at Ida and Jack Sanderson walking their Yorkie down the middle of the road.

"You two are putting the rest of us to shame with all this walkin'!"

"We're like kids again, we're so healthy!" Ida grinned. "You should come with us some time."

"The only exercise I'm getting is from walking from the fridge to the stove." She patted her backside. "It shows too!"

They laughed and waved, then continued up the hill while Adele hustled in the other direction, toward Main. She turned on Juniper Drive and walked down into a cul-de-sac where a semi-circle of shingled cottages stood, Reverend Carter's home on the corner. The bushes in front of the cottage needed some attention, and the over-sized terra-cotta planters on the porch were now containers of dirt. Adele made a mental note to come back and plant something in them. Even the tiniest bit of color could brighten things up.

Judging by the appearance of the house, things needed to be brightened.

She knocked on the door and waited. Nothing. She knocked again. Still nothing.

Finally, she walked around the side of the house. The back yard faced the woods at the top of the Dunes. Perhaps Reverend Carter had decided to take in the lovely scenery from his three-season room. She rounded the corner and saw a tall Adirondack chair at the center of the back yard. Reverend Carter sat in the chair, staring into the woods, a mug in his hand. Suzanne's funeral had set him back, but he hadn't been himself for months now.

"Reverend?" Adele stepped toward him. He sat stock still. A flash of panic swelled inside her. "Michael?"

Finally, he looked at her with empty eyes. "Adele," he said, his voice raspy, almost a whisper. "I wish God would just take me." Reverend Carter turned his gaze back to the woods.

Adele set the cake down on the ground and knelt beside him. She'd watched his mistakes tear him apart—a man who knew the Lord so well—and she'd always wondered why he didn't accept God's forgiveness. Why did he choose to punish himself when he knew better than anyone that God's grace is more than sufficient?

She laid a hand over his. "How long have you been out here?"

"Since yesterday."

"Since you saw Campbell?"

He nodded.

"How about we go inside? You must be hungry."

"I'm fine, Adele. Don't worry yourself about me."

"We need to talk."

Like a child, the man stood and did as he was told. She took the empty mug and followed him through the back door. Once inside, she saw the magnitude of his pain. Garbage littered the kitchen counters. Dirty plates and silverware were piled high in the sink.

Judging by the odor, the garbage hadn't been taken out for days. Probably since he heard about Suzanne's death.

"I made you crumb cake. Me-maw's recipe. You know how good it is." She watched as he stood, almost in a daze, as if he didn't know what to do with himself.

"I think maybe a shower. I'll go shower. I'll be fine. You go." He waved her off and vanished up the stairs.

This was worse than she thought.

She rolled up her sleeves and got to work. It hadn't been too many months since the last time she paid him this kind of visit. After Suzanne left her house, she came to see her old friend. Found him in a similar state. He hadn't been taking care of himself for a while now.

She washed dishes, took trash to the garage, and put away everything she could in the cupboards. As she worked, she prayed for her friend. In the years since he lost his wife, she'd watched out for him now and then. If she didn't, the pastor would live off frozen dinners. She cared about him, and she knew God wouldn't want him to beat himself up like this.

By the time she'd finished, Rev. Michael Carter had returned, showered and clean, but the water couldn't wash away the sadness that filled his face.

Years of remorse had broken his spirit.

"You didn't have to clean up in here, Adele. I'll get it together eventually." He avoided her eyes as he glanced around at the now clean kitchen.

"Don't be silly. That's what friends are for. Nothin' wrong with gettin' a little help now and then." She cut a slice of cake and set it in front of him. "I made some coffee." She poured a mug, hoping it would rouse him from his trance-like state.

"Thanks, Adele." She knew his appreciation wasn't relegated to a slice of cake and a cup of coffee, but she simply smiled.

Silence fell between them, and Adele suddenly didn't feel right about telling him to go to Campbell and make things right. She'd planned to tell him to stop beating himself up for a twenty-five-year-old mistake, but he almost seemed too fragile to hear it.

"What's she like?"

His question caught her off guard. Her face must've shown it.

"She's a pretty thing. Doesn't look exactly like Suzanne, but still stunning, don't you think?"

A glimmer of something flashed in his eye—hope? nostalgia? pride?

"I do. My son does too, I think." Adele took another bite. "I imagine she could have her pick of young men."

He didn't respond.

"She might need a little guidance, though. From a wise old man like yourself."

"You're not fooling anyone, Adele."

"What?" Adele knew she didn't feign innocence very well, but she tried.

"You think this will be an easy fix, like the end of a Hallmark movie, but people aren't as forgiving in real life as the movies paint them out to be. She will be hurt when she finds out what we did. There's no 'happily ever after' here." He pushed his plate away.

"She's a lot like Suzanne." Sadness filled the room at the mention of her name. Adele reached in her purse and pulled out a small slip of paper. She slid it across the table. "You can do what you want with this, but I thought you should have it."

"What is it?"

"Her contact information."

He stared at the paper, unmoving.

"She's a good kid, huh?"

"A great kid." Adele spent the next several minutes telling him her impressions of Suzanne's daughter. His eyes lit as he listened. "She strikes me as the kind of person with a great capacity for forgiveness."

His face fell. "Some things don't deserve to be forgiven. I know you understand that, Adele."

She looked away.

"It's your choice, Michael. You can wallow in your own self-pity like you've been doin' for the past Lord knows how long, or you can hand it over to that God who you claim to know so well. He doesn't want you to carry this burden anymore. His yoke is easy and all that jazz." She stared at him. "At least that's what my pastor used to say."

Michael smiled. "Leave it to you to throw my own sermons back in my face."

"Call her." Adele stood and covered the cake. "That's yours." She nodded at the cake. "Make me proud and eat it all."

She turned to leave.

"Adele?" The Reverend's voice stopped her. "What if she doesn't want to know me?"

She shook her head. "She does. Even if she doesn't know it yet. Just reach out to her. Take a chance."

TWENTY-TWO

Campbell

For hours, Campbell walked up and down the beach, sat on the park bench and watched seagulls, studied the lighthouse from every angle. The sunset came and went, and still she sat, questions tumbling around in her head like clothes in a dryer.

She dialed Information.

"City and state?"

She searched her brain. She had no idea if the man lived in Sweethaven or Harbortown or Timbuktu. "Um. Sweethaven, Michigan?" It was worth a shot. "Could I have the number for Tony Angelotti?"

"I'm not showing a listing for an Angelotti in Sweethaven."

"Could you try Harbortown?"

"Nothing, ma'am. I'm sorry."

"All right, thank you." Campbell hung up, frustrated.

Was she willing to risk more hurt—more pain—if it would lead her to her father?

She got back into her car and drove aimlessly. When she'd woven her way back to Main Street, she glanced at the clock. The time had flown. It was already 10 p.m. She hadn't even told Adele where she was going; could she even think about going back there? She certainly wouldn't win any etiquette awards with her poor manners lately. The old-fashioned street lights cast golden hues across Elm Street, and Campbell decided if Adele's house had a light on, she'd knock. If not.... She hadn't quite thought that far ahead yet.

Campbell parked across the street from Adele's cottage, which was dark except for the flickering blue light of a television in the front room. She supposed that counted as a light on. Maybe Adele liked to stay up late watching old movies. Like Mom.

Quietly, she got out of the car. Only one way to find out.

She crept up the stairs and listened at the door. Before she could knock, the porch light came on, and she jumped like a burglar caught with a fistful of jewels. The lock clicked. Too late to run away now.

The door opened, and Luke stood on the other side.

Did he live here? He hadn't stayed there the night before.

Strange how his lazy smile comforted her.

"Hey." He pushed open the screen door.

"I'm sorry to show up here so late."

"Don't be silly, come in." He held the door open with his backside and she passed by him, then stopped in the quiet entryway of Adele's house. "We were wondering when you'd be back."

Campbell glanced at him and wondered if he'd been waiting up for her, hopeful she'd return. She quickly pushed the thought aside. It had been inconsiderate of her not to call Adele. She'd been so confused by what she'd discovered, but that was no excuse to be rude.

"What are you doing here?" She wondered if he shouldn't be the one asking her that question. She wrapped her arms around herself.

"I came over for dinner and I guess I'm the last to leave. The TV's out at my place." He shrugged. "Mom's old. She goes to bed early."

She smiled. "I'm gonna tell her you said so."

A soft silence fell between then. She noticed it lacked the awkwardness of forced conversation.

"Come in, sit down." He must've sensed her insecurity.

She'd reached a crossroads and now she had a choice. She could keep probing—keep searching for answers. Or she could leave and continue to live in ignorant bliss. There was something to be said for make believe.

He walked into the living room, clearly expecting her to follow. "Come on, you'd really be helping me out with the old lady."

"I *am* tired. Maybe I could just sit down for a while." She followed him into the living room.

"Do you want something to drink?" Luke had turned off the TV and now folded an old afghan that had been strewn across the couch.

"No, I'm fine. Thanks." All day without eating, and she still had no appetite. Campbell sat in the oversized chair and watched him stick the blanket in a basket behind the couch. "Were you sleeping? Did I wake you?"

"I might've dozed off a little." Luke sat down in the recliner.

"Do you sleep here a lot?" He'd mentioned his own place, but now she wondered if he was too embarrassed to tell her he lived with his mother.

"No, I don't live here." He laughed, as if he'd read her mind. "Mom asked me to come to an estate sale with her tomorrow morning. You know she has an antique store on the edge of town?"

"She mentioned it, yeah."

"She buys these crazy heavy pieces and then doesn't have any way to get them home. That's where I come in." He grinned.

"So you're the muscle of the operation."

He raised his eyebrows. "Yeah, I kinda like that."

She smiled.

"It's just easier to sleep here. Besides, I might get a home-cooked breakfast out of the deal."

She grew quiet as exhaustion set in. With all the driving and the funeral and the secrets and the questions, she'd managed to completely wear herself out.

"You have something on your mind." It was a statement, not a question.

"I have a lot on my mind." She sighed.

"Anything I can help with?"

Campbell told him what she'd found out that morning.

The ticking of the clock above the mantel filled the otherwise silent space.

"So you've got a benefactor?" Luke asked after a few too-long moments.

"You don't think my grandfather…?" She couldn't even say the words. She felt ridiculous suggesting that a man who didn't even want her in his family would actually find a way to take care of her.

He leaned back on the couch. "There's only one way to find out."

She met his eyes. "No. I can't *ask* him."

"Why not? You have nothing to lose."

"I can't. I can't face that man." In a flash, she returned to the night before, standing face-to-face with her grandfather—a perfect stranger.

But she had no proof her grandfather had paid for the house or put money in the account.

"I think you should pay the old man a visit," Luke said. "I've known him for years, Campbell, and I think you'd regret it if you didn't get to know him."

Anger rose from a place down deep. "I'm not the one who tried to get rid of him, remember?" She hated that a man she'd never met could inflict a wound that still hurt after all these years. "Look, knowing that man is up the street changes nothing for me. I'm still as alone as I was yesterday and the day before."

"But he *is* up the street. What if he wants to get to know you?" Luke's quiet tone told her he didn't mean to hurt her. He couldn't possibly understand.

She hesitated and then said, "I can't, Luke. I guess I was hoping I could ask your mom. Maybe she knows something—maybe my grandfather mentioned it to her. She said they were friends."

Luke nodded.

"I just want to know whose money it is before I decide whether or not I'm going to keep it."

He leaned forward, elbows on his knees. "You are crazy. It's *your* money."

"Not yet it's not."

"Your mom obviously put it aside for a reason. She wanted you to have it. She didn't want you to struggle. It's a gift—just take it. Doesn't mean you owe him anything."

She looked away. Didn't it? If she took his money, wasn't she saying she forgave him?

She hadn't. Not now. Maybe not ever.

TWENTY-THREE

Adele

Adele awoke before the birds. She flipped on the lamp by her bed, said a prayer, and then hurried to get ready. She'd been looking forward to the Marvin Estate Sale ever since she heard old Dirk Marvin—Lord rest his soul—had taken his last breath.

Luke's empty room told her he'd either gotten himself up already or he hadn't slept there after all. Surely he knew how important this sale was to her. She wouldn't be able to move that old credenza by herself.

She resisted the urge to push open the door of the guest room and check on Campbell. She didn't fault her young guest for keeping her whereabouts yesterday to herself—she had a lot on her mind, after all. Still, Adele had found herself nodding off in the chair waiting for her to return before she finally gave in and went to bed.

Downstairs, she spotted someone on the couch underneath the old afghan she'd made after she had Luke. Had Luke slept down here? Probably fell asleep watching SportsCenter again. But as she entered the room she realized the blond head underneath the covers wasn't her son.

Campbell? What on earth was she doing on the couch?

The smell of coffee pulled her attention to the kitchen where two long legs stuck out behind the doorway.

She cleared her throat.

Luke glanced up. "Mornin', Ma."

"You're up early." She couldn't remember the last time he'd woken up before her. She sat across from him.

"You said you wanted to leave by seven. Figured I needed a good jolt of caffeine if I'm gonna keep up with you all day." He grinned at her. She still saw the kindergartner in that grin. Warmed her heart.

Campbell appeared in the doorway, looking disheveled and tired. Luke looked at her and then at Adele.

"Hon, come sit down. Want some coffee?"

Campbell sat in the chair between Adele and Luke.

"It's not a latte, but it's caffeine," Luke said as he poured her a cup. Adele's eyebrows shot up. By golly, her son seemed more smitten with this pretty little blonde than he had the day before.

"Honey, I'm so glad you're here." She covered Campbell's bony hands with her own and flashed her a smile. The girl's face brightened, but only for a moment.

"Let me get you some coffee cake." Adele cut two good-sized pieces and put them on her favorite plates, vintage gold-rimmed floral saucers.

"This is Me-maw's recipe," she told Campbell. "You would've loved my Me-maw. She was somethin' else."

Luke rolled his eyes. "Here we go." Luke frowned and ran his hands over his belly, which, if she was honest, hardly existed. He'd eaten her out of house and home for years and still maintained all those muscles. The injustice of it didn't escape her as she glanced down at her thighs spilling over the sides of the chair.

Apparently they wore cinnamon streusel differently.

Campbell took a bite. "I went to Harbortown yesterday. I ended up at the community college."

"Oh?" Adele didn't know whether she was surprised or impressed by Campbell's gumption. Maybe a little of both.

"I have a name."

Adele set her fork down. "A name?" She studied Suzanne's daughter. Had she found her father?

"Tony Angelotti."

Adele stared at her for a long moment and then burst out laughing. "Tony Angelotti."

Campbell's eyes darted to Luke, then back to her, and Adele tried to regain her composure. "I'm sorry. It's just, I know Tony. Well, I did."

"You do?"

"He's not your daddy, darlin'."

"But, how do you know?"

The heartbreak on Campbell's face halted Adele's amusement. "He's older than me, for one thing. Tony fancied himself an artist, but the truth was, the man had no talent."

"That's what the professor said."

Adele covered Campbell's hands with her own. "I'm sorry, sweetheart. But be thankful. Eliminatin' names from your list is just as important as addin' 'em."

Campbell's shoulders slumped as she took another bite of streusel. "Any word from Meghan? Did she respond to my mom's note?"

Adele knew Campbell would eventually start asking about Meghan. Why had Jane and Lila come back but not Meghan? Why were they congregating at her house if Meghan wasn't even there? Why had she allowed so many years to pass without speaking to her own daughter?

"I don't know if we'll hear from Meghan anytime soon. I don't know if she can get away. She's so busy." Luke's raised eyebrows tormented her from across the table. She cleared her throat.

Campbell frowned. "That's too bad. It would be good to have

the entire scrapbook put together. It seems strange she wouldn't at least call."

How did Adele explain her greatest heartache without reliving the sins of the past? "It's complicated."

"Seems like everything is complicated, doesn't it?" Campbell's sad eyes gazed down at the table. "Would you be able to call her maybe? See if she's coming? I'd hate to miss her if she does show up."

Adele glanced at Luke. "Have you talked to your sister lately?"

"Been about a month."

"What aren't you telling me?" Campbell asked.

Adele grabbed the coffee pot off the counter. "I need a fresh cup." She poured more coffee into a nearly full mug.

"Adele. What's going on?"

"It's hard to explain, hon."

"Try." Campbell stared at her.

"Well, I haven't talked to Meghan in a long time. We had a sort of fallin' out, I guess you'd say."

"How long?"

"Six years."

Campbell's eyes widened.

Adele sighed. "Suffice it to say—I am not her favorite person. And all of my attempts to make things right with her have gotten me nowhere. She's stubborn, like her daddy."

Luke scoffed.

Adele shot him a look. "Fine. Stubborn like me."

"But she still doesn't know Mom's gone," Campbell said. "Don't you think we should tell her?"

Adele did think they should tell her. She'd been thinking about it since she first found out about Suzanne, but hadn't worked up the courage. "I suppose we should think about that."

"There's still a chance she'll show up, right? I mean, Blossom Fest lasts all week. Maybe she'll come?" Campbell's eyes were full of hope. Naïve, Adele thought.

"We'll see." Suddenly, Adele didn't feel hungry. She didn't know what she feared more, the idea of being face-to-face with her daughter or the realization that if *this* didn't bring her home, it wasn't likely that anything would.

TWENTY-FOUR

Campbell

Adele glanced at the clock. "We should get going, Luke. Would you like to come along, Campbell? It's an estate sale, so it won't be thrilling, but they can be fun."

"I don't know if that's my kind of thing, but thank you."

"Come on," Luke said. "You can keep me company. I *know* it's not my kind of thing, but I don't have a choice." Luke smiled an almost sympathetic smile. Did he feel sorry for her? Did he feel the pain oozing from every fiber of her being?

"That's okay, thanks." She had to admit, she wanted to spend the day with him. She didn't want a repeat of yesterday, wandering the beach alone, directionless.

"I'll throw in a free latte. With whipped cream."

She met his eyes. "Well, if you put it that way…"

Adele clapped. "Oh, good. Thank you, son, for speaking her language. Now, run get dressed, darlin'. You look like you just woke up."

"I did just wake up."

"That's my point. Hurry it up. We've gotta beat the crowd. Especially Harriet Dillon. That woman had her eye on Old Man Marvin's grandfather clock and I want it. If Harriet wants it, she's gonna have to buy it from me." Adele rushed out of the room.

Campbell laughed, thankful the tension in the room had dissipated. "All right, I'll hurry." Before she could leave Luke grabbed her hand.

"I'm sorry about that," he said. "She and Meghan have been carrying this grudge for a long time. I think she makes herself busy by fixing everyone else. That way she doesn't have to face up to her own issues."

Campbell's shoulders slumped. "It's okay."

"No, it's not. She doesn't mean to be flip. I hope you know that. She just—she's tried to make amends with Meghan, but my sister is even more stubborn than she is. She refused to speak to her. Said she couldn't trust her anymore. "

Campbell knew she should be thinking about something other than the way his hand felt wrapped around hers, but she couldn't concentrate. Questions about Meghan and Adele flittered around in her mind, and she couldn't seem to lasso a single one in. "It's fine, Luke, really. I'm fine."

He stood, still holding her hand. "Let me know if that changes, okay?"

She nodded. Words escaped her.

"All right, you should hurry. If I know Mom she's probably already in the truck."

A horn sounded from outside.

They laughed.

"I told ya. She's serious about these antiques."

Campbell hurried to get ready, and after a few short minutes, she met Luke and Adele in the driveway. Adele hopped down and let Campbell sit in the middle.

She climbed up and inhaled the scent of Luke's woodsy cologne.

Not everything in Sweethaven confused her. Some things

seemed straightforward. Like these budding feelings she couldn't contain when she sat next to Luke.

The truck bounced on the brick road as they headed out of town, toward what Adele described as the Estate Sale of the Century.

"I teased Old Man Marvin I was gonna walk away with that clock when he wasn't lookin'. It's beautiful. It's gonna be heavy. Luke, we're going to need more than just you to move that thing."

"I figured," Luke said. He seemed to be half-listening.

"Are you payin' attention? I need you to pay attention." Adele leaned forward and glared at him.

"I'm right here, Ma. Can't hardly ignore you." He grinned at Campbell.

Campbell enjoyed the playful banter between Luke and his mom all the way through town, then out past Adele's shop and finally down a winding road called Kennedy Hill. They turned on a long gravel driveway, passed through an open wrought-iron gate, and spotted several cars parked in the grass around the old house.

"Is that Harriet's old Buick?" Adele squinted in the morning sun. "If she beat me here, Luke, you are in trouble."

"What'd I do?" Luke looked surprised.

"You drive slower than Me-maw."

Campbell laughed.

"Okay, that's not Harriet. You're lucky, son," Adele said. "Just drop me off here and go park."

"So bossy today, old lady." Luke slowed the truck.

Before he'd come to a complete stop, Adele opened the door and hopped down. Campbell watched her trot up to the front where a short line had begun to form.

"Look at her. There's no stopping her." Luke leaned over the steering wheel. "She's on a mission."

"How does this work? Does she have to beat everyone here in order to get what she wants?"

"She gets first dibs if she's first. There's a whole set of rules to this stuff."

"I thought it was like a garage sale."

"Don't let my mom hear you say that." He laughed. "You'd get an earful."

She focused on the driveway as Luke pulled into a makeshift parking space alongside the outermost car.

"We can hang out here for a few minutes. We probably should've driven separately—it's going to be a long day," Luke said. "I don't think she'll even need me for a couple of hours."

"We should go get that latte you promised," Campbell said, in dire need of more caffeine. Sleeping on Adele's couch had made for a fitful night.

He grinned. "Good idea. That'll give me a chance to check in on Delcy. I scheduled extra help, but I'd feel better knowing things are okay. Let's go tell Ma so she doesn't freak out if she sees the truck leaving." He popped open the door and hopped out.

Luke offered her a hand to help her out of the truck. She took it, setting off unfamiliar sparks inside. Her simple feelings threatened to become more complicated the more time she spent with him.

She reached the ground safely, and he squeezed her hand twice before letting it go. She pretended she didn't miss his touch as soon as they disconnected.

"Do you come to a lot of these things?" Campbell asked as they walked toward the line of people.

"I've been to my fair share. When I moved back here it was one of my tactics to get back on Mom's good side. You think she's sweet, but you don't want to cross her." He smirked.

"Why were you on her bad side? Don't all moms want their kids to stay close? My mom was thrilled that I stayed close. She used to beg me to move back in with her after I got my own place." Her voice wavered, and she decided not to replay that conversation with her mom.

He ran his hand over the stubble on his chin. "It's complicated," he said. He glanced down at her as a slow smile spread across his face. "Just kidding." He bumped into her with his shoulder.

"Very funny." She returned the smile.

"I went to school and got a great job in the city."

"You? A city boy?"

He shrugged. "I know, hard to believe, right?"

"What kind of job?"

"I was an architect. Worked for a great firm."

"And?"

He stuffed his hands in his pockets. "Long story short? I couldn't cut it."

She quieted. "I don't believe that."

"It's true. I hated that lifestyle. Hated the fast pace. Hated working such long hours. Hated all of it."

"So, you wanted a simpler life. Doesn't mean you couldn't cut it."

"Same thing, really."

"No, it's not. You made the choice to come back."

"And my mom thought I was throwing everything away. All that school—all that supposed talent I had."

"Ah. Well, I can see why she felt that way." Campbell glanced at Adele. She'd secured a good spot in the line and now chatted with some of the other poor saps waiting for the sale to start. "She wants you to have more than she had."

Luke laughed. "Not exactly. My mom had a pretty good life. She gave it up—decided to move here. I guess I thought she'd understand."

"She moved here for you guys?"

"For Meghan. I wasn't born yet."

"But she didn't want you to stay here?"

"There's not a lot of opportunity in such a small town. She didn't realize she'd raised me to be the kind of person who loves the simple life. That's the price of growing up in Sweethaven." He looked at his mom. "But I wouldn't be happy anywhere else."

What did it feel like to be so tied to a place? To have roots and history? She didn't have that with a town. With her mom's house, maybe, but not the suburbs. Or the city.

She liked the idea.

They'd almost reached Adele when Luke grabbed her hand. "You know what, on second thought, we don't need to tell her what we're doing. She knew I owed you a latte."

"What? We're almost there." Campbell laughed, but then she faced the house and saw Adele talking to an older man. A familiar man. Her grandfather.

Like characters in a slow-motion replay, the two of them turned toward her.

There was no turning back.

Had Adele lured her here on purpose? Or called him to tell him to come?

Luke fidgeted and placed a hand on her shoulder. "We can go," he said quietly. "Let's go."

She stood still. Shock prevented her from moving or speaking.

Adele took a step toward her, but she held up a hand to stop her.

"You did this on purpose," Campbell said, hurt crushing her.

The old man turned away, as if it was too painful to look at her. As if he was ashamed of her.

"I didn't. I promise, Campbell. I didn't know your grandfather would be here, but here we all are, so why don't I introduce you?" Adele stood only a foot away now, and Campbell could feel anger bubbling inside.

"I should go," the old man said, still not looking at her.

"Or I should. Wouldn't that be better for you? For me to just disappear?" Campbell glared at the man.

"Campbell, don't." Adele took a step closer.

"It's not your place, Adele." She turned back to her grandfather. "Tell me it's not true. Tell me you didn't punish my mom for having me. You hung her out to dry, and she was just a kid."

The man turned away, still avoiding her eyes.

Campbell looked at Adele. "I told you this wasn't what I wanted." She rushed toward the truck on numb legs.

"Ma, how could you do this?" Luke's voice verged on angry.

"Hon, I swear, I didn't know..." Adele's voice faded into the background as Campbell got farther and farther away.

The sound of footsteps behind her told her Luke was following her. Before long he fell into step beside her.

"I'm so sorry," he said. "I had no idea he would be here. I've never seen him at one of these things before."

"Maybe your mom invited him."

"She likes to meddle, but I really don't think she'd do that to you."

Campbell hated the tears that welled in her eyes and the unwanted baseball that had plopped itself squarely at the center of her throat. She tromped toward the truck, wishing she could run into the open field until it met the water and then swim somewhere far away.

She reached the truck and pulled the door open. Luke climbed in the opposite side but didn't turn the engine on.

She stared out the window.

"Are you okay?"

"Just take me back to your mom's so I can get my stuff. I should leave for real this time."

Silence filled the cab of the truck.

Finally, she risked a look at him. His worried eyes stared intently at her.

The weight of his concern nearly paralyzed her. She had experienced nothing but rejection when it came to the men in her life. Why should she expect anything different from Luke? She mentally chastised herself for even thinking about a guy so soon after her mom's death.

"Campbell, you can't run away."

She didn't respond. He couldn't possibly understand.

"I admit, that was uncomfortable, but he does have answers to some of your questions. Maybe he's sorry for the way things have turned out."

"He didn't look sorry to me." Her voice cracked, and she swallowed her pain. "This is too hard, Luke. If seeing that man makes me feel like this, I'm not sure I can handle seeing my father. I don't know if it's worth it anymore."

He stared at her for a minute. "Look, I promised you a latte. And I'm not going back on my promise. After that, if you want to leave, I'll drive you back to my mom's myself." He reached across the seat back and let a hand rest on her shoulder. "Sound fair?"

No. None of this sounded fair. It wasn't fair that she didn't have two parents to love her. It wasn't fair that her mom had died. It wasn't fair that the man responsible for Mom's misery stood only yards away, and it wasn't fair to know he never loved her.

But she didn't say so. Instead, she nodded and continued staring outside, away from the crowd gathering at Old Man Marvin's Estate Sale.

* * * * *

"The table in the back is the best one. Go ahead and sit down and I'll get the coffee."

Campbell sat in the corner and looked around The Main Street Café.

Only a few minutes passed before Luke returned. "Delcy's making the drinks. How are you doing?"

She didn't answer.

"You haven't said a word since we left."

"I'm just processing, that's all."

"It's a lot to process."

She sighed. "You can say that again." She ran a hand through her hair, smoothing out the back, wishing she could disappear, curl up into a ball, and go to sleep until all of this went away. Wake up with a new life.

"The way I see it, you have two options. You can run away and never know the answers to any of your questions. Or you can face him. You've done nothing wrong." He stopped and looked at her. "Maybe there's a reason you've run into him twice now. Maybe Reverend Carter knows who your dad is."

At that, she met Luke's eyes. She'd considered that, but if her mom's friends didn't know, why would her grandfather? Unless he'd forced it out of her mom. Would Mom have buckled under that kind of pressure?

"Maybe you should talk to him. Find out what you need to know, then close that chapter for good. No law says you have to have a relationship with the man."

A young girl with crazy, cute curls and mocha-colored skin walked over to the table and set two huge mugs of coffee in front of them.

"Campbell, this is Delcy; Delcy, Campbell."

"Nice to meet you." Delcy smiled. "Don't let this guy talk your ear off. He likes to hear the sound of his own voice."

Campbell laughed. "Nice to meet you too."

Delcy left Luke with a sheepish expression on his face.

"She's my best friend's little sister. Might as well be my little sister. She graduated from college last year—needed some time to figure things out."

"We have that in common."

"That and you're both full of attitude." He laughed and took a drink of the frothy latte.

"You really think I could just ask him my questions and that'd be it? What if he doesn't want to talk to me?"

"We're back to that, are we?" He grinned. "Yes, I think so, but would it be so bad to hear him out? Maybe even forgive him for being stupid?"

"Be pretty hard. You saw him back there. He wasn't exactly excited to see me."

"I think he was just surprised." He sighed. "And probably embarrassed."

The fear of being rejected by him reared its ugly head, clamoring to be entertained, but she forced it away, replacing it with a new thought. *Choose, for once, to believe the best about someone.*

It took all she had.

TWENTY-FIVE

Lila

The tangy scent of barbecue struck Lila's nostrils as soon as she opened Adele's back door. "Hello? Adele?" The screen door slammed behind her.

"I'm in the kitchen, darlin'." Adele stood at the counter, a floral apron tied around her midsection and a wooden spoon in her hand. "Makin' the barbecue for tonight. Figured I needed to do one thing today that wasn't a total disaster."

Lila frowned. "What do you mean?"

"Come in, hon, you don't need to hear about my troubles."

"Don't be silly. Pour me a glass of sweet tea and we'll have a chat." Lila scooted one of the kitchen chairs out and took a seat.

Adele looked surprised.

"I'm turning over a new leaf," Lila said. "Trying to be more sympathetic."

"Sweethaven has bewitched you, darlin'." Adele poured two glasses of tea and sat across from Lila. "I'm so mad at myself. Campbell ended up coming back late last night."

"She did?" Lila hadn't expected that. She figured they'd run the poor girl off for good.

"She did. And then she came with me and Luke to an estate sale this morning and ran into her grandfather." Adele's face fell. "I think Campbell thought I set her up, you know, brought her there on purpose because I knew Michael would be there."

Lila watched the older woman. "Did you?"

"Of course not," Adele said. "But just knowin' she's out there thinkin' I did, it's just tearin' me up. I was so off my game I didn't get anything at the sale. That wretched Harriet Dillon even snagged the most beautiful grandfather clock right out from under my nose."

"I'm sure Campbell will be fine once you explain things to her," Lila said. "Where is she now?"

"With Luke, I think."

"*Oooh*." Lila flashed a smile. "What cute babies those two would make."

"Don't get your hopes up. Luke falls hard, but it never seems to take."

"He just hasn't found the one."

"Aren't you romantic?" Adele set her tea down and stared at her.

Lila's attempt to laugh came across as more of a scoff. "Not really," she admitted. "Probably part of my problem."

Adele stared at her for a few seconds and then smiled. "Well, at least you're honest. Every now and then, a true confession's good for the soul."

Lila stopped. "Adele, you're brilliant."

"Why, thank you." She looked puzzled. "What'd I do?"

"Can I look through the scrapbook pages?"

Adele looked down at the artwork stacked in a neat pile in front of her.

"I just remembered this goofy thing we used to do. 'True Confessions.' We'd write our deepest, darkest secrets in really small letters on the other pages so no one would ever find them unless they knew they were there."

"Clever." Adele pushed the stack toward Lila and leaned in closer.

"You put them back in order?" Lila started flipping the pages.

"I started to—was that wrong?"

Lila smiled. "No, it was really thoughtful of you. And it'll make this so much easier." She started at the back and scoured the pages for hidden messages.

Lila sifted through the pages carefully. If only she could remember where they'd inserted those hidden messages. Finally, after combing through several pages, she spotted it. "I think I found something." Lila stuck her index finger on the scrapbook. "Look."

"Darlin', if you think I can read that small scribble, you are outta your mind. Just tell me what it says." Adele pulled four apples from the fridge and set them on the counter.

On the side of the page, one of the girls had hand-written bubble letters to spell out the title "The Boon Docks." Inside the bubble letters was one of Suzanne's hidden "true confessions."

"It says, 'I have a secret crush. No one can ever know. He's around all the time, and it's getting harder to pretend.'"

Adele frowned.

"I was thinking about it this morning. Who did we know back then? And then I remembered about Mark Davis."

"Mark Davis? The doctor's son?"

Lila nodded. "He, Tom, Nick, and that other kid, Gunther. They were always around. Especially the last couple summers we all spent together. Jane had a terrible crush on Mark. And you know Jane— she was so painfully shy. Suzanne warned me to stay away from him—said he liked me, but maybe she wasn't looking out for Jane. Maybe she was looking out for herself."

"You think Suzanne and this boy carried on a secret affair?"

Lila laughed. "I don't think I'd call it an affair. She was only seventeen."

"What would you call it then?"

Lila shrugged. "A mistake."

"At any rate, how do you intend to prove it?" Adele sat down.

"I'm not sure. I thought I'd start with Jane. I mean, she and Mark were good friends. Maybe he told her."

"True, but don't you think she would've mentioned it by now?"

"I don't know." Lila stood. "I'm going over to Jane's house. Want to come with me?"

"No, but invite her here for dinner. Her family too if they've arrived. I told her already, but she won't come unless we bug her."

"Her family's coming?"

"Might already be here."

Lila left Adele's and drove toward Jane's house. How familiar it felt to be back in town after all these years. It amazed her how easily she fell back into the Sweethaven groove, where life was slower paced and laid back. She'd forgotten how much she needed that. Several people had gathered in the Square to set up for the Blossom Festival. By the weekend, this place would be filled with tourists and visitors and summer residents, all out to enjoy the music and food, the vineyards and orchards, the charm and beauty of the place she'd abandoned all those years ago.

In that moment, she decided never to ignore Sweethaven again. Tom might not enjoy it as much as he used to, but being back here, Lila knew she needed it in her life. Mama and Daddy had offered her the lake house years ago, but she'd refused. Tom wouldn't come with her so what was the point? It had been so important to him to get out of his hometown—to make something of himself. Why didn't he want to come back now that he'd accomplished that goal?

She picked up her cell phone—just out of curiosity—but she hadn't missed any calls and Tom hadn't left her a message. As she drove, the same question kept running through her mind: where did they go wrong?

TWENTY-SIX

Jane

Jane hung up the phone and stared at the clock. Graham said they'd just exited I-94 onto Main Street and were only a few minutes away.

She held the small blue scrapbook in her hands. It had been therapy, making that book. She'd done it alone, in the dark of night, without the daughters she usually scrapped with. She'd created it to comfort herself, but now it had the opposite effect on her. Rather than soothing her, it drew every ounce of stuffed-down emotion to the surface—the ones she usually buried with chocolate cake and sugar cookies.

She lifted the cover and saw his face smiling at her. He'd been only six years old, with a wide gap in his mouth where two front teeth used to be. Beautiful boy. Fresh tears sprang to her eyes. She sniffed and wiped them away. Six years had passed and she'd carried the pain of losing him like a satchel on her back.

A honk sounded outside, and she snapped the scrapbook closed. The minivan pulled into the driveway. Jane hid the book at the bottom of her suitcase. She checked her mascara in the mirror and paused at the sight of her ordinary features and chubby cheeks.

She forced a smile in an attempt to prepare for their arrival. After all, she welcomed the distraction of their presence. No more agonizing silence.

She walked to the front door and opened it just in time to meet her girls as they came up the front steps.

After pulling them both into a tight hug, Jane pulled back and looked at the two of them. Beautiful girls. Both brunettes with Graham's icy-blue eyes. Did they remember that day as clearly as she did? Did being back here dredge up the past like raw sewage in a backed-up gutter?

Emily walked past her and set her bags down in the entryway. Jenna locked eyes with her for a long moment, and Jane finally had to break the gaze. She knew Jenna felt responsible. She knew the pain that guilt brought with it. They had that in common.

She strengthened herself for her daughter's sake and hugged her again. Sam's shouts as he ran up the walk interrupted the moment, and Jenna pulled away. She gave her mom one last knowing look before she headed toward the bedrooms.

"Mom, this is so cool!" Sam's little-boy voice echoed through the entryway, and within seconds the house that had taunted her with silence had filled with squeals of joy. He ran past her and explored their cottage—their home away from home, the place he'd never been allowed to visit.

Graham stood in the doorway, his arms loaded with bags, and stared at her.

"It feels so wrong," she said.

He took a step in and dropped the bags. "Alex wouldn't want you to stay sad forever."

"But being here—in this place—the last place where we were all a family..." Jane stared at him through tear-filled eyes.

She remembered reaching the top of the dune leading down to the beach, the red and blue ambulance lights twirling and flashing, sending panic straight into Jane's soul. When she saw the girls standing in the sand, holding each other and crying, she broke into a run. Lucky barked. Meg, soaked to her core, stood on the beach, hovering over a small circle of paramedics.

As she approached, Jane saw they were surrounding Alex, who lay limp on the hot sand.

"Mom!" The girls ran to her.

Jane fell to the ground. "Alex?" She crawled closer, barreling her way through the paramedics. One of them administered mouth to mouth, but Alex didn't respond.

"God, no," Jane prayed.

Emily cried and clung to Jenna.

The EMT stopped trying to breathe for Alex and looked at the other paramedic. He shook his head.

"You aren't going to stop, are you?" Jane's voice sounded shrill in her own ears. "You can't stop! That's my son."

She watched as they loaded Alex's tiny body into the ambulance.

Meghan took a step closer and put a hand on Jane's shoulder. Jane shrugged her off and glared at her. "I'll never forgive you."

The paramedic extended a hand in Jane's direction. "Ma'am, we've got to close this now."

Jane watched as they continued CPR, but the life had gone from his body. In that moment, she knew.

Her son, her Alex, was gone.

TWENTY-SEVEN

Lila

Lila pulled onto Lilac Lane and drove past the cottage where Mark Davis had lived, just down the street from Jane. Did his family still own it? They were seasonal, so it's not likely they would've sold it unless they had to.

Jane's family cottage sat at the center of a cul-de-sac, its back yard jutting up to the lake. Her family had never had money. How they came upon the quaint white cottage with black shutters had always been a mystery. Jane seemed to think someone left it to her grandparents in their will.

Lila saw two cars in the driveway, the one Jane had been driving and a blue minivan. So that's what Jane had become. A soccer mom. She'd expected nothing more from her friend. No one had. Jane was built for motherhood.

Which is why it had to have been that much more painful to lose her son.

Despite the passing judgment, Lila envied Jane's life. Her friend had everything that mattered—and Lila had everything else.

She knocked on the door, and a little dark-headed boy opened it and stared at her with big blue eyes.

"Hi." Lila smiled.

"Mom, there's a lady at the door."

"Sam!" Jane's muffled voice trailed outside. "You are not

supposed to open the door to strangers." She spotted Lila. "Oh, thank heavens it's just you."

"You know her?" Sam stared at his mom.

"Yes, Sam, this is my friend Lila."

He shrugged. "Guess she's not a stranger then."

"Go play." Jane swatted his behind with a dishtowel. "He's all ham, that one."

Jane unlocked the screen door and let Lila in.

"Are you really worried about strangers in Sweethaven?" Lila asked.

"No, but we won't be here for very long, and if he gets used to it here, he'll do it at home. And he can't do it at home."

"Right." That had never even crossed Lila's mind. She really would've made a lousy mother.

"You want something to drink?" Jane turned and headed toward the kitchen.

"Isn't it weird? Being in this house as the grown-up?" Lila followed her.

Jane opened the fridge and looked inside. "I was just thinking that same thing. All those years I spent here with my mom and dad—and now I'm the mom and Graham's the dad. I still feel like I'm nineteen most days. Only with a spare tire around my midsection." She laughed.

"How long will you stay?"

"I'm not sure. Graham insists on taking the kids to the Blossom Festival. You know how I feel about this place. I was ready to leave before I even pulled into town."

"Still?" Lila took the tall glass of lemonade Jane offered.

"Still. It's not the same." Sadness filled her eyes.

"At least Meghan's not here. I mean, that would make it harder, right?"

"I don't know. Sometimes I wonder if she *was* telling the truth.

If she watched him go under and there was nothing she could do. Those rip currents can get pretty crazy out there, and Alex was kind of a daredevil. The girls don't even remember. They just remember turning around and he was gone. Just like that."

"I'm so sorry, Jane. I should've called."

Jane held a hand up to stop her. "It's okay. I'm getting better. I spent the first couple of years angry. Even after I had Sam. I was still angry. Sam was a surprise. Right after Alex's funeral, I found out I was three months pregnant. I felt like God gave him to us to replace Alex—and that didn't seem fair."

Lila wished she understood. A bitter taste filled her mouth. How dare Jane talk about it being unfair when God had given her so many children? All she'd asked for was one. One. Was that too much to ask?

"So, I punished God for a while. I was so angry that He took my baby. But eventually, I realized God has a bigger plan. I don't know why Alex died that day—and you better believe I'm going to ask God when I get to heaven. But for now, I have to trust what I know about God. That He's good. And His ways are always right. I couldn't stay angry with Him. Not after all He's given us." Jane looked at her. "Who am I kidding? My head knows those things, but my heart still isn't quite convinced."

Lila sipped her drink. The silence gave her a few moments to reflect. Four miscarriages. Two almost-adoptions. All the fighting between her and Tom. Two people with nothing in common but an address.

She had many reasons to be angry with God.

"Sam's a doll," Lila said.

Jane's face brightened. "He is, isn't he?"

"And I like the minivan."

Jane laughed—loud—and grabbed Lila's hand. "I've missed you, my friend."

The words threatened to melt her, and Lila didn't often melt for anyone. She pushed the sentiment aside and focused on why she'd come.

"I found something I wanted to show you." She pulled the Boon Docks page from her bag and set it on the table.

Jane gasped. "This was in Suzanne's stack."

Lila nodded. "Yes, and look in the title. Look close."

"My goodness, did you find a true confession?" Jane picked up the layout and squinted to read the tiny print. "It's not one of mine, is it? I'd be mortified to read what I wrote then. My eyes are getting old. I can hardly read this."

When she finally read the sentence, her face went pale. She looked at Lila, horrified. She'd obviously put it all together.

"It was Mark Davis."

Jane's expression changed. "What?"

"Don't you remember? He was always hanging around that summer, but you had a crush on him—that's why Suzanne couldn't tell us. Because if she did, you wouldn't have forgiven her and you two were so close."

"We were close," Jane said. "But I don't think she and Mark—"

"Jane, it makes perfect sense. She and Mark were always flirting. I know you thought maybe he liked you, but—"

"I didn't. I never thought that."

Lila tossed her a look that said *Come on, Jane.*

"I hoped. But I didn't think that. Boys didn't like me like that. Not until Graham."

The back door opened and two beautiful teenage girls entered. With long dark hair and naturally tan skin, they were built like athletes. And they both belonged to Jane.

"Mom, that coffee shop downtown is awesome. I got a latte for like three bucks."

"That's great, Em. Emily, Jenna, this is my friend Lila."

Two gleaming white smiles greeted her. "Nice to meet you," they said practically in unison.

"Is it okay if we borrow your car?" The older girl, Jenna, flipped her hair behind her shoulder. "They're doing a fish fry down at the beach."

"You're going to the beach?" Jane's eyebrows drew downward and pain haunted her eyes.

"We were thinking about it," Jenna said.

"It's a youth fish fry, Mom. Put on by the Sweethaven Chapel. I don't think you have to worry about anything." Emily's voice dripped sarcasm.

Waves. Currents. Darkness. Plenty for a mom to worry about. At least, Lila imagined there was.

"I don't know about the beach, girls."

"Da–ad." They both looked at their father.

Graham stood off to the side, his arms loaded with groceries. "We'll discuss it and let you know." He tossed a glance at Jane then set the groceries on the counter.

The two sisters looked at each other, exchanged eye rolls, then left the room.

"Graham. Not the beach," Jane said.

"Hon, they'll be fine." Graham rested his hands on Jane's shoulders and then looked at Lila. "Lila, it's good to see you again. How've you been?"

"Can't complain." Lila admired Graham's eyes. Jane had really struck gold with this man. Tall, good-looking, stable, caring. Even in the way he looked at Jane, Lila could see how much he loved her. No one would say that of her and Tom.

"All right, I'm going to go check out the grill situation for dinner tonight." Graham gave Jane one last squeeze.

"Oh, I almost forgot. Adele wanted me to remind you about her barbecue tonight. Pulled pork sandwiches with coleslaw and the works. Don't make me go alone, okay?"

"Works for me," he said. "Adele can cook for me anytime."

"Okay," Jane said. "We'll go. The thought of not having to cook again tonight is pretty appealing."

"Good."

"Then I'm going to go find Sam and see if he wants to go ride his bike or something. It's a nice day out there." Graham started for the door. "See you tonight, Lila."

Lila watched him leave. "He's a good guy, Janie."

"I know. The best guy."

"You're lucky."

"He's so good all the time. He forgave a lot easier than I did."

"I've had four miscarriages," Lila whispered. "And two babies were almost mine, but both birth mothers changed their minds after they were born. I've had more almost-children than anyone I know."

Jane's shoulders slumped, her expression changed. "I'm so sorry, Lila. I should've been there...."

Lila shook her head. "No. We're not going to do that to ourselves." She smiled, but she knew the smile did nothing to mask the sadness she felt. "I *haven't* forgiven, though. I'm still angry. I never got to have a family. The one thing Daddy couldn't buy me. Ironic, huh?"

"You've lost so much. I'm so sorry."

Sitting in that kitchen with Jane's support and the weight of her secret out in the open, peace began to creep into Lila's spirit. It inched in, a little at a time, and curled up inside her like a stray kitten at her feet.

It was a peace she hadn't known in years. A peace she couldn't have purchased—not for any price. A peace she hoped she could hang on to.

TWENTY-EIGHT

Campbell

Campbell stared at the bottom of her empty coffee cup, wishing she had more caffeine. More time. More courage.

Luke stood at the counter going over instructions with Delcy. She watched his easy way with customers, Old women smiled and laughed as soon as they saw him. Harried young moms carting small children and in dire need of coffee fixes seemed to soften in his presence.

He glanced in her direction, checking up on her. She straightened in her seat. He could probably see right through her.

He walked toward her table. "Let's go for a walk." He held a hand in her direction.

She stared at it. When she finally took it, he laughed. "No, I need your mug."

"Oh." Her face ignited. If only there was a hole to crawl into.

"But I'll take that too." He grabbed her other hand.

With her hand in his, she walked out of the café, aware of the many pairs of eyes that watched them go.

"There'll be talk." He pushed the door open.

"They'll get the wrong idea." From the sidewalk, she glanced in the window. Four older women sat at a table watching them. When their eyes met Campbell's they quickly turned away.

Luke's eyes stayed intently on her. "What would be the wrong idea?"

She shrugged. They took a few steps down the block, out of sight of the nosy Sweethaven clan. "You know, that you're off the market. Then you might lose business."

"That *would* be pretty terrible."

"I'm sorry I misunderstood back there." Campbell stared down the street.

"Don't be." He stopped walking and looked at her. "Listen, I know you've got a lot on your mind, so let's do something fun."

"Like what?"

"You have your camera?"

She lifted the oversized bag that hung on her shoulder and patted it with her other hand. "Always."

"Good. I promised to take you on a tour of Sweethaven, and I'm starting with the place I think you'll like the best."

"Okay—" She hesitated. It seemed unreal that only an hour ago she'd been ready to hit the road.

He turned to face her, took both her hands in his. His face grew serious, and she felt her eyes widen. Her stomach fluttered at his touch.

"I don't want to pretend like all of this stuff is just going to go away, but maybe it'll help to get it off your mind for a while. Is that okay?"

Her pulse quickened. She hated that she liked him so much, so soon. He seemed to understand her already, even better than she understood herself.

She finally nodded. Then, gently, he pulled her close, wrapped his strong arms around her, and held her head to his chest. As she listened to his heart beat in her ear, he smoothed her hair and rested his chin on the top of her head.

He didn't say anymore, but his touch spoke loud and clear. *You're going to be okay.*

When she pulled back and saw that her tears had moistened his gray T-shirt, she knew all attempts to hold back her tears had failed.

"I'm sorry." She wiped her face dry.

"Don't be. I can handle a few tears." He let go of one of her hands and kept the other one firmly wrapped in his. As they walked, she started to feel the ball of stress in her stomach slowly unravel. Like a soothing balm, the beauty of Sweethaven spoke to her soul. It medicated her, took the sting out.

As they passed Sweets of Sweethaven, the smell of donuts wafted onto the street. "We're stopping here, right? Is this the place you thought I'd love?" She inhaled the delicious aroma of the old-fashioned bakery.

He shook his head. "We'll stop there later. There's somewhere else I want you to see."

They passed a small hardware store and finally stopped in front of the Sweethaven Gallery.

She'd visited many art galleries in Chicago and didn't expect much from one nestled in this tiny beach town in Michigan. She realized as she peeked through the door that her elitist attitude had been unjustified.

Four small awnings topped the vertical windows of the second floor. A wider, matching awning hung above the oversized front window. The brick building had a solid, old feel to it, confirmed by the 1854 date embedded in the masonry near the front door.

"I think you'll like it in here." Luke led her inside.

An older woman with reading glasses propped on her nose and a paintbrush in her mouth sat at an easel behind a long counter. Engrossed in her work, she didn't look up as they entered, reminding Campbell of Mom's concentration when she worked.

"Deb?" Luke walked toward the long wooden counter.

The woman startled and looked in their direction. "Luke." She set her brush down and walked around the counter to greet him. She pulled him into a quick hug and then turned her attention to Campbell. "Who's your friend?"

"This is Campbell Carter," Luke said. "You remember her mom, Suzanne?"

Deb let out a high-pitched "Ohhhh," and clasped her hands in front of her face. "I do remember Suzanne. She was one of my best students. How is she?"

Campbell fidgeted with the bag on her shoulder, unsure of how to break the news. "Actually, she passed away a few days ago."

Deb's face filled with horror. "What?" She shook her head. "She was only, what? Forty-one? Forty-two?"

Campbell nodded. "Forty-two."

"What happened?"

"She had cancer."

Luke shifted.

Deb took her glasses off and wiped a tear from her cheek. "That's just so unfair."

"Campbell's a photographer. I thought you might show her around the gallery."

The woman regained her composure and put an arm around Campbell. "A photographer? So you inherited your mother's artistic genes?" She squeezed her tighter. "She loved to spend time here during the summers. Such a shame when she stopped coming to Sweethaven. My whole world got a little darker."

"I'm sorry." Campbell felt solely responsible for the darkness in this stranger's world.

"Don't be silly. She went off and got a real life. Good for her. I would've loved to see her before she passed away, though."

"Deb, do you happen to know if she had a boyfriend the last

summer she was here? I know she took an art class at the community college, but the teacher had no records. I thought maybe someone she met there?"

Deb scrunched her forehead. "Do you mean Jared Kimball?"

"Jared Kimball?"

"He's still in the area. In fact, he has a piece in the studio right now." Deb walked over and stood in front of a dark painting.

"What is it?"

Deb tilted her head. "I'm not sure. He was always a troubled boy. A local. Suzanne must've felt sorry for him. She kind of took him under her wing."

Campbell shot Luke a look. His eyes widened, and she knew they were thinking the same thing.

"Deb, do you think they could've been dating? Secretly, maybe?"

Deb frowned. "I suppose it's possible. Lots of girls fall for the dark, brooding artist type. Why do you ask?"

"I'm looking for my father."

Deb sighed an "Ohhh."

"How old was she when she and this Jared person hung out?"

"Gosh, I'm not sure. Fifteen, sixteen maybe?" Deb took her glasses off and let them fall on a chain around her neck.

"Not seventeen?"

She frowned. "Could've been, I suppose. You could always look him up. He lives over on Petunia Place."

Campbell's stomach lurched. Did she have the courage to approach another stranger and ask if he was her dad? "Maybe. Thanks."

"But Campbell, if you decide to do that, make sure you take Luke with you." Deb walked toward the front of the gallery.

"Why?"

"Like I said, Jared was a troubled kid. He never really found his way. He's a talented artist, but he's had a few run-ins with the law. I just wouldn't want you to approach him on your own."

Great. So the only lead Deb had for her was an emotionally unstable criminal?

Campbell looked away.

"I'm sorry." She squeezed Campbell's hand.

"Don't be silly. I'm ready for the grand tour."

Deb walked Campbell back to the front door and turned her around. "To get the full effect, we have to start at the beginning. Notice the floors? Those are all original. The building was built in 1854. I wanted to take it back to that time with our renovations."

"It's really beautiful," Campbell said.

"It is, isn't it? I love the tin ceilings."

Campbell looked up. Exposed pipes matched the high white tin ceilings. Light burst through the front windows. They passed a baby grand piano, and she perused the art on the long white wall. Piece by piece, she soaked it in, let it feed her creative soul.

"It's been so long since I've been in a gallery," she said. "My mom and I used to go all the time."

"These are mostly local artists, like Jared, but we have a few from Chicago and around the country. I've been thinking about adding more photography in here. You should bring in your portfolio." Deb stopped in front of a small painting of a ballerina.

"Really?"

"I'd love to see it."

Campbell smiled. She knew the gallery was small, and Sweethaven wasn't Chicago or New York, but it also wasn't *The Buzz*. It was real art. If she hung there, it'd validate her talent. It was a start anyway.

"I'll bring it by." Campbell was already running through photos suitable for her portfolio.

"The sooner, the better. I don't know how much longer I'm going to keep this place open." Deb walked to the next painting and stared at it.

Campbell frowned and looked at Luke. He leaned against the counter but offered no explanation.

"What do you mean?" Campbell asked.

"I'm too old to keep doing this. I love this gallery, but do you know I have never been to Italy? Life is too short not to take breaks every now and then." She looked at the painting in front of her and sighed. "I've always wanted to go to Italy."

"Why don't you hang your mom's paintings in here?" Luke's voice filled the cavernous space.

"Your mom still painted?" Deb turned to her with a smile. "I would love to see."

Luke walked toward them. "Better yet," he said, "why don't you take pictures of the things she painted and you could hang them side by side? Like a mother-daughter art show." He held his chin up, looking pleased with his own brilliance. "She has canvases of all the places her mom loved here in Sweethaven."

Campbell smiled. "That's not a bad idea."

"It's a brilliant idea." Deb beamed. "It may be the last show I do; let's make it a good one. A tribute to Sweethaven. When could we do it? Too bad we didn't have it ready for the Blossom Fest this weekend. We get so many out of towners."

Luke's raised eyebrows challenged Campbell from across the room.

"Could we open it in a few days? The festival is all week, right?" Campbell asked.

Deb shrugged. "Sure, why not?"

Campbell fished her camera from her bag and shot a couple of pictures of Deb's glowing face. "I've gotta run. I've got pictures to take."

TWENTY-NINE

Campbell

The streets of Sweethaven shone with new promise as Campbell set out to capture the charm in pixels and prints. Before she started, she needed to look at Mom's canvases again. Thank goodness she had brought them with her.

Luke drove her to Adele's house and helped as she lugged the oversized trunk out of the backseat of the car.

"How'd you even get this in here?" Luke set the trunk on the patch of grass next to her parking spot.

"I'm a lot stronger than I look." Campbell grinned.

"I'll keep that in mind."

She popped the trunk open and started pulling the canvases out, propping them against the car. One by one, she showed them to Luke, and when he recognized the spot, she wrote it down on her list.

"Are you sure you don't mind showing me these places?" Campbell asked.

"You'll never get this done on your own—not in two days," he said.

"That doesn't answer my question."

"Are you kidding? Gets me out of the café. Better views. I love this stuff."

She narrowed her eyes at him, trying to decide if he was telling the truth.

"What? I'm serious. If I didn't, I'd draw you a map."

She laughed. "Fair enough."

"Campbell, what's this?" Luke pulled at a corner of the inside of the trunk's lid, where the covering had peeled away.

Campbell moved in closer. "Looks like the backing on the lid is loose." She picked at it with her finger.

"Looks intentional."

She pulled at it for a few more seconds, then stuck her fingers inside.

"Wait." He tipped the trunk on its side, careful not to let its contents spill onto the street. As he did, something brushed across her fingers.

"There's something in there." Campbell wiggled her fingers until finally she grabbed hold of something solid underneath the lid. Carefully, she worked it out, pulling it through the opening she'd created.

"What is it?" Luke righted the trunk and sat down on the curb next to her.

Campbell ran her hand across the front of a sealed envelope. "It's a letter. To my grandparents. From my mom." She looked at him. "Returned to sender." The stamp on the front of the envelope told her the letter hadn't been delivered. Her grandparents had sent it back. Unread.

"Are you going to open it?"

She handed it to Luke. "You do it."

"What? No. It's personal."

"Right. So, maybe I should just leave it alone." Campbell set the letter inside the trunk.

Luke stared at her for a few seconds and then pulled at the hole in the cover.

"What are you doing?" she asked.

"I'm wondering if there's anything else in there."

Campbell watched as he made the hole larger. "We could cut it."

But even as she was getting the words out, he pulled the cover off and exposed the trunk's secret underbelly. A stack of letters, identical to the one they'd already found, fell into the base of the trunk alongside something else—a small stack of scrapbook pages. Pages her mom had kept hidden.

She picked one up and studied it. A photo of the Sweethaven Dock adorned the left center of the page. Underneath, her mom had painted a design, and beside it, she'd written a long journal entry.

Mom's handwriting hadn't changed over all these years. It read:

Strange thing happened last night. Fought with Cathy— as usual. Dad's getting more and more upset that I refuse to call her Mom anymore. She thought I was sleeping, but I left. Like in a movie, I climbed out the window and shimmied down a tree. Didn't even know I could do that. Cut my thigh in the process.

I wish I could've taken a picture of the sky. Pitch black. No moon. Stars dancing like crystals playing with the sun- light. In seconds, I forgot why I was angry in the first place.

I went to the dock and put my feet in the lake. The water was cool and it felt good on my toes. I lay down on the dock and found the Pleiades, Orion, and Cassiopeia. I didn't even hear him behind me. He asked if he could sit with me. Said he had a lot on his mind. I never really paid attention to him before. I mean, we're friends, sure, but not really. He's preoc- cupied. This is our last year before we're officially grown-ups.

We didn't talk at first. Just stared at the sky. He found the Milky Way. How'd I miss it? He asked me what I was doing out there so late at night and I told him. I told him the truth. Even my friends don't know how bad things are at home, but I spilled it all. Maybe it felt safer since it was so dark. I'm going back tonight. I'm embarrassed to say it, but I hope he's there again.

Campbell's heart threatened to pound straight through her chest. She stared at the page, reading the last paragraph two, three times.

Had the answers been with her the whole time?

She flipped through the pages quickly, scanning the journaling for any mention of a name, but there was none. Only "he" and "him" over and over again. Her mom had been purposely vague, but why? Could it be Jared Kimball?

"If your dad had a troubled past, I can see why your mom would've kept it a secret if she had something going with him. Her parents wouldn't have approved."

"I need to think about this." Campbell had tried to imagine introducing herself to Jared Kimball, but in her mind she always stumbled over the part where she asked if he had a relationship with her mom. Did she even have the courage to keep pursuing this?

"You can't quit now. It's what you came here for. If you go back home now and you don't find out, you'll always wonder."

Campbell looked away.

"Look, we'll just close it up." He shut the lid of the trunk. "We'll go shoot pictures and you can come back to this whenever you decide it's time. But just think about it, okay?"

She nodded.

He opened the passenger door to the truck and motioned for her to get in. They drove downtown, and he parked outside the Sweethaven Train Station.

"Um, I don't think a train is going to work for this trip," she said.

"Have a little faith, will ya?" He turned the engine off, jumped down, and walked over to her side of the truck.

She watched him, unmoving.

He opened her door. "Seriously, it'll be fine," he said. "Come on."

"You do know I have a deadline now, right? And it won't be daylight forever?"

"Come on, trust me."

She took his offered hand and stepped onto solid ground. When he didn't loosen his grip, she felt that flutter back in her stomach.

"You sure you wouldn't rather read those letters?" He prodded now. Perhaps he was more curious than she was.

"I'm positive. Stop asking me." She smiled, and they crossed the wide sidewalk in front of a yellow wooden building with hunter-green trim.

"Wait, I've seen this before." The building reminded her of a photo she'd seen in the scrapbook of her mother and her three friends peeking out the back of an electric trolley.

They crossed the tracks and walked up to a window that had been cut out of the side of the building. Behind a counter sat a man, reading a newspaper and chewing on a toothpick.

"Hey Russ," Luke said as they approached.

The man didn't respond.

She glanced at Luke, who seemed unfazed by the lack of interest.

"Hey, we were hoping you could take us for a ride. A couple stops so my friend here can take some photos. It would only take about an hour."

He was so optimistic.

Russ shuffled his papers as he tried to turn the pages, but he still didn't respond.

"Free coffee for a week," Luke offered.

That warranted a sideways glance, first at Luke and then at Campbell. Russ's brow furrowed, and his eyes turned to slits as he sized her up. "Two weeks."

"Ten days."

"Deal." He closed the paper and folded it in half twice. "Who's your friend?"

"Campbell Carter."

"Related to the Reverend?"

The question caught her off-guard. Until that week she hadn't been related to anybody but her mother.

"Suzanne was her mother," Luke said.

"Was?" Russ tossed the toothpick from side to side with his tongue.

"She passed away just a few days ago," Campbell said.

He frowned. "Shame. I always liked that one. Used to let her ride around for free."

Why did fond memories of her mother nick her heart like a too-sharp razor on loose skin?

"We're in kind of a rush," Luke said.

"Don't start bossing me around, Mr. Coffee." Russ lifted the counter and locked the door. "I'll get there when I get there." Judging by his slow movements, it might take awhile.

Luke tossed Campbell a look that told her their banter was playful, and she followed them down the platform to where an electric trolley was parked.

"I took your mom and her friends on our very first ride." Russ stepped into the trolley and sat behind the wheel. "The trolley hasn't been here forever, but the day it opened, those girls hopped on board, all four of them with their own camera. You'd have thought they were the tourists."

"They were good friends, weren't they?" Campbell had never

had those kinds of friends. Her friends had been fair-weather. She brushed the thought away.

She snapped a picture of her view from inside the trolley, Russ's profile off to the left, his worn wrinkles deep and telling. She imagined it in black and white.

Luke showed her the places her mother had painted, and she photographed those, but as she worked, a different idea welled inside her. She had her own story to tell through images: the story of Sweethaven through the eyes of a stranger. A tiny seed of excitement had burrowed down deep inside her and now twisted and turned and begged to be watered. The creativity seed.

She couldn't ignore it. Her hair blew away from her face as they rode down Main Street.

"Just tell me when you see something you want to look at." Luke draped his arm on the back of the wooden bench where they sat in the rear of the trolley.

The same two old men she'd seen together once before sat on a park bench at the corner of two downtown streets. The trolley moved slowly enough now that she could raise the camera and zoom in to capture the smiles of the two old codgers. *Click.* They spotted her and one of them waved. Another *click.*

Luke waved back. "That's Charlie and Dale. They're both widowers. Both been coming to Sweethaven since they were kids. They retired up here. When the weather gets nice, they spend all day on that bench. Notice they've got their sack lunches and a big thermos of coffee."

She focused the camera again, zooming in on wrinkled hands wrapped around a thermos lid of a steaming drink. *Click.*

From behind the camera she waved as they passed by, and the men laughed. "Make us famous," one of them shouted.

"That was Charlie," Luke said.

As they rode along, she clicked off a few shots of the entire downtown area through the open window at the back of the train.

She could almost picture her mom, Jane, Lila, and Meghan riding bikes down the brick road to the candy store to fill a bag with jelly beans and then dashing off to the soda fountain for root beer floats. Her mother had walked these streets.

For that matter, so had her father.

Her thoughts turned to the hidden scrapbook layouts she'd found. The words on the page told of the beginning of a crush, or at least an infatuation. Who was the boy who stole her heart? A dark art student? A gangly admirer? What if the pages placed her no closer to the truth?

An even scarier thought popped into her head: what if they did?

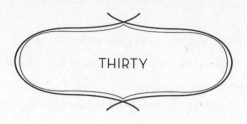

THIRTY

Jane

Jane watched Lila pull out of the driveway and disappear down Lilac Lane. She'd been asked to locate Mark Davis—a task that wouldn't be difficult but seemed completely ridiculous.

Off the hook for dinner, she walked out back, wondering if she should think about planting some flowers this year. Mom had always kept up on the flowers. Their yard had exploded with color every year. Now it looked dry and empty.

Who was she kidding? She didn't need to landscape the yard of a house she had no intention of revisiting. Her conversation with Lila left her analyzing her own heart. She'd made peace with God, but she still carried a grudge against Meghan. The thought shamed her. Logic told her it wasn't her friend's fault, but blaming Meghan meant not shouldering all the blame herself.

Because trying to carry that burden had nearly killed her.

Graham tossed a ball to Sam in the back yard. Sam whipped it back and pelted his dad in the leg.

"Good aim, buddy. Next time, maybe not so hard." Graham threw it back.

Jane sat in a lawn chair and watched for a few minutes, thankful the trees obstructed the view of the lake.

"All right, let's take a break, Samster," Graham said.

"Okay, I'm going to play my DSi." Sam ran toward the house.

"Half an hour, buddy," Jane called after him.

Graham settled into the chair next to her and stared until he had her attention.

"What?" She knew the look on his face meant trouble.

"I didn't say anything." He took her hand. "How are you doing?"

She sighed. "I feel like this trip has set me back months. I was doing so well."

"No, you just stopped thinking about it all the time," Graham said. "And now, it's smacking you in the face."

"Punching me in the gut is more like it."

He stayed quiet.

"Lila thinks she found Campbell's father."

"Really?"

"I don't buy it, but she's convinced. She wants me to find out if this guy's family still owns the house down the street."

"Why you?"

"Because our families were friends."

"And why would it be such a secret if it was this guy?"

"Because I had a huge crush on him." Jane giggled. She looked at Graham. "He was so dreamy."

"I don't want you talking to this guy," Graham joked.

"I just think Lila's got the wrong person."

"You have another idea?"

She shrugged. "I don't know. Maybe. Maybe not." She paused. "We may never know now."

"True."

Empty flowerpots flanked the back door. "I know we're not coming back here, but do you think I should plant some flowers in the yard?"

He looked at her. "Why couldn't we come back?"

She shook her head.

"The kids love it. Emily and Jenna could use a little small-town life. Maybe a couple of weeks this summer would do us all some good."

"I don't want to talk about it, Graham. Forget I said anything."

"Just think about it. I believe it's good for us." He took her hand. "All of us."

But thinking about it meant thinking about the lake. And thinking about the lake meant thinking about Alex. And thinking about Alex meant being in pain.

And that's why she hadn't wanted to come back here in the first place.

* * * * *

Campbell

Against Deb's better judgment, Campbell had looked up Jared Kimball in the Sweethaven phone book and now pulled into what appeared to be his driveway. The GPS had led her to a gravel road on the outskirts of town. When the voice told her to turn right, she nearly missed the turn for all the overgrown brush that covered the driveway.

The car bounced down the gravel drive until she turned a corner and a tiny white house came into view. Outside sat a late-nineties–style Nissan with rust above the tires. Campbell took a deep breath and willed herself to calm down.

The curtains on the second floor moved, and a yellow-headed little girl appeared between the two sheers. When she met Campbell's eyes, surprise crossed the little girl's face and she disappeared back behind the curtains.

Campbell walked up to the house and knocked deliberately on the door, wondering if there were any more children hiding inside.

And then she wondered if they were her half-siblings. She'd always imagined having a sister.

The sound of the door jolted her back to reality, and Campbell waited for Jared Kimball to appear, but when it popped open, a tired-looking woman stood there, scowling at her.

"Can I help you?" She bounced a curly-headed baby on her hip.

"I'm looking for Jared Kimball."

Her expression changed, and she looked Campbell up and down. "Has he gotten to you too?"

"I'm sorry?"

"Where'd he pick you up, the bar downtown? Or are you the girl from the smoke shop?"

"No, I've never met Mr. Kimball." Campbell wrung her clammy hands.

"Obviously not." The woman laughed. "If you had, you wouldn't be calling him 'mister.'"

"I just wanted a moment of his time. Is he here?"

The baby fussed, and the woman hollered inside. "Libby, get down here."

The little girl Campbell had spotted in the window appeared in the entryway, and the woman handed her the baby. "Take your brother into the kitchen."

The little girl could barely manage the weight of the baby, but she hobbled away, leaving the two women alone on the front step.

"I haven't seen Jared in…oh, probably ten days now. Said he was going out for some smokes and he still isn't back. I guess he drove 'own to Florida to get his cigarettes or something."

Campbell nodded. "I understand."

"What do you want him for?" She squinted, still seeming suspicious of Campbell.

Campbell knew telling this woman her real reason for coming was out of the question, so she searched her mind for another explanation. "It's nothing, really. I heard he might've known my mom—a long time ago. They were art students together."

"Yeah, Jared always said he was an artist."

"Well, I'm sorry to bother you."

"No bother. You want me to give him a message—if he comes back?"

Campbell opened her mouth to respond but quickly thought better of it. She shook her head. "No, that's okay, thanks."

"Suit yourself."

Campbell got back in her car and stared at the run-down house. The little girl reappeared in the window and stared at her like a prisoner craving the sunlight. Campbell waved at her, but the girl disappeared without returning the gesture.

She started the car and drove back toward town. Perhaps it was better not to find out if Jared Kimball was her father.

THIRTY-ONE

Lila

Lila sat in one of the overly soft armchairs in front of the faux fireplace at the Main Street Café. She clutched her Chanel bag and watched the door. She'd asked Campbell to meet her there, but she hadn't said why.

"Couldn't we just talk tonight at dinner?" Campbell had asked.

"I think it would be better if we spoke in private." Her cryptic response must've piqued the girl's curiosity.

Unfortunately, the only information Jane had found in the past two hours was that the Davis family still owned the cottage down the street and that Mark was expected in town for the Blossom Festival.

This revealed nothing about his relationship with Suzanne. It was all just a hunch.

"You shouldn't tell her until we know something," Jane said on the phone.

"She has a right to know it's a possibility. I would want to know," Lila said. "We told her we'd tell her if we thought of anyone."

"And if it's not him?"

"Face the facts—she kept the secret for a reason."

Jane's heavy sigh told her she didn't buy it, but Lila didn't feel like forcing the issue. All she could do was present Campbell with the facts. She could do what she wanted with the information.

The bell over the door rang as Campbell walked in. Luke

lowed behind her the same way boys used to follow Suzanne.
ma said ordinary boys wanted someone approachable and
rage—someone who didn't challenge them. "But you don't want
ordinary boy, Lila. You deserve someone special."

Lila shoved the memory aside and waved in Campbell's
ection.

Campbell walked toward the armchairs while Luke spoke with
of the girls behind the counter.

"Lila, what is it?" She sat down and stared—her eyes wide and
ectant. Second thoughts rushed to Lila's mind.

"It's…"

"My father? What'd you find out?"

Lila never empathized with the women in Macon. She pur-
ely kept her distance from them. But the women here pulled her
nd she genuinely cared what happened to them and how they
Campbell's heart lay on the line here, and she knew she could
it in two if she weren't careful.

'It's just a hunch." Lila proceeded with caution. "It could be
ing."

Who was she kidding? All the qualifiers in the world wouldn't
Campbell from getting her hopes up. She'd spent her whole life
ut a daddy.

I thought of someone who was around a lot that summer. He
wns a house here. In fact, Jane found out he's going to be here
eekend."

mpbell's face went pale.

is was a mistake. Lila should've listened to Jane and dug
a little more before telling Campbell anything.

may be nothing, but I thought we should check it out. I can
for you if you want me to."

Campbell stared at her. "I've got a few leads I'm looking into too. I'd love to hear what you found."

Lila took the scrapbook page from her purse and showed Campbell the confession. "His name was Mark Davis. He was Jane's neighbor, and she had a huge crush on him for a few summers in a row, really until she met Graham. Your mom would've never done anything to hurt Jane, but—"

"It does look like Mom's handwriting," she said.

Lila leaned back in the chair. "I know this is hard for you so take your time with it. I was thinking Jane and I could get in touch with him if you'd prefer. We can let you know if there's anything to it."

"So is there anything besides this confession to make you think it was this Mark guy? Did my mom spend any time with him?"

"We all did," Lila said. "Jane knew him best, but boys were naturally drawn to your mom. I don't think she meant for it to happen, but if it did, I can see why she'd want to keep it a secret."

"Because of Jane."

Lila nodded and ran a hand through her hair as she looked around the café. Being back in Sweethaven unearthed every regret she'd worked hard to bury. She'd convinced herself those three girls meant nothing to her. It'd made it easier to walk away, but it wasn't easy, and she had suffered for it. She'd masked her loneliness and covered it with pride.

Had Suzanne suffered for it too?

"If he's coming this weekend, could you point him out to me?" Campbell asked.

"Sure, and I'll see what else we can dig up." Lila leaned forward. "I hope it was okay for me to tell you—even though it's not certain."

"Of course. I'm glad you did. I was starting to get discouraged."

Campbell picked her bag up off the floor and then turned back to Lila. "Thanks for letting me know."

Lila smiled and watched as Campbell walked toward where Luke stood waiting for her. He leaned against the counter nonchalantly, but Lila could see plain as day that he'd fallen for this girl—hard.

He had that look in his eyes, the same look she'd seen in Graham's eyes. Concern. Worry. Love. Had Tom ever looked at her that way?

She pulled her cell phone out and tried to reach him one more time. Still no answer.

This time, she decided to leave a message. "Tom, Suzanne died. She was gone before she could make it here. I'd really like to talk to you."

As she spoke, her mind wandered. Maybe he was at the attorney's office, working out the details of their divorce.

"Could you possibly call me back?" Anger wound its way around her heart.

Or maybe one of the flight attendants had caught his eye. She slammed the phone shut without saying good-bye and forced the thoughts away.

THIRTY-TWO

Campbell

Luke waited for her by the counter, anticipation in his eyes. "Well?"

"She thinks she figured out who my father is."

"Really? That's great." His smile faded as he read her expression. "Why aren't you smiling?"

"Just nerves." She forced a smile. She hadn't told Lila about Jared. Maybe a part of her was too afraid to find out the truth.

"What if he didn't know you were his?" Luke asked, pulling her from her thoughts.

"You mean, like, my mom never told him?"

He shrugged. "Could've been. If it was that big a secret. There's got to be a reason she kept it to herself. Maybe she didn't even tell the guy."

"I guess." She almost hoped that was the case.

"Who'd she say it was?"

"Some guy named Mark Davis."

"Dr. Davis? Really?"

"You know him?" A twinge of hope flickered in her mind, but she forced it away. She could not get excited about a maybe. All the childhood fantasies of fathers she never had rolled into one giant ball of humiliation and taunted her.

"Sure. He's here every summer. A lot. He's a big-shot cardiologist or something."

"He's coming this weekend for the Blossom Festival."

"He's a good guy. Has three kids, I think."

"And a wife?"

He nodded. "Melissa. Nice lady."

Campbell looked away. If she confronted this maybe-father, she could ruin things for his real-life wife and family.

"You want to get back to the photos?" Luke glanced outside. They'd cut their tour short when Campbell got Lila's call. "I had to promise Russ another week, but he said we could come back."

"I think maybe I need to be alone." Sorrow wormed its way into her belly as she said the words. It wasn't what she wanted. She wanted to hop back on the trolley, tour Sweethaven with this handsome guy, and take pictures of all the places her mom had painted. Land and buildings rich with history—*her* history.

She did not want to watch his face fall or his smile fade.

"I'm sorry, Luke. I think I have some things to sort out."

"I understand. Will you be at my mom's for dinner? She's throwing a pre–Blossom Festival bash and she wants you to come. I think Jane's whole family will be there and Lila's coming…"

"Sure. I can do that." She forced a smile. "Thanks for understanding."

They stared at each other for a few seconds that felt a lot longer, and finally Campbell looked away.

"I guess I'll see you tonight," he said.

She nodded and walked outside.

As nervous as she was to meet Dr. Mark Davis, her conversation with Lila had given her hope. A big-shot cardiologist or a deadbeat dad: one of these men had to be her father. She wanted to cautiously entertain the idea that in a matter of days, she could find out his identity. The sun shone down on her face, and she reveled in having an open afternoon. No commitments—only her and her camera.

As she walked toward the lake, her mind wandered. She took her shoes off, feeling the warm sand soft beneath her feet. In the distance, she glimpsed the lighthouse her mom had painted. The carousel. The boardwalk. The places of her mom's youth.

And her dad's.

Zoom. Click. Click. Click. Her camera captured the sights.

The more time she spent here the harder it got to ignore the fact that she had another parent. Somewhere. And for years she'd been trying on different dads in her imagination, but none of them had stuck.

What would it be like to find him? What if Dr. Mark Davis had her upturned nose or her blond hair? What if he had long, thin fingers like hers? What if his three kids were her half-siblings, and they invited her to be part of their family?

Or what if his wife left him because he'd never told her the truth about having a daughter? She'd already ruined enough families—she didn't want to risk ruining another.

But you deserve the truth too.

The names Jared Kimball and Mark Davis rambled through her head. Someone had to know the truth.

Seagulls chirped overhead. She imagined the beach was filled with people during the summer, but now it was virtually empty. A man threw a Frisbee to a golden retriever, a young woman jogged on the sand near the water, and an old man sat on a bench just ahead in the distance.

An old man. Tall. Lanky. Familiar.

Her grandfather.

He didn't see her. She could run the other way, but something stopped her. This man could have the answers she needed. Would he turn and walk away from her after the way she'd spoken to him at the auction?

Her words rushed back and heat crawled up the back of her neck. She had to find out for herself.

But the nagging question of the money rose in the back of her mind. And what if he had forced her mom to tell him who had gotten her pregnant?

But Lila and Jane will find out the truth. You don't need him.

She could ask him and then go. Luke was right—she didn't have to have a relationship with him. She'd ask him the question and that'd be it.

Simple.

But as she got closer, as he looked up and saw her approaching, she realized there was nothing simple about it. In all her years of imagining the perfect father, she'd never considered a grandfather. She'd never entertained the idea that her mom hadn't told the truth.

He stared at the ground, as if he couldn't bear to look her in the face.

The closer she got the more she wanted to turn around. Run away. Get back in her car and never come back to Sweethaven again.

But she had questions. And he had answers, so she kept walking.

"Would you like to sit?" He looked at the bench next to him. His quiet voice surprised her. He seemed...broken.

She willed herself not to feel sorry for him after what he'd done to her.

They stared at the water as it lapped the shore. Birds hopped on wet sand. A man with a metal detector passed by and waved. The man at her side lifted a hand in recognition.

The tense silence stretched between them like a tightrope pulled taut. Her mind whirled with questions.

"It's beautiful here, don't you think?" He focused on the lake.

A quick glance at him and then back to the lake. She didn't respond.

"I moved here year-round when Cath—your grandmother—died. People thought I was crazy, but they'd never been to Sweethaven. What do you think of it?"

She shifted in her seat and straightened her shoulders. She didn't want to have a conversation with him. She didn't want to enable him to ease his guilty conscience with a quick chat about the weather.

"It's nice." She wished she'd spent her summers here, running the beaches with girlfriends and learning how to scrapbook their memories with Mom and her friends, but his actions had prevented that.

"I was sorry to hear about your mother."

"Did you pay off Mom's house?" she blurted.

He turned to her. "What?"

"The house is paid for. Was it you?"

She could see by the look on his face he had no idea what she was talking about.

His shoulders slumped, and he sighed. "I wish I could've done that for you. We never had much extra money."

She bit the inside of her lip to keep from crying, but her eyes betrayed her and clouded anyway. If he hadn't given them the money and paid for the house, then who had? Certainly not Jared Kimball.

She stared at the water. A young family walked on the long dock that led to the lighthouse. The mom held the hand of a toddler, and the dad carried an older child on his shoulders. From a distance, they looked like the family she'd always imagined having.

Too late now.

"I'm sorry." Her grandfather's frailness surprised her.

She turned to face him, and he looked away.

"I'm sorry for everything."

He wasn't talking about the house. Or the bank account.

Conflicted feelings rose inside her. Part of her wanted to tell him she forgave him. That's how her mother had raised her.

"You can't hold onto this stuff, Campbell," she'd said. "The bitterness will kill you."

But some things couldn't be forgiven with two simple words. Surely Mom understood that or she would've made amends before she died.

Reverend Carter's eyes welled with tears that glistened in the light of the setting sun. "I have so many regrets."

Starting with her birth.

"Your mom came by to see me the day she was here, in Sweethaven. She said she forgave me. She'd had a good life and raised an incredible daughter. It shamed me that she'd offer her forgiveness when we were so terrible to her. We'd tried to get her to give you away."

Campbell chewed on her lip.

"Your grandma was so embarrassed. She couldn't get past that pride and focus on what Suzanne really needed." He shook his head. "And I went along with it. Suzanne was so belligerent, so strong-willed, but I know she was terrified. I should've been there for her."

She couldn't think about that right now. She didn't want to be the priest at his confessional.

"You don't know who my dad is, do you?"

He shook his head.

She stared at him for a long moment, determined to discern if he was telling the truth.

"I tried to get her to tell me. I wanted to wring the kid's neck. She wouldn't say a word. I thought she'd have told you though."

"She didn't get a chance."

Campbell stood.

She couldn't help him. She couldn't take his regret away. Nothing she said would make what he'd done disappear. His actions had wounded her—as much as she hated to admit it—and sticking around for a second dose seemed like a stupid thing to do.

He didn't have the answers she needed.

"I have to go." She didn't move for a long moment. He stared at the water. She should have more to say. She should be able to forgive.

But she just wasn't ready.

Not yet.

Maybe not ever.

THIRTY-THREE

Adele

With Luke's help, Adele hung paper lanterns in the grand oak tree in her backyard. They positioned her favorite long table underneath and decorated it with sprays of twigs and tulips. Swathes of floral fabric hung at the front of the table, held together by small bouquets of white flowers.

Inside, the pulled pork simmered in the Crock-Pot, cooked first in vinegar and then bathed in homemade barbeque sauce. It should be falling apart by the time her guests arrived. Two large pitchers of sweet tea sat on either side of the long table. The coleslaw was finished and the apple dumplings almost done.

Now to clean herself up. Her guests would arrive shortly. She hadn't seen Jane's family in years, and she'd told Lila to invite Tom, but judging by the reaction she'd gotten, she didn't expect him. Campbell hadn't been around all day, and the quiet house begged to be filled with laughter again.

The phone rang, cutting through the silence.

"Hello?"

Nothing.

"Hello?"

Just as she was about to hang up, the person on the other end cleared her throat.

"Hello?"

"Mama?"

Meghan.

Her face warmed, and tears sprang to her eyes.

At the sound of Meghan's voice, Adele's mind conjured images from that day six years ago—a day filled with regret.

"Mama, something happened to Alex," Meghan had said, her face stained with tears.

"What's wrong, Meg? What happened?"

Her daughter's face fell then and instantly Adele knew. The unthinkable. "What'd you do?" Her words escaped before she could stop them, and the hurt registered on Meghan's face in an instant.

"It was an *accident*," she said, her eyes pleading.

"Is he okay?"

Meghan shook her head. "I don't think so, Mama."

Adele's pulse raced, her heart beating at lightning speed. Without thinking, she grabbed Meghan's arm and searched for track marks, then studied her eyes for signs she'd been using again.

Meghan recoiled. "You think I'm high?"

She dropped Meghan's arm. "I don't know what to think, Meghan."

"I'm clean. I told you." Meghan stared at her, probably searching her face for signs of an ally. "You don't believe me." She looked away.

"I just have to be sure, Meghan. After everything, I have to be sure. If that boy is gone—" Adele's voice caught in her throat. "If it's *your* fault, I need to know."

Meghan's shoulders dropped as the air escaped from her body. Adele watched as pain filled her eyes and, without a word, she turned around and walked out of the kitchen, then out the front door without even a backward glance.

Adele watched as she drove away, unaware that her daughter would cut off all contact for years.

She thought about that moment every day, and now, with Meghan on the other end of the phone, the pain rushed back and her chest filled with the pressure of regret.

"I got a letter—from Suzanne."

"I know, hon. We hoped you would show up for Blossom Fest." She tried to keep her tone light, in spite of the weight that buried her.

"Probably not a good idea."

Adele took a deep breath. "Hon, Suzanne didn't make it. Her daughter sent those letters to you girls. She died a few days ago." What she wouldn't give to hug her daughter right then.

Meghan paused. "She's gone?"

"I'm sorry, darlin'."

Silence fell between them. They had so much to say. And in less than an hour, her house would be full of people, but her daughter wouldn't be one of them.

"Come home." Her heart spoke the words. Meghan's kids were in Sweethaven—with their daddy. Adele always wondered how her daughter went such long stretches without seeing them. If it weren't for their other grandmother, Violet, Adele would spoil them every chance she got.

After a long pause, Meghan sniffed. "I can't, Mama."

"You can. Everyone misses you. We all want you here. With us."

Regret wove its way through her heart. She should've called and told her about Suzanne as Campbell had recommended.

"I went through my scrapbook pages," Meg said. "I found one I did about you and that Tammy Wynette song you used to sing to me at night. Even when I was in high school."

Adele remembered. The tune of "Bedtime Stories" drifted into her mind, and a smile passed her lips.

Softly, she sang the chorus into the phone and realized Meg was singing with her. She wiped a tear away as the music closed the gap between them, just as it always had. The years she'd wasted now filled her with remorse. Why had she stopped trying to make it right? She never should've given up. You don't give up on your kids—no matter what.

"I close my concerts with that song," Meg said.

"You do?"

"Every one."

Adele smiled through her tears. "I'd love to hear that someday."

"I'd love that too, Mama."

Mama.

"Meg, I'm sorry. For everything."

"Oh, sorry Mama. My manager's calling on the other line. I gotta run."

"Meghan, wait."

"I'll call later, okay?"

Adele couldn't speak. She didn't know how to say good-bye again. "You promise you'll call?"

"I promise."

Adele hung up, and tears poured down her cheeks. It was the kind of gut-wrenching cry she'd only experienced a handful of times in her life.

The front door opened. "Adele?" Campbell's voice rang through the entryway and reached her in the kitchen, but she couldn't respond. She didn't trust her own voice to hold.

She sniffed and wiped her eyes and nose, praying she'd done a decent job of putting herself back together.

"I'm back." Campbell entered the room.

"Oh good, Luke told me about the gallery. Did you get what you needed?" Adele stared out the window at the back yard. She knew she should clear up what had happened at the estate sale, but she couldn't muster the energy.

"I think so."

Adele finally turned around and recognized the heavy sorrow on Campbell's face. "What's the matter?"

"I ran into my grandfather."

Adele's stomach flip-flopped. She knew Michael's regret intimately—it easily rivaled her own. Maybe she couldn't fix everything with Meghan, but could she help Campbell understand?

"And?" They sat at the table.

"I asked him about the money. The house, the checking account. He didn't know anything about any of it."

"I didn't think he would."

Campbell's face fell. "Then who?"

Adele raised her eyebrows.

"You don't think…" Campbell's voice trailed off.

"Who else?"

"So he does know about me—he just decided to pay us off instead of actually having a relationship with me." Sorrow swept across her face.

"Hon, I'm sure there's a reason." She closed a hand over Campbell's.

"So he must be wealthy—like, a doctor maybe?"

"Why would you think so?"

"Lila thinks she knows who my father is. A man named Dr. Mark Davis. And then there was some art student named Jared Kimball. The woman at the gallery said they spent time together."

"I remember Mark. I run into him on occasion. Doesn't really resemble you, but I don't suppose people would think either one of my kids belong to me. Jared Kimball, though. He's a local. Pretty sure he's not your daddy."

"What makes you so sure?" Campbell chewed the inside of her lip.

Adele sighed. "Your mama came over here late one night, frantic over an art student who'd gotten the wrong idea. I think he'd been following her around town. Scared her pretty good." Adele studied her hands. "Meghan tried to tell her she couldn't be so nice to everyone all the time. I'm guessing he was the one. He's a troubled man."

"Was that the same year?"

Adele squinted and stared at the ceiling, as if the answer hung in the heavens. "No. It was the summer Meg got her license. They were sixteen."

"So it wasn't Jared Kimball." Her chest filled with relief. "So, Dr. Mark Davis?"

Adele raised one eyebrow.

"I guess the only thing left to do is to ask him." Campbell ran her hands through her hair.

"How was your grandfather?"

She frowned, then shrugged. "Apparently he's sorry."

"Darlin', what that man has been through—"

Campbell looked surprised, but she didn't respond.

"Some regrets are too big. You just don't understand how much he needs your forgiveness. We're all just mistakes with feet anyway."

Campbell's eyes narrowed as if she were putting the pieces of a puzzle together in the air. "This isn't about me and my grandfather at all, is it?"

Adele looked away. "Of course it is." The lie smacked at her like a child throwing a tantrum.

"What happened with you and Meghan?"

Adele sighed and then told her the whole sordid story from top to bottom. "I'm a fine mess of a woman, Campbell Carter."

"So, you need me to forgive my grandfather to give you the hope that one day Meghan can forgive you."

Adele recoiled.

"I'm not Meghan, Adele, I can't forgive you for her."

Adele gasped.

"I'm sorry. I shouldn't have said that," Campbell said. "I'm sorry. It's just—this is all getting to me, that's all."

"Of course I want her to forgive me. It's all I've ever wanted—to make sure she knows how sorry I am." Adele wrestled with the anger and sadness that sprang to life inside her. "I just hung up the phone with her."

"With Meghan?"

Adele nodded, begged herself to keep it together.

"And?"

"I am full of regrets. I thought I was helping her. But her sobriety was pretty new. The lifestyle she'd been living—it didn't lend itself to trust. But my accusations—my disbelief of my own daughter—that's what made her leave. She knew I suspected she'd been using that day, and that hurt her. If I could take it back, I would."

Campbell's face softened.

"Just like your grandfather. I know how sorry he is. I've seen it."

"What he did—"

"Was no worse than what I did. I accused my own daughter of the unthinkable. I might as well have told her that boy's blood was on her hands." The memory of that day skittered through her mind. She pushed aside the image of Meghan's face. "It was my fault she left. I forced it—just like your grandparents forced your mom. And yet, you're sitting here, holding my hand."

THIRTY-FOUR

Campbell

Campbell stood in Adele's guest bathroom. After a day spent mostly outside, she felt grimy and needed to clean up. She splashed water on her face and dabbed it dry. A glance in the mirror left her with a deep ache. The quiet house scratched at the pain she'd buried for days.

She closed the toilet lid and sat down, her head in her hands.

"God, this doesn't make any sense," she said out loud. "Why am I even here?"

She'd meant *here* as in *Sweethaven*, but once the sentence had been spoken, a bigger meaning came into play. Why was she here? So far, her life had brought nothing but ruin.

She startled at a noise in the hallway and wiped the tears from her face. She tried to focus on the positive—at least she had more answers than when she'd first arrived.

Back in the guest room, she noticed that the trunk sat in the middle of the floor. Luke must've brought it in. Subtle.

She changed clothes and reapplied her makeup, but the trunk tormented her. She flung the lid open and pulled out one of the letters her mother had written to her grandparents.

She tore open the envelope.

Dear Mom and Dad,

I wanted to write you a quick note to let you know how we're doing, and to see if maybe you'd like to see us again soon? Campbell is starting to walk now—or at least trying to. She's really cute and smiles all the time. I would love for you to get to know her.

I've decided to enroll at the community college here. I got a scholarship and some financial aid, so I hardly have to pay anything. I'm going to study art and become a teacher. I think I'll be really good at it.

Here are a couple of photos from Cam's one-year photo shoot. I think she has Dad's ears, what do you think? ☺ Take care, and please call. I'd love to hear from you soon.

Love,

Suzanne

Two wallet-sized photos had fallen to the ground when she opened the letter. Her mother had tried to make contact, but her grandparents had returned the letter unopened. All the letters. Judging by the postmarks, it looked like Mom stopped trying after Campbell turned five—old enough to start asking questions. Mom hadn't cut them off—they'd cut her off. And she'd made up that story about their death so Campbell wouldn't be hurt knowing her own grandparents didn't want her.

She wiped the tear that had fallen down her cheek and returned the stack of letters to the trunk next to the scrapbook pages her mother had hidden away. Those pages could tell her the truth about Mark Davis.

The stairs creaked, and she shut the trunk. Adele appeared in the doorway. "Just checkin' on ya, hon. Everyone's downstairs, but I didn't want to serve the food without you."

The welcome distraction she needed.

"I'll be right down," she said.

She shoved the trunk out of the way and walked downstairs.

Luke saved her a spot next to him at the table, and she wished she didn't have so much on her mind. It would've been lovely to spend the evening marveling at his tan skin or his stubbled chin. Or the way he paid attention to her without being smothering.

"I took the trunk to your room," he said. "Just in case."

"I saw that. Thank you." She didn't really feel thankful, though. Part of her wished she could dump that trunk in the lake and never open it again. But another part of her—the part that needed answers—was grateful for his thoughtfulness.

Dinner played out like a well-rehearsed scene in a movie. Old friends reconnected. They laughed. They passed good food around for second—and third—helpings. Campbell documented it all with her camera. And while they had all been strangers to her this time last week, she reveled in the quiet familiarity of her mother's friends.

The night waned, and people dispersed. Graham and Luke talked at length about the best golf courses in the area. Jane's daughters headed out for a fish fry down at the beach, and Sam tossed the ball to Mugsy, who stared at it and laid her head back down.

The four women huddled at the table over coffee and apple dumplings.

"Everything was just wonderful, Adele." Jane sipped the hot coffee.

"It really was, thank you for including me," Campbell said.

"Don't be silly. You're part of the family now. All of you are—so you better not be strangers." Adele took a bite of her apple dumpling. "I just wish Meghan could be here." She looked away.

"I could've sworn I saw Nick in the grocery store earlier," Lila said. "I can't believe he lives here now."

"Yeah, after they split up, he moved back here." Adele sighed. "Their twins divide their time between here and Nashville. When Meghan's on tour, they stay with Nick and his mom. I'm worried, though; Violet Rhodes has never been right in the head."

"I remember," Jane said. "Poor Nick, growing up with her for a mother."

"I bet I have stories that could rival his." Lila laughed.

"What did you mean 'when Meghan's on tour'?" Campbell asked.

Adele set her drink on the table. "That's right, you don't know. Meghan is Meghan Rhodes. The country singer."

"What? Why didn't you guys tell me this?" Campbell shook her head. "She's famous."

"Yes, she is, darlin'," Adele said.

"Really famous." Campbell glanced at Luke, who had also managed not to reveal who his sister was. She mailed a letter to a famous singer, and she didn't even realize it.

"Let's change the subject," Adele said. "Where are we at with your daddy-search?"

"I found some more scrapbook pages." The words escaped before Campbell had a chance to decide if she wanted them to.

"You did?" Jane set her mug down.

"They were hidden in the trunk. With letters Mom had written to her parents."

Adele let out a slight gasp.

"The letters had been returned—unopened."

"What in the world was wrong with Suzanne's mom?" Jane shook her head. "I don't understand how a mother could intentionally stop speaking to her own child."

Campbell glanced at Adele, who looked away.

"I'm so sorry, Adele, I didn't mean—" Jane's cheeks went red.

"No, darlin', you're right. It's no way for parents to carry on with their children. Yet, here I am." She paused, as if trying to decide whether to go on. "I made a grave mistake with Meghan, and she's makin' me pay for it. I have to let her work it out for herself and pray that the good Lord brings her back to me."

Campbell smiled softly as her eyes met Adele's.

"Campbell, what did the pages say?" Lila asked.

"I only read one of them. It was from the first night she met a boy out on the dock. She said she'd had a huge fight with her parents and she snuck out. He was there. They talked. Sounded innocent, but I think you might've been wrong. Whoever this guy was— I think maybe she loved him."

Lila and Jane exchanged a look.

"Do you still think it could've been Mark Davis?" Campbell tried to read them both.

Jane shrugged. "It would really surprise me if it was."

"It seems the most logical possibility," Lila said. "Mark was so good-looking and we all knew he'd end up rich like his father. I think in some way we all had a crush on Mark Davis."

"Lila!" Jane threw her napkin at her.

"What? I'm just telling the truth. Not like *your* crush on him, of course." Lila laughed.

"Maybe it was Gunther," Jane said.

Confused glances criss-crossed over the table. Then Lila burst out laughing. "I am *sure* your mom had better taste than that. Mark Davis is definitely the best option."

Campbell went to bed that night replaying the conversation in her mind. She'd spent hours editing photos, but even that distraction couldn't keep her mind from wandering. As she tried to sleep, her thoughts returned to the pages in the trunk. The words her mother had written. Quietly, she opened the lid and fished the stack from inside.

One by one, she read the pages her mom had hidden. Like a delicious romance novel, the pages chronicled not only a love story, but a friendship—between two people who felt misunderstood everywhere but on that dock in the middle of the night.

One of the pages described a conversation they'd had about their fears of moving beyond high school—something that supported the argument that it was Mark Davis and not an older man. Another page mentioned her friends and how she needed to be careful to keep from wanting anything but friendship from this boy because it could erode the relationships that meant so much to her. Another clue that it was Dr. Davis.

One page, written in white paint pen on a dark navy sheet of cardstock, had been titled "The Night Everything Changed."

Her mom had drawn stars and a sliver of a moon on the background. The dock led to a boat, and in the boat, her mom had drawn two people. The journaling read:

Tonight he arrived with a yellow rose. Maybe I wanted it to mean more than it did. Maybe it wasn't a symbol of his undying love—just something pretty he found on the way to the dock.

I didn't mean for this to happen. I know better. We had the perfect friendship—one that I could count on, different from my girlfriends, and I ruined it. I let us ruin it. We had gotten so close, but I think we both got confused. I let myself fall for someone that was never supposed to be mine to begin with. And I made a huge mistake. He told me he was sorry. He'd never meant for it to happen either. My heart is broken.

Everything will change now. We'll never be the same.
But I'll never forget it. Not for as long as I live.

Mom *had* loved him. Whoever he was. He broke her heart.

Campbell cried, not just for herself, but for her mom—who'd never found someone to replace the love she knew in Sweethaven.

THIRTY-FIVE

Campbell

Sunlight poured in the windows, rousing Campbell from sleep.

She looked at the scrapbook pages strewn across the floor. She must've dropped them when she drifted off. She'd discovered more evidence to prove Lila's theory. A wave of fear shot through her body. Dr. Davis could be in town at that very moment.

She curbed the emotions, trying to forget she had a grandfather to attempt to forgive and a maybe-father to confront.

So far, every effort to ignore those facts had failed.

She threw off the covers and hurried to get ready. After one final glance in the mirror, she went downstairs. The house was quiet. Even Mugsy was gone.

Tonight she'd pick up her prints and take them to the gallery for framing.

She walked down Elm Street to Main and turned toward downtown.

Campbell took a couple shots of the flurry of activity in Sweethaven Square as residents decorated the gazebo. She walked down a busier than usual Main Street until she reached the Café.

Inside, her eyes grazed the crowd until she found Luke behind the counter.

As he glanced up and met Campbell's eyes, his smile widened and he waved. The little old lady he waited on followed his stare until she spotted Campbell, gave her the once-over, and then wiggled her eyebrows, teasing Luke. His face flushed red, and he handed the woman her drink.

"Did you get all your shots edited?"

"I finished them around two, but I took more this morning."

"Did you send them to the place I told you about? I called my buddy Jeff—he's going to rush them through for you."

"Yeah, I e-mailed them. Thanks, Luke." Had anyone ever been so nice to her?

"My pleasure. Listen, I know you've got a lot on your mind, but I thought you might want to know that Dr. Davis is here."

Campbell's pulse quickened.

"Right over there." He pointed to a man sitting at the high counter against the wall. The man was reading a newspaper and drinking from a disposable coffee cup. His back was to them so she couldn't make out his features.

Campbell switched her bag from one shoulder to the other. She knew an opportunity had presented itself. Her maybe-father was only a few feet away. She could potentially sit down and have a conversation. Maybe God had opened a door for her. But that was silly. Why would God do that?

"He's by himself," Luke said.

"Should I talk to him?" Campbell's mouth went dry like someone had swabbed the moisture away with thick strips of cotton.

Luke laid a hand on her shoulder. "I think you're the only one who can make that decision."

Sometimes she hated being a grown-up.

"All right," she said. "Wish me luck."

She hitched the bag up higher on her shoulder and walked toward Dr. Davis. She left a seat between them.

Dr. Davis concentrated on his newspaper. He wore reading glasses and a thick gold band on his left ring finger.

She imagined herself as a little girl, showing him crayon drawings or telling him fairy tales. She imagined him taking her to the beach and building sand castles on the shore. Or coming home with a puppy in his arms—a dog he'd picked out just for her. She'd name the dog Ollie and teach it to catch a Frisbee in mid-air. She'd call home from college after a particularly difficult exam and her father would tell her to "stay the course." He'd say, "You can't give up after the first hard test, Cam." He'd call her Cam because that's what fathers do. They give their daughters nicknames like *Sweetheart* and *Peanut-girl* and *Squigs*.

She chewed the inside of her lip as she tried to work up the courage to speak. She must've been staring because Dr. Davis, her maybe-father, gave her a sideways glance. She smiled and looked away.

"Here's your latte." Luke must've have witnessed her crashing and burning.

"Thank you, Luke." Her voice was quiet.

"Dr. Davis, how's that coffee?"

The man smiled up at Luke. "Can't find a better cup anywhere, Luke. I dream of this coffee when I'm back home."

"Good to hear it." He paused and looked at Campbell. "This is Campbell Carter. I think you might remember her mom, Suzanne?"

He stared at Campbell, but she could tell by his expression her mom's name hadn't registered.

"She used to come when she was a kid," Campbell said. "She hung out with Luke's sister Meghan and Jane—"

"Oh, Suzi." He laughed. "I remember. I haven't seen her—wow, since I was in high school."

Campbell glanced at Luke. He'd swooped in like a knight and saved her from the fire-breathing dragon.

"How is your mom?" Dr. Davis had folded his paper and now gave her his undivided attention.

Her imagination sprang to life again, this time with a giant pile of autumn leaves. She could smell their crispness. And then she was seven, burying him in the sand, jumping off a diving board into his arms, playing catch in the yard.

She pushed the daydream aside. "She passed away, actually."

He sank back in his chair, slouched at the shoulders, and sighed. "I'm so sorry. She was young."

"Cancer."

He lifted his chin. "Ahh."

"Dr. Davis, I was wondering if you and my mom ever—dated?"

"Suzanne and me?" He laughed. "No. Unfortunately, she wouldn't have given me the time of day."

"So you two never—" She squirmed in her seat. "I'm looking for my father."

His eyes widened.

"My mom's friends don't know who he is and she never told me. Someone mentioned you were around a lot back then."

She recognized the look in his eyes. Pity, clear and unrestricted. He felt sorry for her.

Humiliation stood at the door to her heart and knocked. She sighed. Another dead end. Another mistake. Another regret.

"I wish I could help you, but it wasn't me. I was pretty hung up on Jane back then if you want to know the truth. Suzanne always tried to talk me into asking her out, but I was too chicken. The next summer, she'd already started dating the guy she ended up marrying."

"Graham."

Dr. Davis nodded. "How old are you?"

"Twenty-four. She got pregnant here, the summer before her senior year."

He shook his head. "You know…" His eyes glazed over as if he were remembering something.

"What is it? Do you know who it could be?"

He hesitated for too long a moment and then re-focused his eyes on her, quickly looking away. "No, I'm sorry."

"Dr. Davis, if you know something, please tell me. I have no one else."

The harder she looked for her father, the angrier she grew with her mother for keeping this secret. What could be more important than leaving her with a father, rather than leaving her alone?

The bell over the door rang, grabbing Dr. Davis's attention. His face lit, and Campbell turned to see a petite blond woman wearing black capris and a black and white striped shirt. A small, curly-headed girl who appeared to be about six or seven held her hand.

She probably built sand castles with Dr. Davis in the summer and snowmen in the winter.

"Daddy!" The little girl ran over to him, and he picked her up and squeezed her tight.

Awkwardness descended on Campbell, and she wished she'd never sat down next to him.

His wife stood at his side, her eyes darting from her husband to Campbell.

"Melissa, this is Campbell Carter. Campbell, my wife, Melissa."

Campbell shook the woman's hand and prayed for an easy escape. Whatever Dr. Davis had remembered, she wasn't going to find out now.

"Nice to meet you, Campbell," Melissa said.

"Campbell's mom grew up here. I knew her way back when."

"Oh? Is your mom here now?" Melissa's smile warmed, and she seemed to relax a little.

"No, she died," Campbell said. "Thank you for your time, Dr. Davis."

"Anytime. If I think of anything else, I'll let you know."

She nodded, gave another glance at his daughter, and then left the café, determined to give up looking for her father once and for all.

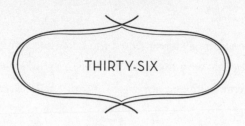

THIRTY-SIX

Jane

Jane awoke early, and the bright spring sun drew her out of bed. Her mental checklist skittered through her mind as she dressed. Orchard. Vineyard. Craft Sale at the Commons. Campbell's art show. Suzanne's memorial. She caught a glimpse of herself in the mirror. Wet eyes stared back at her. She dreaded the moment she officially said good-bye to her old friend.

She hurried into her warm-up pants and a sweatshirt and jotted a quick note for Graham. *Carrot cake is yours for the taking. Went for a walk. Back soon. —J*

Before she left, she checked on her sleeping kids. The girls would sleep till noon if she let them. She wouldn't.

She stepped out the door and inhaled the morning air, and despite all her trying, she couldn't help but replay the horror of the day Alex had died. Behind their cottage, the dune peaked and then sloped down on the other side, leading to the lake. The climb had always been part of the fun for Alex.

She reached the top and stood, the cottage on one side, the lake on the other.

"Come *on*, Mom!" His voice rang in her memory.

She could hear the words, carried on the wind, and they echoed through the air in the very place they had originally been spoken.

She took a couple steps toward the lake but stopped. Could she do this? Alone?

Words from long ago sprang to mind. *I will never leave you or forsake you.*

God's promises. *Do not fear, for I am with you.* She wasn't alone. She'd known that since she was a girl, and God had proven it time and time again.

But this was different. This pain didn't compare to any she'd ever felt. God couldn't take this pain away.

Slowly, cautiously, she put one foot in front of the other.

"Mom! Come on!" Alex's voice, so clear in her memory, drew her onward. She looked up and in the distance, by the lake, she could see him, running along the water. He darted out to meet the waves as they rushed to the shore.

"Alex?" she whispered.

She picked up speed, stumbling down the side of the sandy dune. Her eyes focused on Alex as his screams of excitement filled the early morning air.

"Alex?" Her voice grew louder.

At the bottom of the dune, she planted her feet firmly on the beach.

"Alex, stop! Get out of the water!" She rushed forward, catching a glimpse of his smiling face. He turned to her, his hair wet, and waved. In front of her, the lake crashed, tumultuous and unpredictable.

"Come on, Mom!" He jumped as the waves hit him in the chest.

Jane tried to run through the thick sand, but its resistance slowed her down. Every time the water splashed above his neck, panic rose up and she called out to him. Every time, he emerged, joy on his face, waving and calling to her.

Farther and farther into the lake he moved, but he still bobbed up for air, smiling and laughing.

"Alex, come back!" As she reached the edge of the water her heart pounded in her chest, and her mind raced. Where had he gone? He'd come up every time. And then he didn't.

He was gone.

He disappeared, leaving her bewildered, wet and alone on the shore.

"Alex, I'm so sorry." She fell to her knees.

She'd blamed Meg and God and even Alex all these years, but she knew it was the blame she carried for herself that ate her up inside.

"I'm so sorry." The sobs overtook her then, pulled up the grief she'd buried, and laid it out in the open where it ached and writhed and tore her apart.

The sun shone in the distance, casting a pink glow through the clouds, and she imagined God had given her a glimpse of what Alex was doing right at that moment. Laughing, splashing, playing.

As the tears fell, she allowed herself to feel the pain she'd pushed away all these years. She didn't hide from it or mask it with food or pretend to be fine. For once, she felt it, and she acknowledged the anger that taunted. Deep, unabashed sorrow gripped her gut and tied it in a knot.

Collapsed in a heap on the beach, she finally found the courage to say the one thing she hadn't been able to say since they put her son in the ground six years ago.

"Good-bye, Alex."

A strong hand wrapped around her shoulder, and she didn't even have to look up to know Graham had found her. In her time of utter sorrow, he came to her aid, sat down beside her, and held her while she cried.

"It wasn't your fault, honey," he said. "You couldn't have saved him."

Jane sank into Graham's arms. She stared out over the water and something inside her shifted. Something had changed. The still water now stretched in front of her, glassy and serene like a painting. Alex forgave her. Graham forgave her. God forgave her.

All that was left was for her to forgive herself.

THIRTY-SEVEN

Campbell

The morning of the art show, nerves flickered in Campbell's stomach like jolts of electricity. She sat on the bleachers at the Blossom Fest charity softball tournament, but as much as she wanted to watch Luke play, her mind wandered.

Afterwards, she met up with him near the dugout, praying he didn't ask her what she thought of the game.

"Thanks for coming."

She smiled, shielding her eyes from the afternoon sun. "I wouldn't miss it."

"How about the parade? You still wanna go?" He took his baseball cap off and put it on backwards.

Campbell ran her hand through her hair and forced herself to nod.

He frowned. "You don't want to go?"

"No, I do, I'm just so nervous about the show tonight." She'd gotten everything done, but the thought of actually opening the gallery doors made her insides a jumbled mess.

"The parade will be the perfect distraction," he said. "And the carnival down by the lake. After the show tonight, we might even catch the fireworks."

She nodded. Judging by the look on his face, though, he didn't buy it.

The crowd had started to disperse, most of them on foot. A

vendor stood at the corner selling corn on the cob smothered in a buttery concoction.

"No pressure. We can go eat or…" He studied her face. "I can leave you alone?"

She scrunched her face. "I'm sorry. I'm no fun today."

"I'm just trying to gauge your mood. I haven't got them all figured out yet."

Campbell laughed. They walked past a huge float, covered with flowers. "Wow, I haven't seen a real float in a long time."

Luke waved to a woman sitting on top of it. "It's tradition here. You'll see lots of them. They line up around this block and then the parade goes all the way down Main Street and around. It's quite a spectacle."

"So you're saying I should go?"

"Absolutely." He took her hand in his and led her through the crowd. As they reached the Main Street Café, he waved to Delcy, who sat next to two empty lawn chairs.

"Guess you were counting on my coming, huh?" Campbell looked up at him.

"Wishful thinking." He grinned, and they sat down among the employees from the café. The sounds of a marching band warming up carried across the street. Something about the *rat-a-tat* of the snare drum and the cacophony of warm-up scales brought an air of excitement.

Across the street, tourists and locals gathered in lawn chairs and on blankets to watch the parade. Children sat on the curb, buckets in hand, anxious for the candy that would be thrown their way.

A man burst through the door of the tiny tavern on the corner across the street. He stumbled to the ground and struggled to right himself.

"Not again. Looks like Kimball's up to his old tricks." An older man sitting behind them stared at the intoxicated man.

Kimball? As in *Jared* Kimball?

"It's barely two o'clock in the afternoon. Doesn't he know the streets are filled with children?" the woman next to him responded.

Campbell stared at the man. Unkempt and seemingly disoriented, he fell into the crowd. Another man attempted to help him up, but Jared shoved the guy away. The do-gooder's hands went up in surrender, and Jared stared at him, pushing into him with his shoulder as he passed.

Campbell watched as Jared Kimball disappeared down the street, and her thoughts turned to the small kids she'd seen at his house. If he *was* her father, perhaps she didn't want to know.

Her thoughts were interrupted when a teenage girl thrust a flier in her face. "Come out to the Sweethaven Art Gallery tonight," she said. "The new exhibit opens at seven. It's called 'Treasures of Sweethaven.'" The girl's braces caught the sun as she grinned and moved on to the next person.

Campbell glanced down at the flier and saw one of Mom's paintings beside a photograph she'd taken. "How in the world did Deb get these done so fast?" she wondered aloud.

"Yeah, Luke, how *did* Deb get these done so fast?" Delcy grinned at him, and Luke looked away.

"She might've had a little help." He bumped into Campbell with his shoulder. "They turned out well."

She stared at him.

"What?" He feigned innocence.

"You did this?"

He shrugged. "I might've had something to do with it."

She studied the flier more closely. All the details were included, and judging by the design, they'd been done by a professional and printed in full color. She watched as the girl handed one to everyone in the crowd. How much had those fliers cost him?

"Luke, thank you," she said. "No one's ever..." She stopped. "Just thanks."

He stared at her for a long moment. Her stomach flip-flopped as she wondered if he might kiss her right there, but a young guy who worked at the café walked up and punched him in the arm.

Campbell looked away, back toward where Jared Kimball had disappeared into the crowd.

Would she ever find out the truth? Would she ever get the answers she came here for?

She glanced at Luke.

Or had she been drawn to Sweethaven for another reason entirely?

THIRTY-EIGHT

Campbell

In the back room of the Sweethaven Gallery, Campbell stared at her reflection in a hand-painted mirror. Her sleeveless black dress, cinched at the waist, hung to her knees and showed off her favorite feature—her shoulders. She fixed the clasp of her necklace, which had squirmed around to the front, and ran her hands through her hair.

She exhaled, hoping to dispel the nerves.

Deb poked her head in the room. "You have a visitor."

She stepped aside and Luke's tall silhouette appeared in the doorway, a large bouquet of tulips in his hand.

She smiled.

"I wanted to congratulate you." He offered the flowers.

She took them and inhaled, their fragrance reminding her of her mom. "They're beautiful. Thank you."

He wrapped his arms around her waist and pulled her into a warm hug, and for the first time in a long time, she didn't feel uncomfortable being this close to another person. Instead, she wrapped her arms around his body and pulled him closer.

She rested her head on his chest, the tulips tickling her nose.

"I have to admit, I already looked at your pictures."

She pulled back and gasped. "Cheater!"

"I couldn't resist." His lazy grin teased her. "You're incredible. I especially liked the shot of that good-looking guy on the train."

"Russ?" Campbell grinned.

"The *other* good-looking guy."

"I figured you'd like that one." She looked away. "And I'm not incredible. My mom was incredible."

"She was, but Campbell, you are an artist. Your photos are amazing." He wove a hand around the back of her neck and let it rest there. When their eyes met, she fought the urge to look away.

Her face heated and her heart raced. She'd been here before—why did she still get so nervous?

One look at him answered that question. Big eyes intent on her. Perfect lips. Disheveled hair. No, she'd never been *here* before.

"Luke, I'm going back—"

But he didn't let her finish. He closed the space between them, leaning in to her and pulling her body against his. His lips grazed hers, soft and tender, void of the rush of expectant schoolboys. Their eyes met, the closeness between them taking her breath away. When his lips found hers again, the blood rushed to her face and she parted her mouth to receive his kiss. Longer this time. She tingled all over.

He pulled back and looked at her again. "You were saying?"

"Nothing."

"All right, your public is waiting." He smiled.

"I'm nervous. What if they hate it?"

"Not a chance."

She took another glance at the mirror. "Oh, great, now I need lipstick." She flashed him a grin and reapplied her Brown Sugar #5.

He shrugged. "No apology here."

"Campbell, you ready?" Deb had returned. "People are starting to arrive."

I hope you're watching, Mom.

In the gallery, waiters in white shirts and black ties served appetizers on silver trays. The artwork had all been hung to perfection, the ideal combination of paintings and photographs.

"I'm going to go get us something to drink," Luke said. "You okay?"

She begged her pulse to slow down and nodded.

The door opened, and Jane entered with Graham at her side. Dressed in a black pantsuit and holding her husband's arm, she had a unique glow about her.

Campbell excused herself and waved to Jane.

"This is so exciting," Jane beamed.

Campbell stopped for a moment and soaked in Jane's joy. Aside from her mom, there had never been anyone to share her victories. She'd expected to live this one out on her own, but here she was, surrounded by new friends who felt more like family—all willing to celebrate the realization of her dream. She hoped she could make it through the rest of the night without crying.

Nerves danced in her belly.

The door opened and Adele's boisterous voice rang out over the crowd. "Well, bless my soul." Campbell turned, but as soon as she saw Adele, disappointment filled her chest. She'd half expected her grandfather to join Luke's mom—though she'd given him no reason to make an appearance. Did she want him there?

Campbell's heart raced at the realization. She might never find out who her father was, but she had a grandfather—living and breathing—and only a few blocks away.

"Jane, if you'll excuse me."

"Sure, hon."

Campbell turned off her brain so she wouldn't lose her nerve and escaped out the back, hopped in her car, and drove down Main Street to Elm. She turned left on Juniper Drive, pulled in front of her grandfather's cottage, and turned off the ignition.

One deep breath and she found an ounce of courage hidden behind a gallon of fear. "I can do this," she said.

She walked to the door and knocked, holding her chin high.

When she heard someone on the other side of the door, the tips of her fingers went numb. For a brief moment she wanted to hide, but when she saw her grandfather's face, the nerves settled a bit. He was just a man—a broken man, in fact.

He didn't hide the surprise on his face.

"I'm sorry to bother you," Campbell said. "I know it's late."

"It's fine. Would you like to come in?"

She hesitated for a moment, then nodded. "Thanks."

She stood in the entryway and glanced into the living room. Above the mantel was a row of framed pictures, all of her mom.

"We're having an art show tonight," she said without looking at him. "I came to ask if you wanted to come."

She met his eyes, which were wet with fresh pain.

"It's Mom's art," she continued. "And my photographs."

"I read about it in the paper," he said. "I thought about coming, but I didn't want to upset you. It's not really my place."

She nodded. "I want you to see how amazing she was."

"I already know how amazing she was," he said, his voice barely a whisper. "I'd love to come. Just let me get cleaned up and I'll meet you there in a bit."

"I don't mind waiting."

He stared at her for a long moment. "If you're sure."

"We can go together."

THIRTY-NINE

Campbell

Campbell returned to the gallery with her grandfather at her side, praying no one noticed she'd gone. She walked in, and Luke rushed up to her.

"Everything okay?" he asked.

She nodded. "Just had to take care of something." She glanced at her grandfather and smiled.

"I cannot believe my eyes, Campbell Carter." Adele pulled her into a tight hug. "This is quite something. *You* are quite something. Your mama would be so proud."

"Thank you, Adele. For everything."

Adele glanced at Campbell and her grandfather and shot her an approving look.

"This is quite a turnout," her grandfather said. "I'm going to go get us something to drink."

Campbell nodded and scanned the room. He was right. The crowd that had gathered surprised her. In this small town, all these people had come out to support her—and her mom—and the idea of it humbled her. And she had the people who stood closest to her to thank for that. They'd been vigilant about spreading the word.

After about twenty minutes, Campbell glanced at the door. Her grandfather stood by himself, looking as out of place as a cowboy at a ball.

She shuffled her way through the crowd until she finally reached him.

He handed her a glass of punch. "I didn't want to interrupt. You looked busy over there."

"Thank you. And thanks for coming."

He looked around the room at the art hanging on the wall. His eyes settled on one Mom had painted of the cottage on Juniper Drive. His cottage. "It's beautiful. I always knew she had a gift."

"She did."

"And she passed it on to you." A smile wrinkled the skin around his eyes. She'd never noticed it before, but Mom had his eyes.

She had his eyes.

The pinch of grief stung. She missed her mom.

"I'm sorry, Campbell," her grandfather said. "I just wanted to say that. It's important that you know how sorry I am."

Campbell took a moment to study his eyes. She saw a sincerity there that she hadn't allowed herself to see before.

"Maybe we could go for coffee sometime?" She scanned the room briefly before turning back to him.

He held her gaze, surprise on his face. "I'd like that."

"Can you wait here for one second?" She went behind the counter and found a small stack of letters, many of them unopened, tied together with a satin ribbon. She returned and handed them to her grandfather. "I wanted you to have these."

"What's this?" He held them in his frail hands and studied them.

"Letters my mom wrote to you and my grandmother. They were all returned unopened, but I found them in her things. I thought you should have them."

He gasped. "She wrote to us?" Suddenly, the letters became even more valuable.

She'd suspected it was her grandmother who had kept the rift between them all those years. Sorrow welled within at the wasted relationship—what they could've had if only they'd found a way to see eye to eye. To forgive. To move on.

"I thought you might like to read them."

"Yes. Very much. Thank you for these, Campbell, but after everything we said to your mom, after the way we made her feel, I don't feel like I deserve these."

"She wanted you to have them." Campbell watched as he examined the envelopes in his hand. "For the record, Reverend, I do forgive you."

As she spoke the words, a weight lifted off her shoulders and she began to wonder if it was entirely true. If it wasn't, she wanted it to be. She wanted to learn how to forgive him—and maybe put an end to the pain they'd both been feeling all these years.

"I can't promise we're going to be close. You might not even like me, but I've decided not to hold a grudge."

He smiled. "Thank you." He reached out and put a hand on her shoulder. "Thank you for showing me grace when I don't deserve it."

"None of us deserve it. We're all just a bunch of mistakes with feet anyway." She glanced up and saw Adele moving toward them.

He laughed out loud and seconds later Adele was at his side. "Well, my land, I haven't seen you laugh in years. Campbell, I do believe you've bewitched this man."

The two of them walked away, and Campbell watched as her grandfather showed the stack of letters to Adele. The older woman turned back and looked at Campbell. They exchanged a knowing smile, and she knew she'd done the right thing.

In front of her, the painting of the dock caught her eye. Now that she'd been there, the painting easily transported her to that place.

She could almost feel the warm sun on her shoulders. She closed her eyes and was drinking it in when someone walked up behind her. She opened her eyes, expecting Luke, but instead she found a stranger at her side.

He stood at least a foot taller than her and didn't make eye contact. Instead, he stared at the painting, then finally glanced at her. He cleared his throat and loosened his tie. He looked like a model from an Eddie Bauer catalog. Rugged and handsome. She smiled at him and then caught Deb's eye, who was approaching as she made her rounds around the gallery.

"Are you the artist?" he asked Campbell.

"I'm a photographer. My mother painted these."

"Can I buy this piece?" he asked. The man studied it, his eyes scurrying across the canvas. "I know this place."

"Deb? Looks like you might have a customer," Campbell said. It had always been Mom's dream to sell her artwork, and after carefully marking three of the paintings Not For Sale, Campbell decided she would part with the rest for her mom. She glanced at the painting again and realized it wouldn't be easy.

Deb took her glasses off, letting them hang on a chain around her neck, and held out her hand. "Sir, what can I do for you?"

"Yes, I'd like to buy this one, but…I think I'm here to see you." He looked at Campbell.

"Are you from the press?" Deb asked.

The man shifted.

"Did you need to interview Campbell? I'm sure she's got a few minutes for the press. Who'd you say you were with?"

He glanced at Deb and then at Campbell, a confused expression on his face. "Actually, I'm not with the press."

Deb frowned. "Oh." She peeled a Sold sticker from her sheet and placed it next to the frame. "It will be available to pick up after the show."

"Thank you."

Deb smiled, and then she was pulled away to restock the cheese tray.

"So what did you need to see me for?" Campbell didn't understand. If he wasn't a reporter, why did he need to talk to her?

"Can we maybe go outside?" He shoved his hands in his jacket pockets and for a moment looked like a schoolboy at detention.

"Okay." Campbell followed him outside, where he sat on the bench in front of the gallery. She sat at the other end of the bench and stared at the gazebo one block over, feeling a bit uncomfortable.

"You have your mom's eyes," he finally said.

She looked at him.

"But you have my nose."

Campbell's jaw went slack.

He stayed quiet for a few seconds but it felt like much longer. Across the street, she spotted Lila, carrying an oversized purse and heading their way. She waved.

Campbell barely lifted her hand and waved back, drawing the man's attention across the street.

"Oh no," he said.

Lila crossed the street and stared at the man as she approached. "What are you doing here?"

"You two know each other?" Campbell looked at the man, who wore a sheepish expression.

"*You* two know each other?" Lila said with raised eyebrows. In the uncomfortable silence, she looked back and forth between them. "Tom, what's going on? I've been trying to reach you since I got here."

Campbell stood, feeling suddenly awkward and altogether horrified. "I've got to get back inside. It was nice to meet you...Tom." She forced a smile, but now he was looking the other way. She saw but didn't feel her feet moving toward the gallery. She prayed they didn't buckle under the weight of her horror.

Her mind rewound to the moment she'd first noticed Lila's husband standing next to her and replayed the entire scene.

She glanced back at the two of them, still sitting on the bench, and her thoughts raced through the possibilities.

If she'd understood correctly, things were about to go terribly wrong.

And it was all her fault.

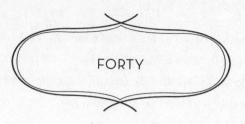

FORTY

Lila

Lila sat next to her husband on the bench, several feet between them.

"Do you want to tell me what you're doing in town?"

"I just got here this afternoon. I had a few things to take care of."

"What could you possibly have to take care of in Sweethaven? Don't you think maybe your wife should be a priority? You haven't answered my calls since I left."

"Do you have any water?"

She narrowed her eyes at him but didn't answer. Then she rifled through her purse and produced a water bottle.

He opened the bottle and drained half of it in seconds.

"How are you?" He stared at her, expecting a response. It had been months—maybe years—since she'd seen the sincerity she saw now. She'd missed that. Tom's genuineness had been part of what attracted her to him in the first place. He didn't act like the spoiled rich kids she knew. He'd always been his own man.

When she said nothing, he cleared his throat. "We need to talk."

Her heart sank, and her stomach churned. Had he come to tell her it was over? Hand her divorce papers and be done with it?

"Lila?"

Her whirling mind had prevented a response. "Okay."

She straightened her shoulders and lifted her chin. *Remember who you are.*

After meeting her eyes for a brief moment, he looked away.

She shifted. Tension hung in the air.

"What do you want to talk about?" She tried to keep her voice light, but the depth of her fear surprised her.

"When I came back from my run, you were gone." Tom picked at the wrapper on the side of his water bottle.

"I know. I'm sorry for that. I should've left a note." She looked down at the oversized diamond that sparkled on her left hand. An upgrade from her first wedding ring. Tom had bought it for her after his last promotion. Silly how she thought a bigger ring said something about them as a couple. She knew now the size of the diamond said nothing about the depth of their love.

"No, I shouldn't have gone running. I knew you were upset by the letter." He shook his head. "I needed to clear my head."

"It's been good to see Adele and Jane again. And I met Suzanne's daughter." Lila swept her long hair back behind her shoulders. "But I guess you met her too." She exhaled.

He didn't say anything.

"I think we may've had a breakthrough in the search for her father." Lila filled the silence with small talk. Anything to pretend her marriage was still intact.

"What do you mean?"

"We found something in the scrapbook that made us think maybe Suzanne and Mark Davis had a secret fling that summer."

"It wasn't Mark Davis."

Lila's heart pounded in her ears, and her throat went dry. "So if it wasn't Mark, then who was it?"

Tom took a deep breath and then exhaled. He looked down at his folded hands in front of him. The color drained from his face. "I'm sorry." The words came out in a whisper.

Lila's mind spun. Her pulse quickened, and a wave of nausea settled in her stomach. She finally found her voice, but an eerie calm had come over her. Just like Mama. "You've been lying to me for twenty-five years. You said you'd never been with anyone else." She looked at him then through clouded eyes. The pain on his face matched the pain in her heart.

How could he do this to her? Had he loved Suzanne?

She fought the tears, the rage, the emotions that warred inside her.

"I didn't lie about knowing she was pregnant. At first, I didn't know. You told me."

"I'm still trying to figure out how you and Suzanne—" She couldn't finish the sentence. "How did I not see it?"

"You and I were so new. We'd only been dating a month. It just...happened."

"Save it, Tom," Lila spat. "I don't need your excuses." She stared in the opposite direction.

"Lila, I'm sorry."

Tears stung her eyes. Her stomach felt hollow, and her palms were wet. For a moment, her own body betrayed her and she couldn't find a breath.

"She loved you," she whispered.

"No. We weren't in love." Tom's eyes pleaded for understanding, filled with tears at his admission.

"You're wrong, Tom. She did love you. Campbell found journal entries about the time you two spent on the dock." Lila felt torn between wanting to read them for herself and wanting to burn them so no one would ever discover her humiliation. "Our whole marriage is a lie."

Her hands rested in her lap, but she couldn't feel them. Couldn't feel her feet on the ground or the legs connected to them. She'd gone completely numb. But the numbness had evaded her heart. She could feel every nick of pain inside.

"No. It's not." Tom moved over next to her. "It's not. You are the one I loved. That's why when I found out about Campbell, I begged Suzanne not to tell you. Not to tell anyone."

"Did she come to you?" Had Suzanne tried to trap him or get him to leave Lila?

He groaned. "Not exactly. It was the summer that you and I got engaged. We were here, in Sweethaven, but you were caught up with wedding plans, and I knew Suzanne wouldn't be back again that year. I couldn't shake the feeling that I needed to find out for sure. So, I called her."

"You called her." Lies piled on top of lies. She fought the urge to stop him, teetering between needing to know the full story and desperately wanting to stay oblivious.

"After I found out about the pregnancy, I wondered, but I kept convincing myself there was no way. I mean, she would've called and told me, right? I pushed it out of my mind, but then we got engaged. If we were going to get married, I needed to know for sure. I had to do some digging, but I found her number and asked her if we could meet."

Lila didn't know if she should be angrier with him or with herself. She'd been so self-absorbed she hadn't even bothered to look for Suzanne's number, and they'd been good friends. But knowing her husband had taken time to locate Suzanne and then called her—only months before their wedding—stung like a Band-Aid being ripped from damaged skin without warning.

"I met her at a park. She had Campbell with her. She had just turned two." Tom's eyes glossed over at the memory. "I didn't even have to ask if she was mine. I could tell by the look on Suzanne's face."

Lila shook her head and closed her eyes—more to keep the tears from falling than anything else.

"We talked for a few minutes, and I apologized to her. She said they were doing really well. Left her parents' house and moved in with a cousin or friend or something."

"You don't even know? You didn't care where your own daughter was living?" Lila chose shame. She'd shame him and make him feel small. Make him feel like every move he'd made had been the wrong one.

"I did." He crossed his arms over his chest. "I told her I could help—with money."

Lila's eyes widened.

"I told her we were engaged and that I loved you and if you found out about any of it, you'd leave. She said she'd carry the secret to the grave." He paused. "And she did. I never thought she would. I thought she'd at least tell Campbell." His voice quivered as he mentioned Suzanne's daughter by name. *His* daughter.

"She didn't get a chance," Lila said.

Lila's fingers turned to ice. Suzanne had kept Tom's secret to spare Lila. She hated the realization, but she knew it was true. Even through her own pain, Suzanne had loved her. And she'd done nothing to deserve that kind of love.

"I started sending her money. I figured it was the least I could do. In exchange, she agreed to keep it all a secret." He stilled. "But I've spent the last twenty years expecting her to show up on our doorstep."

He almost sounded relieved.

"How lovely. The two of you had a secret." Hatred filled her voice, but Lila knew her anger only masked the devastating pain of his betrayal.

"I did it for us, don't you see that? To give us a chance." Tom's eyes pleaded with her.

"You slept with someone else for us? You had the baby that *we* always wanted with someone else for *us*?" Her voice sounded shrill in her own ears. She stood.

"Lila, wait."

She turned to face him. "What do you want?" She tried to sound firm. Angry. But inside, her heart had broken. Sorrow overtook her, but she couldn't let on how desperately she didn't want to lose him. It would only make her weak.

"The same thing I've always wanted. You." His face fell, and even in the moonlight, she could see the pain behind his eyes. "Tell me what to do. I'll do whatever it takes. I just don't want to lose you."

He hadn't been this persistent since the beginning of their relationship. They'd both grown so accustomed to each other, they stopped seeing how special the other one was.

But it was too late to romanticize what they used to have.

Lila took a step closer and forced herself to hold in the tears—just for a few more minutes. "We need to keep this between us for now."

Tom shook his head. "No. I came to make things right. With you *and* with Campbell."

Lila's jaw tightened. She put a hand on his cheek and gently kissed his lips. One last time. "Good-bye." She hoped that would be enough to convince him to keep this nonsense to himself.

She turned around, concentrated on the clicking of her heels on the pavement, held her head high. *Remember who you are, Lila.* Her mother's words rang in her mind.

Remember who you are.

She refused to look back as her greatest fear washed over her.

Lila Adler Olson was undeniably alone.

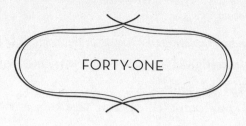

FORTY-ONE

Campbell

The gallery buzzed with excitement, and in spite of the compliments and great reception, Campbell couldn't concentrate on the show. Lila's husband stood outside on the street looking dejected. This was her fault. She'd done this to them. They were breaking up because of her. She practically lunged at Jane and Adele when she spotted them.

"I found him." Campbell's tone sounded detached—emotionless.

Jane's expression changed as she glanced around the room. "You did? Where?"

She hesitated. Finding her father hadn't come without a price. "Lila's husband."

Adele gasped. "Tom?"

"He's here."

Jane's expression went bleak as she pieced it together. "It makes so much sense now," she said. "If Suzanne had fallen for Tom after he and Lila already started dating, she knew it would separate the four of us. Lila would've demanded we choose sides. So Suzanne left, hoping that would hurt less." She shook her head. "And she couldn't tell us who the father was after we found out about the pregnancy because Tom and Lila were really serious by then. I can't believe it." Jane stopped and sighed. "Is Lila here?"

Campbell averted her eyes. "I think she left."

Jane took both Campbell's hands in her own. "I may not be able to stay real late tonight. I have a feeling my friend needs me."

"I understand."

"But for you, I am thrilled. You have your answer. You have a father."

Campbell smiled. She'd gotten her answer, but at what cost? Ruining Lila's marriage was exactly what her mother didn't want to happen. It seemed like Campbell had been tearing people apart ever since she was conceived.

"If it's any consolation, I don't think they were doing very well to begin with." Jane stood beside her.

"It's my fault, Jane. I never should've come here."

"Then we wouldn't know each other. You wouldn't have this wildly successful showing or that handsome man standing back there, waiting until he can have you all to himself." She glanced at Luke, who kept one eye on Campbell as he mixed and mingled with the Sweethaven crowd. "He checks up on you. Like Lloyd Dobler."

Campbell frowned.

Jane looked horrified. "You have seen *Say Anything*, haven't you? I'm getting so old."

Campbell laughed. "Of course. My mom and I watched it together."

"That makes me so happy."

After a beat of silence, Campbell shook her head slowly. "I never should've come here. This is going to ruin everything."

Adele wagged her finger at Campbell. "It's not your fault that your mama fell for her best friend's boyfriend. It's not your fault you wanted to meet your daddy. It's not your fault you found him. Do you hear?"

But Campbell could see by the look on Adele's face that this

situation had her every bit as worried as it had Campbell. Neither
of them wanted to hurt Lila. Lila and Jane were her mom's friends—
her friends now. She couldn't betray them like that.

Jane's expression turned serious. "Don't be sorry you came here,
Campbell. I have a feeling this is just the beginning." Jane wrapped
her arm around her and squeezed her tight. "Sometimes we all need
a little kick to force ourselves to deal with our stuff. In case I don't
see you later, let's plan to meet at the café tomorrow, after the memorial. What do you think?"

Campbell nodded. "Sounds good."

She spotted Tom Olson looking at a painting, but his thoughts
seemed far away.

"I'll be right back."

Jane took Campbell's hand and squeezed it, and Adele offered
her a firm nod.

Campbell approached Tom, but when he didn't register that
she was nearby, she wondered what to do. Should she say "dad"?"
Instead, she cleared her throat, jarring him from his thoughts.

"Lila didn't know, did she?" Campbell asked. Judging by the
expression she'd seen on the woman's face, Tom's admission had
certainly come as a surprise. Surely Lila had been in the dark—she
wouldn't have sent her to Mark Davis on purpose.

The humiliation of that moment returned and Campbell forced
the memory away.

"No. I just told her." His eyes remained on the painting.

Campbell stared at the floor. "I'm sorry."

He sighed a heavy sigh. "Don't be. You didn't do anything wrong."

"The money—that was you?"

He nodded.

"You didn't have to do that."

"I had to do something." Sadness filled his face. "I didn't know about you until after Lila and I got engaged. I'm not proud of the way I handled it. I was a jerk, Campbell. I told your mom I'd buy her a house and give her money, but only if she didn't tell Lila."

Campbell looked away, fighting tears.

"She wasn't going to tell Lila anyway, but her not telling you— I think that was because she didn't want to subject you to me. I think I really hurt her that day. I've always regretted it."

"But not enough to make it right?" Campbell bit the inside of her cheek.

"The more time that passed, the harder it got." His trail of excuses grew cold.

"I get it." Campbell watched as his eyes filled with tears. If he'd admitted it to Lila, she would've left him. He loved her. It made sense now. Mom kept the secret to spare her friend the pain. She'd been protecting Lila, but she'd also been protecting *her*—from a father that couldn't give her anything but money.

The memory of the scrapbook pages she'd pored over the night before came back to her. Mom had loved him. She would've kept his secret simply because he'd asked her to.

"This painting reminds me of your mom. We spent a lot of time on the dock. We were good friends."

"I know. I read about it." Campbell looked at the painting and imagined the dock at dusk. She could almost see the full moon, feel the warm summer air. It was the perfect spot for wishing on stars. "You broke her heart," she said. "She loved you."

Silence fell between them. She'd found him. Or rather, he'd found her. Her father. Someone she resembled. Someone whose nose she had.

"You're a very talented artist," he said. "You should be proud."

Tears filled her eyes and as she blinked, they ran down her cheeks. She quickly wiped them away. "Thank you."

He turned to face her. "I want to make this up to you."

Was there still time for that? Inside, her heart felt squeezed between two clenched fists.

He shoved his hands in his pockets. "I understand if you're too angry, and I know I can't change what a jerk I was, but if you're willing, I'd like to get to know you."

Another tear fell. "I'd like that, I think." The image of her seven-year-old self, hair curled with rollers, a tiny bit of lip gloss on, wearing a frilly white dress, sprang to mind. It was the image that often came to mind when she imagined a father—only this time, in the dream, the father had a face. A smile. Strong arms to pick her up and twirl her around.

"I really am sorry," he said. "For not being there. It was…"

"Complicated. I know." She forced a smile. "I understand." She understood why he'd asked her mom to keep their secret, and his choice made her respect her mother even more. She'd been completely alone, and she still made a beautiful life for the two of them.

Knowing he hadn't wanted her stung, but looking at him now, she felt compelled to finally believe the best about someone. Even though he didn't deserve it.

Luke returned to her side, a look of concern on his face.

She wiped the tears from her eyes and forced a smile. "Luke, do you know Tom Olson?"

"Not formally." Luke looked at him.

"He's…" Campbell looked up at Tom.

"…an old friend of her mother's." Tom extended a hand in Luke's direction.

"He's my father," Campbell said.

Luke's eyes darted to Tom, then back to her. "Are you okay?" Luke turned to her.

"I think so." She smiled—this time without having to force it.

"It's good to meet you, Mr. Olson."

Tom smiled. "Good to meet you too."

"She's a special girl, your daughter," Luke said.

Tom glanced at her, then back at Luke. "I believe you're right." In all her years of imagining her father, she'd never properly anticipated the mix of emotions she'd feel. She'd so desperately wanted a dad all this time, but she couldn't pretend he'd come to her gift-wrapped in a perfect package.

Campbell inhaled and took a moment, just like Mom used to tell her to do. "Don't let the precious moments pass you by, Cam. Take snapshots in your mind. Seal them in good and tight. These are the things you'll carry with you. These are the moments that will keep you young."

She looked around the gallery. Like a camera in slow motion, she took the snapshots with her mind and sealed them in tight.

This was the night she found her father.

The night she forgave her grandfather.

This was a moment to carry with her—a moment to keep her young. And she would never forget it.

But a question nagged at the back of her mind. *What about Lila?*

At that moment, the door swung open and the street lights illuminated the dimly lit gallery. Lila entered, wearing an elegant navy cocktail dress, low and loose on one shoulder and belted in the middle. Sparkly silver heels elongated her legs, and she looked every bit the beauty queen she'd always been. Tom excused himself just as Adele, Jane, and Graham appeared next to Campbell and Luke.

* * * * *

Lila

Lila spotted her friends and waved in their direction. A master of disguise, she wore that fake smile with a genuineness no one would question. When none of them waved back, a sick feeling bubbled in her stomach.

"What's wrong?" Lila did her best to make sure her eyes flashed, the way they did in beauty pageants when she was younger.

Jane looked at Campbell, who looked away.

"You guys? What is the matter?" Lila waited for an answer, then spotted Tom at the back of the room.

"We know." Jane's lips trembled. "About Tom."

He'd gone ahead and told them. The betrayals just kept coming. Lila's heart rate quickened. She took a step backwards, but before she could go, Jane grabbed her hand and squeezed.

"It's okay," she said. "It'll be okay."

"No, it's not." Lila straightened her shoulders. "I'm leaving him." She'd decided in that moment, as she spoke the words.

"Lila, wait." Jane squeezed her hand. "Don't do anything crazy."

"What's crazy about leaving a marriage that's a complete lie?" Lila kept her voice low, careful to make sure no one else heard her falling apart.

"He loves you. That part isn't a lie." Jane seemed so sure, but she didn't know them anymore. They weren't those two lovesick kids they were all those years ago.

Lila shook her head then pasted that smile back in place. "I'm sorry I can't stay, Campbell. I think I need to go home." She looked past her and met Tom's eyes. Her breath caught in her throat. "I'll get in touch with you tomorrow." She walked to the door, longing to unleash her emotions somewhere dark and solitary.

Outside, a cool wind chilled her arms and she tried to rub the goose bumps away. Her attempt to convince Tom to keep this mess between them had failed. She had no say anymore—and that alone was reason to walk away.

She'd return to the lake house, pack her things, and leave in the morning.

And with any luck, she'd never have to come back to Sweethaven again.

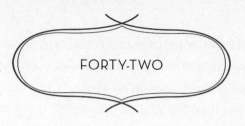

Campbell

The meadow behind Sweethaven Chapel sparkled in the early morning sunlight. The beads of dew that clung to blades of grass reminded Campbell of the newness of every morning, the newness that came with each day. Life held endless possibilities—even in a small town like Sweethaven.

She walked toward the marker Adele had made in memory of her mother, noting how different she felt now than she had only days before at Mom's proper funeral. In just a few short days, she'd learned more about her mother than she ever could've imagined and, in turn, more about herself.

She stared at the memorial plaque on the ground in front of her. It was nothing special like the headstone they'd had made at home. Just a simple reminder that Suzanne Carter had lived and that she would forever be remembered by those who loved her. Campbell knelt and ran a finger over the dash between the two dates on the plaque, thinking of all the memories it represented. The life she had lived. The people she had loved. The community she had inadvertently created by starting a scrapbook so many years ago. Her mom had taken the most difficult of circumstances and turned it into a beautiful life for the two of them, and she knew there had been many sacrifices to make that happen.

Something behind her jarred her from her thoughts. She turned and spotted Lila walking in her direction. Her face looked worn, devoid of makeup, as if she'd spent a very restless night. Campbell's heart clenched as she imagined Lila's pain.

"Good morning," Lila said. "Am I early?"

"A little bit," Campbell said.

"I didn't get much sleep last night. I was tired of staring at the walls in that old house." Lila glanced down at the plaque. "That looks really nice."

"I didn't know if you'd come."

Lila glanced at her and smiled—a forced smile if Campbell had to guess. "Why would you think that?"

The silence between them pulled like a tightrope, and Campbell wished she knew how to comfort her mother's friend. "I'm sorry," she finally said.

"For what?"

Campbell was surprised by the tears that welled in her eyes. "For coming here and searching for my father." She paused. "For being born."

"No." Lila turned to face her. She stood tall, her shoulders back, a new resolve bolstering her expression. "Don't you ever apologize for that. Remember who you are. You are Campbell Carter. You are extraordinary. And the circumstances of your birth do nothing to change that. If I'm being honest, I wasn't going to come this morning, but I wanted to make sure you understood that. It's important."

A month's worth of tears washed down Campbell's cheeks. Tears she'd been unable—or unwilling—to cry. Tears she'd held back for who knew what reason. And for the first time, she imagined she *wasn't* a mistake.

"But you and Tom—"

"Were having our share of problems long before you came into the picture. We'll be fine. Together or apart, we'll be fine. I do wish your mother were here, though, so I could give her a piece of my mind."

Campbell laughed. "I have a feeling she's listening."

Lila raised an eyebrow then looked around.

"Go on," Campbell said. "No one else is here."

Lila turned and looked at the little plaque. She reached in her purse and fished around until she finally produced a small photo of the four girls down on the boardwalk, ice cream cones in hand. She knelt and set it on the plaque. "Suzanne Carter, I am too late to strangle you, but if you were here right now I would, I swear it." Lila spoke in a hushed tone. "I lay awake all night wondering how on earth you could've done this to me. We were best friends. I was so jealous of you. I always thought you had it too easy." She sighed and glanced at Campbell. "Obviously I was wrong about that.

"I understand falling for Tom. He was so gorgeous and sweet and always seemed to have the right words to say. I don't blame you for that. But...you should've told me. You shouldn't have kept this from me all this time." Her voice broke, and she paused. "I think you kept the secret to keep me from getting hurt, but in some ways, this hurts so much worse."

Campbell listened quietly, trying not to intrude. She studied the ground and wished she could somehow comfort Lila, but she knew she didn't really understand her pain. She took a step closer, and a figure to her left drew her attention.

Tom.

Dressed in dark jeans, a blazer, and a button-down, he also seemed to wish for a way to comfort Lila. His eyes fixed on her, he hardly moved.

How much had he heard?

Lila slowly stood, still staring at the photo. "I don't hate you,

Suzanne," she said. "Even after everything, I can't help but love you for helping shape who I am." She wiped her tears.

Tom took a step closer, and Lila startled. When she turned to face him, her face went white as a sheet.

"What are you doing here?"

"I came to see you," he said.

Campbell quietly turned and walked away, out of earshot, where she could wait for the others to arrive. Her presence, no matter how kind Lila had been, was a constant reminder of all that had gone wrong.

* * * * *

Lila

Lila turned away, and he took a few steps closer, settling in the space at her side. She wrapped herself tighter in her jacket and fiddled with the belt.

"I thought about you all night." Tom watched her. "I know it sounds crazy, but having this out in the open feels like a huge weight has been lifted."

Lila scoffed. "I bet."

"You have no idea how this has torn me up inside. I think we should start over, with a clean slate."

"I don't know if I'm ready to talk about this yet, Tom. I think I might need some space."

"Space? What do you mean by 'space'?"

"Time apart. I was thinking I'd spend the summer up here. You go back to Georgia and we try things apart for a few months." The decision had come to her in the wee hours of the morning.

Sweethaven hadn't hurt her—Tom had. And coming back seemed far more comforting than spending an entire awkward summer back in Macon where she'd have to face the curiosity and gossip of the city's social elite.

He let out a stream of air and ran his hands through his hair. "I don't want that."

She risked a look at him. Would she lose her resolve? "It's really not up to you."

He stepped in front of her and forced her to look at him. "I made a huge mistake twenty-five years ago. I'm begging you to forgive me."

Pain pushed the tears down her cheeks. She stared into his eyes and knew she saw sincerity there. He'd never been one to lie to her, and she had no reason not to believe him. But he *had* lied, simply by keeping this from her. And a lie by omission was still a lie. Wouldn't she be weak if she simply accepted the apology and moved on?

She wiped her cheeks dry and looked away. "I don't know if I can forgive you. At least not yet. Every time I see Campbell, I'll remember how I feel right now." She looked at Campbell. The girl was half her husband—but not half *her*. As she looked closer, she saw the resemblance between the two of them. Why hadn't she seen it before? Had a part of her always known? Maybe she'd begun to believe lies she told herself. "Every time you try to become a father to the only child you'll ever have, I'll stand in the wings and watch like a pathetic understudy."

"It doesn't have to be like that. You can be a part of it. You can get to know her too."

"I'm not ready for that. I'm so angry every time I look at you." She stopped and met his eyes. "You broke my heart, Tom." She took a deep breath. "I need space. Just give me the summer."

He hesitated and shook his head.

"Please."

"Are you leaving me?" Tears filled his eyes, and Lila fought the urge to pull him into her arms and hold him tighter than she ever had.

"I don't know yet," she whispered.

He reached out and placed a hand on her cheek. "Please don't. I'll leave you alone, but I'm waiting for you." He leaned down and brushed his lips softly over her forehead.

She blinked back fresh tears but said nothing.

As he walked past her, back toward the chapel, she inhaled his scent, clean and woodsy and distinctly *Tom*. Her tears came quicker now, and she wished she could've maintained the wall she'd built so carefully over the years.

This pain, though, hurt too badly to mask and too intensely to hide.

She heard the sound of people gathering behind her, and she quickly, quietly slipped away to put herself together. As she did, she glanced in the distance, where Tom had stopped to talk with his daughter, and the pain, with the precision of a sharpshooter, shot straight back into her heart.

No, forgiveness wouldn't come easily—if at all.

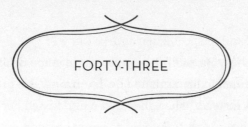

FORTY-THREE

Campbell

Luke had closed the patio at the Main Street Café, sectioning it off specifically for those who'd attended Campbell's mother's memorial service. The service had been light-hearted, yet poignant, and it seemed to give her closure the funeral hadn't. Surrounded by friends who days ago had been strangers, she put to rest not only a mother who had meant the world to her, but the questions that had plagued her ever since she was a little girl.

Tears fell throughout the entire gathering, not only tears of sadness over all she'd lost, but also tears of gratefulness for all she'd found.

Now, standing in the doorway of the café looking around the patio, she couldn't help but smile. Friends and family gathered together, eating, celebrating, and sharing the stories that had brought them together in the first place. At the center of it all was the scrapbook.

Adele had put it back in order, had it bound in an album, and put it on display now for all to see. Meghan's pages were still missing, but so many stories were well-preserved thanks to that collection of cardstock, stickers, and, most importantly, words.

Luke wrapped his arms around her and hugged her from behind. "This is pretty spectacular."

"It really is," she agreed. "Thank you for opening your café to us."

"I wouldn't have it any other way."

She turned to face him.

"You're kind of spectacular too, ya know."

She laughed. "Is that the best you could come up with?"

"I've been working on that one all morning." He grinned. "Fine. Let's try this instead." He leaned down and kissed her—right there in the doorway of the café—and for only seconds she wondered if anyone watched. One glance into his eyes, though, and the rest of the world seemed to disappear. She kissed him back, savoring the way his skin smelled, knowing that she very well could have met the one person who could steal her heart.

"Stay for the summer." He pulled back to face her.

"Where would I live? My job, I—"

He stopped her with another kiss. "Just think about it, okay?"

She nodded, dazed. Coming to Sweethaven for the summer would give her time to figure out her next move. What if she actually did it?

She watched him walk away, smiling when he glanced back before disappearing behind the door.

Still reveling in his kiss, she started to walk as an arm linked through hers. "My darlin'." *Adele*. "The honor of your presence is requested at a very special table near the front."

Campbell smiled. "What are you up to?"

"Not a thing." Adele walked her through the people and led her to the largest table on the patio. On it sat three gift bags. "Have a seat. I'll be right back." Adele started to walk away. "And no peeking," she called over her shoulder.

In only a few minutes, she returned with Jane, who sat next to Campbell and smiled. "Do you know what's going on?"

Campbell shook her head. "No idea. Have you seen Lila?"

Jane frowned. "Not since the memorial service. Do you think she's going to come?"

"Maybe. I still feel terrible."

Jane laid a hand over hers. "Sweetie, stop beating yourself up. I've learned the hard way that is no way to live."

Adele returned and sat on Campbell's other side. "I can't find Lila. Jane, can you call her?"

Jane pulled her phone from her purse and dialed. "Voice mail." She left a brief message and hung up.

"I wanted us to all be here together, but it looks like the Southern belle is late to the ball. I wanted to do something to show you girls how much I have loved having you back, and I wanted to remind you what it was that brought us all here in the first place, so I put together gifts for each of you."

"Can we open them?" Campbell took hold of her bag.

"Of course, Miss Impatient." Adele laughed.

Campbell pulled the bag onto her lap and removed the pink tissue paper. Inside was a stack of cardstock, scissors, a paper cutter, a pack of patterned paper, and a small box of photos.

"I had the photographer from the art show make a few prints for me this morning," Adele said. "I thought you might want to get those memories down in a scrapbook of your own."

Campbell shot her a look.

"I know, you aren't a scrapbooker, but maybe you could just give it a try?"

Jane held a similar package. Her photos were from the barbecue at Adele's—mostly of her family and a few of the four women together. "Adele, this is so thoughtful. Thank you."

"I know The Circle isn't the same, but I thought maybe we could start something new. Our own circle. If you'll let an old lady join, that is."

Jane reached out and took Adele's hand. "I can't think of anything I would like more."

Campbell smiled. "For you, I'll give this a try. But only for you."

Lila's silver Mercedes pulled into the handicapped spot in front of the café. She quickly parked, bypassed the front door, and walked through the gate to the patio.

"Lila, you need to move that car," Adele said. "You're not handicapped."

Lila waved her off. She sat in the empty seat at the table and picked up the gift bag that obstructed her view. "What's this? Presents?"

They all watched Lila.

"Adele, is this from you?"

"It's just a little somethin' to remind you of your trip."

She looked through the contents of the bag, stopping at the photos, most of which were from the night of the barbecue. She held up one of the four of them and smiled. "What are the odds we all look good in the same photo?"

Jane put a hand over Lila's and stopped her charade. "Hon. How are you?"

Lila's eyebrows raised. "I'm fine, why wouldn't I be?"

"We're just worried about you is all." Adele watched her.

"Marriages end every day. It's not breaking news."

Campbell's heart sank. Tom had told her Lila planned to spend the summer in Sweethaven, but she'd practically forbidden him to come. Her heart twisted with guilt. Partly because she'd caused this rift and partly because she'd imagined spending time with him that summer. Sweethaven was closer to Chicago than Macon, Georgia.

Jane leaned forward over the table. "People throw marriages away too quickly these days."

"I can't stay after what he did." Lila looked at Campbell. "No offense, Campbell."

Campbell looked away.

"How weak would that make me?"

"Honey, leaving isn't the stronger choice. Stayin' is," Adele said.

"What's that supposed to mean?"

"Any weakling can walk away from a marriage when things get tough. It takes a truly strong woman to stay and fight for what's hers." Adele folded her hands on the table. "You take it from someone who knows."

Lila held her gaze for a long moment, and Campbell prayed the older woman had gotten through to her.

"Just think about it, Lila. Don't do anything rash." Jane glanced at Campbell. "I have some news," she said. "Adele, you're going to be seeing a lot more of me. Turns out the Sweethaven Chapel needs a pastor for the summer, and Graham is working it out so he can take the position."

Campbell appreciated the change of subject.

Adele's eyes widened. "Jane, that's wonderful. Are you sure you're gonna be okay here all summer?"

"I think it'll be good for me. And for the kids. It'll be different. I don't know many people here anymore." Jane smiled.

"Oh, you'll fit right back in, darlin'." Adele glanced at Campbell. "What about you, hon? What will you do now that Sweethaven is in your blood?"

Three sets of eyes waited for her answer. She glanced through the windows and inside the café to where Luke alternately served drinks and glanced in her direction. What if she *did* come back here? She could give herself the summer. Just the summer. A summer to take pictures and explore new places and make new friends…maybe to fall in love?

"I think I may spend my summer here too," she said.

Adele let out a little squeal, followed by Jane's excited "Yay!"

"Maybe taking a little time to figure out where I want to land is a good idea." Campbell loved their enthusiasm over her decision. It solidified her choice. Because in Sweethaven, she felt anything but alone.

"You are more than welcome to stay in my house," Adele said. "But if you do, I'm gonna have to change the rules for my handsome son. I have a feeling he'd move back in with you around." She patted Campbell's hand.

"I'm coming back too." Lila stared at them.

Jane grabbed her hand. "And Tom?"

Lila met her eyes. "I'll think about it, Jane."

Relief settled on Campbell's shoulders knowing Lila might give her father another chance. Regardless, she'd already started concocting a plan to get the two of them back together. She knew Tom loved Lila—she just needed to help Lila get over her pride and see that for herself.

"Are we really all doing this?" Jane giggled. "We're all spending the summer in Sweethaven?"

"The good Lord's answered my prayers." A smile spread across Adele's face.

"Since we're all going to be back for the summer, why don't we reinstitute a new chapter of the Sweethaven Circle?" Campbell looked at them, one at a time.

Jane let out a slight gasp.

"No." Lila held her hands up in front of her and shook her head. "Your mom already swindled me into doing that once."

"But look at how fun it's been to relive your memories through that book," Campbell said.

"I love the idea," Adele said.

"I'm in," Jane said. "I'm still not promising anything artistic, but

I'll give it a try." She giggled. "Lila?" She moved closer to her friend. "Come on. We could have a whole section all about you."

Lila laughed. "Fine. I'll do it. But I have veto power on any photos that show my wrinkles."

"Lila, you're talking to a Photoshop master over here," Campbell said. "I'll be sure to make you look like the goddess you are."

They sat for a moment, a contented silence winding through them, and Campbell couldn't help but romanticize the summer that loomed on the horizon. In a matter of days, she'd grown to love these women and this town—and everything it represented.

Her soul felt at peace.

And that peace was worth far more than anything she could imagine.

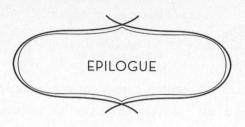

EPILOGUE

Adele

A month had passed since she'd seen the girls, and now that June had arrived, excitement fluttered in her stomach. One by one, they'd all be arriving and she'd have nearly three solid months of constant joy. She'd already planned out every weekend's meal and hoped to convince Lila, Jane, and Campbell to attend monthly scrapbooking crops with her in The Commons. They all claimed not to be scrapbookers, but she'd find a way to convince them.

It had been months since her social calendar had been so full.

In the backyard, her grandchildren tugged at Mugsy's ears in spite of the poor mutt's protests. "Finn, not so hard with her. She's as old as the hills," Adele hollered out the window.

Finn's four-year-old face scrunched in disappointment. It tickled Adele to see his personality start to bloom, even if she did see his mama's stubborn streak in him. Nadia ran underneath the sheets that hung on the line, her giggles wafting in through the open windows.

The doorbell rang, and Adele glanced at the clock. Too early for Nick to pick up the kids. Maybe one of her girls had gotten in early as a surprise.

She wiped her hands on a towel and tried to calm the excited butterflies that zipped around in her stomach.

She reached the door and pulled it open, expecting Lila, Jane, or Campbell.

But as her eyes registered what she saw behind the door, her heart skipped a beat and she struggled to find her breath.

"Meghan?"

Her daughter leaned against the porch railing and stared at her.

"Hi, Mama," she said. "I'm home."

AUTHOR'S NOTE

A couple of years ago, some very sweet friends gifted us with a long weekend in their cottage in a place much like Sweethaven. A community where the houses are passed down through the generations, rich with history and filled with stories. It was there that I began to imagine the women of this small town coming together in the Commons for evenings of scrapbooking while the summer sun waned over the lake and their children caught lightning bugs in the field out back.

Suddenly, I wanted to live in this place. With these women. And I wanted to uncover their secrets. To dive into their friendships and see how they'd begun, how they'd changed and evolved through the years. I wanted to give place to the preciousness of friends who knew me while I was still discovering who I was, and to explore the power of the bonds that are formed in those earliest years.

But most of all, I wanted to take a look at the redemptive qualities of unconditional love. Friends who let you make mistakes—who look on you with love when you do, who forgive and go on loving you anyway. Those kinds of friendships are so hard to find, but when you find them, they are better than gold.

Pulling in my love of memory-keeping was an absolute must, since at my core, I have always been a scrapbooker. Because of this, I have a record of many of the most important milestones in my life. And I've discovered, like the women of Sweethaven, that those records can remind me of what's really important. They act as therapy in the darkest hours. They serve as keepsakes when my memory fails. And they help my children understand a little more about their mom in a way no conversation ever seems to be able to.

I realize not everyone is a born scrapbooker, but I encourage you to share your stories—using whatever method you choose. Journal them, scrapbook them, record them on video—whatever works for you. Because in the end, our stories are what will help us live on.

I can't thank you enough for reading this book. I'm overflowing with appreciation and excited to connect with you. I hope you'll visit my blog at www.courtneywalsh.typepad.com and maybe even let me in on one or two of your stories. There's nothing that I would love more.

ABOUT THE AUTHOR

Courtney Walsh is a published author, scrapbooking expert, theater director, and playwright. She has written two papercrafting books, *Scrapbooking Your Faith* and *The Busy Scrapper*, and is currently working on her third. She has been a contributing editor for *Memory Makers Magazine* and *Children's Ministry Magazine* and is a frequent contributor to Group Publishing curriculum, newsletters, and other publications. She has also written several full-length musicals, including her most recent, *The Great American Tall Tales* and *Hercules* for Christian Youth Theatre, Chicago. *A Sweethaven Summer* is her debut novel.

Courtney lives in Colorado with her husband and three children. You can visit her online at www.courtneywalsh.typepad.com.